D0461188

TWISTED CREEK

TWISTED CREEK

JODI THOMAS

BERKLEY BOOKS, NEW YORK

THE BERKLEY PUBLISHING GROUP
Published by the Penguin Group
Penguin Group (USA) Inc.
375 Hudson Street, New York, New York 10014, USA
Penguin Group (Canada), 90 Eglinton Avenue East, Suite 700, Toronto, Ontario M4P 2Y3, Canada
(a division of Pearson Penguin Canada Inc.)
Penguin Books Ltd., 80 Strand, London WC2R 0RL, England
Penguin Group Ireland, 25 St. Stephen's Green, Dublin 2, Ireland (a division of Penguin Books Ltd.)
Penguin Group (Australia), 250 Camberwell Road, Camberwell, Victoria 3124, Australia
(a division of Pearson Australia Group Pty. Ltd.)
Penguin Books India Pvt. Ltd., 11 Community Centre, Panchsheel Park, New Delhi—110 017, India
Penguin Group (NZ), 67 Apollo Drive, Rosedale, North Shore 0632, New Zealand
(a division of Pearson New Zealand Ltd.)
Penguin Books (South Africa) (Pty.) Ltd., 24 Sturdee Avenue, Rosebank, Johannesburg 2196,
South Africa

Penguin Books Ltd., Registered Offices: 80 Strand, London WC2R 0RL, England

This is a work of fiction. Names, characters, places, and incidents either are the product of the author's imagination or are used fictitiously, and any resemblance to actual persons, living or dead, business establishments, events, or locales is entirely coincidental.

TWISTED CREEK

A Berkley Book / published by arrangement with the author

PRINTING HISTORY
Berkley edition / April 2008

Copyright © 2008 by Jodi Koumalats.
Cover art by Jim Griffen.
Handlettering by Ron Zinn.
Cover design by George Long.
Interior text design by Laura K. Corless.

ISBN-13: 978-0-7394-9575-9

BERKLEY®
Berkley Books are published by The Berkley Publishing Group,
a division of Penguin Group (USA) Inc.,
375 Hudson Street, New York, New York 10014.
BERKLEY® is a registered trademark of Penguin Group (USA) Inc.
The "B" design is a trademark belonging to Penguin Group (USA) Inc.

PRINTED IN THE UNITED STATES OF AMERICA

Chapter 1

If rotten luck were a man, I'd have a stalker. In college I used to wait for just one of those "many blessings" my grandmother promised would fall down on me. All I got was a string of loser boyfriends and part-time jobs going nowhere. But that didn't stop me from rounding every corner, hoping luck would be waiting with open arms.

During my junior year, about the time I thought my goal of teaching art might come true, my grandfather died, pulling any hope of finishing college out from under me. Since then, I've been tap dancing on the bones of dreams thinking I could make it rain.

Autumn in Memphis made me believe nothing would ever change. It had been almost five years since I'd left school and moved back in with Nana. We were no better off than we'd been that day when we'd returned home after my grandfather's funeral to find the eviction notice. But we were together and for Nana that was enough. She was a solid in my life, always there, always caring.

On the outside I felt young. But inside—the part of me who clapped believing in fairies and danced down the Yellow Brick Road—was slowly petrifying into a cynic. I was aging on the inside, giving up on dreams.

Today felt like one more nail in my coffin. I could almost smell the lilies.

Pulling my van into the front yard of the duplex I shared with my grandmother, I concentrated on guessing what color they meant to paint the place and tried not to think about my boss at the greenhouse. He'd threatened to fire me for the third time. I'd been the low employee on the totem pole before and knew last-hired would be first to go when business turned bad. With winter coming on, the plant business was bound to turn bad.

I might have consoled myself that the nursery job wasn't where I wanted to be anyway. It wasn't where I belonged. But if I admitted that, I'd have to ask the next question. Where should I be? Most of my life I'd felt like the last guest at a dinner party. I kept circling the table looking for my seat as all the food disappeared.

Nana, my grandmother, opened the door of our place as I grabbed the mail out of the box. "How was work, dear?" As always, Nana reminded me of a hundred pounds of bottled sunshine.

I forced a smile. "Well, I didn't kill any patients today." I rubbed the tag on my uniform smock that read "Allie Daniels, Plant Doctor." "But it was touch and go with an ivy determined to commit suicide."

Nana grinned and followed me through the tiny living area, where I slept, and into the kitchen. "I'm sure you do the best you can."

Flipping through the mail, I mumbled, "It may not be

good enough. There's talk of layoffs." I paused, noticing a letter from Texas amid the bills. I stared at the fat envelope with interest. Though Nana had grown up there, she'd been gone too long for any relative or friend to be writing. I balanced the envelope on my palm, weighing it.

"You got to open it, Allie, if you plan to read it," my grandmother said as she prepared our dinner—a can of pork and beans over toast.

I twisted a strand of my sun-bleached hair behind my ear and shrugged. "It can't be bad news, Nana. Surely nothing terrible can travel three states to get us." We'd been on the move for almost five years—first Kansas, then Arkansas, and now Tennessee. I'd hear about jobs opening somewhere with better pay and Nana would pack. We'd learned our lesson when Grandpa died. It didn't pay to get too attached to a place or to people. The duplex was only ours while we paid the rent and people tend to forget they know you when times get hard.

Nana called us "corner peepers," always thinking something better lay just around the bend. Every time we moved, I'd notify the post office in Clinton, Oklahoma, where I'd grown up, just in case someone was looking for us. No one ever had. Until now.

"What's it say, child?" Nana's voice had taken eighty years to mature into pure twang.

At twenty-six, I no longer considered myself a child, but I knew I'd always be one to her. "It's from a lawyer in Lubbock." I raised an eyebrow as I unfolded the papers. Nana loved me to read the mail, even flyers addressed to Occupant. I read the first paragraph, then frowned.

Nana leaned over my shoulder as if she could see the type without her glasses.

I straightened. "It seems this is the fourth address he's tried."

Nana dried her hands on her apron. "Well, whoever it's from is persistent. What could he want with us?" I could hear the unsaid words in her deep breath that followed. We'd had bills find us before and somehow we'd managed to pay them.

I read the entire first page before I whispered, "I've inherited Uncle Jefferson's lake property out on Twisted Creek."

Nana looked up at me, her light blue eyes as clear with reason as ever. "You don't have an Uncle Jefferson, Allie. Your mother was my only child."

I knew the whole story. Nana had my mother during her change of life, and my mother had me at fifteen with half the freshman football team denying ever having known Carla Daniels and the other half smiling. Nana took over raising me when my mom left for college.

In truth, I barely remember Carla. She was always forgetting she had me. I was an embarrassment to her, like teenage acne, and she usually tried to cover me up. When she moved out at eighteen, no one was surprised she forgot to pack me along. About the time I started first grade, my mother was off to New York and a career. For a while she came home at Christmas, then she claimed she needed a chance to see the world. I'd only talked to her twice since my grandfather had died and I moved home. Both times my mother treated my call as if I were a telemarketer.

Nana lost all interest in the letter that made no sense. She set the table with cloth napkins and a plastic centerpiece as if we were dining on something other than a can of beans. Just before she sat down, she passed the wind chime hanging over the sink and brushed it lightly with her fingers. The hollow chimes I'd heard all my life tinkled through the kitchen.

I smiled at the sound and continued to read through the

letter from the lawyer in Texas. When I flipped to the third page, a slip of paper drifted out and floated to the floor. Picking it up, I stared at a check for five thousand dollars made out in my legal name. In the bottom left corner, someone had typed "for traveling expenses."

"Somebody must be playing a joke on us." I handed Nana the check.

Nana pulled her glasses from her apron pocket and examined the paper. "It's a cashier's check. I've seen a few before, and they are good as cash."

Taking another look, I reread the letter. "This can't be for real, can it?"

Nana divided the beans onto two plates. "The part about Uncle Jefferson can't be, but the check might. You could always go over to the bank and see. The Hamilton Branch is open until six."

I glanced at the beans and decided to drive over and verify. What did I have to lose but a few minutes? The supper would taste pretty much the same cold. "I'll be right back."

Once en route, I called myself a fool for wasting gas to go to the bank. But once in a while I wanted to believe in a dream if only for a short drive. I had thought I'd find Mr. Perfect in college, marry rich, and build Nana a little house by the tennis courts. When that didn't work, I was sure I'd find a great job even without a degree if I looked hard enough, and we'd travel together seeing places Nana used to tell me about. But I'd never found any job except the ones I took to pay the bills.

Maybe—just once—a surprise could turn out to be something grand.

I walked into the bank trying to think positive, but at ten till six, the tired teller didn't even smile at me. She stared at the check and said she'd have to get it okayed.

I waited, angry at myself. You would have thought all

those childhood years of daydreaming of how my mother would come after me in a big car would have taught me something. I had envisioned those dreams down to the gold buttons she'd have on her sleeves and the way the car horn would sound. I even spent days deciding which toy she'd be carrying when she stepped onto Nana's porch. I guess I thought the details could make the fantasy real, but it only made for cluttered disappointments.

Straightening my smock, I tried to look as if I didn't feel out of place. Everyone around me had on business dress. A few of the tellers were already closing up. The guard moved to the door and began letting out the last customers. As the bank emptied, his smile widened and his "good evening" grew louder.

I waited. What would I say if the girl came back and told me the check was a fake? Could I be arrested? I should have taken one less art class in college and at least one law class. What I was doing was probably called . . . passing a hot check. Or maybe aiding the criminal who wrote the thing. I could almost see myself being handcuffed and led away while Nana waited at home with the pork and beans.

I heard the clank on the front lock. They'd locked me in. It was too late to run.

"Miss," the teller snapped. "Miss?"

"Yes." I gulped down panic.

"It appears this check is fine. Would you like me to deposit it into your account?"

I nodded.

She handed me a pen. I signed, turned, and prepared to make my break.

The guard unlocked the door and held it for me. "Evening," he said as I passed.

"No," I corrected. "*Good* evening." I would have tipped him if I'd had any change. I ran for the van and drove home feeling like I'd just finished a bit part in a movie, and this was all make-believe.

Only I had the receipt in my hand. Someone I didn't know had just given me money. No, not just money, but five thousand dollars. I almost wished I'd asked for it in ones.

I didn't turn loose of the bank slip until I was back in the kitchen. I moved the plastic flowers and laid it between us as I sat down.

Winking, I giggled. "I always did love dear Uncle Jefferson."

"It's real?" Nana whispered as if saying it too loud would make the possibility disappear.

"It's real," I answered. Part of me knew it was too good to be true, but I needed hope desperately.

Nana shook her head. "Money don't just fall out of the sky. There must be a catch."

Much as I hated to, I agreed with her. No one had ever given us anything. Somewhere, if we took this money, there would be the payback. I reread the lawyer's letter while I ate. It looked cut-and-dry. A man named Jefferson Platt, who the lawyer thought was my uncle, had left me his property on Twisted Creek. Nowhere was there a small clause that said "This offer is only good for . . ."

Nana lifted the deposit slip. "What should we do, Allie?"

I thought of all the options. Ignore the letter. Stay here and look for another job. We could pack and try Kansas City again; I'd found a good job there last winter working in a shoe store. Or . . .

There was that corner again waiting just beyond my

view. I knew what I had here. Minimum wage with winter coming on. A van in need of tires. Nothing left to sell for extra money. "We go to Texas." I tried to sound positive one more time.

Nana grinned, turning her face into a river of wrinkles. "It'll be good to be back home. I haven't seen Texas since the summer I turned sixteen."

I couldn't resist smiling back. I'm not sure how she always managed to do it, but my nana could look on the bright side of a tornado. She had that sparkle in her eyes sometimes that seemed to say this life she lived and worked in was simply a stage; her real world, where her heart lay, was somewhere else. Good times or bad, both were simply acts in the same play to her.

I wanted to go to Texas to see if this inheritance was real, but I already knew deep down that it couldn't be.

So, why go?

I straightened, a weary soldier answering bugle call. Because there are times in your life when any somewhere looks better than where you are, and this somewhere made my grandmother smile.

That night, while Nana watched *Survivor*, I paid off every bill I owed. Almost half the money was gone by the time I finished, but I would be leaving Memphis with my head up. I wrote the landlord a note and told him to keep the hundred-dollar deposit since I wasn't able to give him any notice. He'd been kind, letting me pay a few weeks late once when Nana got sick and my entire check went for a doctor's visit.

An hour later, from my bed on the couch, I listened to Nana's snoring and tried not to get my hopes up. I knew it made no sense that some stranger would leave me something. There had to be a catch . . . a trapdoor I'd fall into any minute. I got up and called the bank, punched in my checking account number and password.

The money was there.

I tried to go back to sleep. What if the five thousand was all there was? What if the property was worthless and I made a twelve-hour drive to find out I had nothing waiting?

Moonlight from a rip in the curtain shone across the living area and onto the kitchen counter. A roach crawled along the beam of light, searching for crumbs.

I laughed. What did I have to lose? I was going to Texas. There would be jobs there as well.

By dawn I was packed. We ate breakfast with the deposit slip still between us. I left at eight and drove to the nursery to turn in my uniform. The boss smirked at me, but I only told him to have a nice day and waved. I heard once that you should always be nice to people you dislike; it confuses them.

When I got back to the house, Nana was ready. A box of kitchen staples and her tattered suitcase waited by the door.

My grandmother wasn't a collector and told me many times that the only thing of value in her life was me. We had no pictures or keepsakes from her past or my childhood. All she ever moved besides essentials were her Bible and her wind chime.

Like hopeful fools we loaded our belongings once more and left the key in the mailbox. The same bored girl at the bank counted out my money. I debated asking for it in ones, but settled on twenties. I left twenty dollars over what I'd used to pay bills so the account could stay open.

The teller blinked a smile as she handed me almost three thousand dollars.

I smiled back and walked out of the bank with more money than I'd ever had in cash.

It felt good.

I felt rich.

And I started to believe that maybe I really did have an Uncle Jefferson.

Chapter 2

Twenty-four hours later, after driving all day and spending the night in a Motel 6, I was ready to meet the lawyer and inherit my property. I held my disposable coffee cup in one hand as I drove toward the offices of Garrison D. Walker, Attorney-at-Law.

"Maybe you knew Uncle Jefferson, Nana? Maybe he was a friend of your family from way back?" We'd played this game for a hundred miles with no luck.

Nana shook her head. She'd been a tenant farmer's wife all her married life, and once my grandfather died she'd lived with me. She could count the number of people she'd called friend on her fingers. And as for Nana having a rich, secret lover hidden away somewhere, that was about as likely as magnolias in Alaska.

"I knew a Jeff once, but he went by the name of Red 'cause he had hair as red as an apple," she mumbled around a donut. "He took me to a dance that summer I spent time in Texas. My mom sent me to stay with my brother Frank's wife, who was expecting. She'd taken a summer house for one week when Dallas was burning up 'cause being big pregnant is hot on a body even in the winter. She drove up to Oklahoma and picked me up, then we wandered around the most nothing land until we found the place she'd rented."

Nana smiled as the wind tickled through her short gray hair. "All the boys had been called up after Pearl Harbor. My mom wanted me to stay with Mary until school started. She weren't but a year older than me."

I remembered the story and didn't want to hear the retelling of how Frank was killed in the war and his wife died in childbirth. "Tell me about this Red you met," I encouraged.

Nana licked donut icing off her fingers. "He was real nice. We talked almost all night, every night that week. He was turning eighteen in the fall and couldn't wait to join up."

"Why didn't you marry him?" I winked at her.

She laughed. "I was already engaged to your grandpa. My folks had promised we could marry as soon as I finished my eleventh year of school. They said your grandpa was solid on account of him being older than me and already a farmer." She popped another donut and turned to look out her side window. "Some folks didn't think so, but those men who stayed to farm did their part in the war, too."

I frowned. If Nana didn't have anyone in her past, it had to be me. But who?

I'd had my share of boyfriends in college, but most had wanted to borrow money from me, not keep in touch because they planned to name me in a will. Once I moved back home, I hadn't known a single man in the county I wanted to have a cup of coffee with, much less get involved with romantically. When the few single guys my age did come around, they lost all interest as soon as they discovered Nana was part of the package.

Glancing at Nana, I smiled. She'd been a real help and didn't even know it. A man who couldn't love Nana, too, wasn't worth having.

Nana refolded the map she'd been trying to get back in its original shape since Oklahoma City. She stuck it over the visor where I'd put the lawyer's letter. Nana had read it aloud so many times during the trip, we could quote almost every line. She hummed as we passed through the streets of Lubbock.

This morning, we'd had our motel showers and hot coffee. It was time to meet with Garrison D. Walker and solve the mystery. I tried not to hope for anything. If the inheritance was nothing, we'd already had an adventure, and I could look for a job here as easy as I could have in Memphis.

I turned off of Avenue Q onto a tree-lined street named Broadway. Finding the lawyer had been no problem, thanks to the directions he'd left on the back of his letter. When I called to tell him we were coming, he sounded excited. Maybe he was glad to be rid of his responsibility with the will.

A very proper secretary welcomed us. She offered us a seat and disappeared through one of the mahogany doors behind her desk.

"Don't say anything about not knowing Jefferson Platt," I whispered to Nana, who was busy pulling the tag off the outfit I'd bought her at a Wal-Mart last night. I thought if I was going to inherit something we should look like we didn't really need whatever it was. We'd found dresses for both of us for under a hundred dollars. Nana's was navy, made to look like a suit with a white collar. Mine, a shift that buttoned down the front, was the pale blue of a summer day. Like everything I bought, it seemed a few inches too long, but we hadn't had time to hem it.

"I won't say a word," Nana mumbled. "It's not right to talk about the dead, dear." She'd managed to pull the tag off, but the plastic string still dangled from her sleeve.

I think the world of my nana, but she is a woman far more comfortable in a housecoat than a suit. "All dressed up" to her meant taking off her apron. She helped me through those first two years of college by cooking at the elementary school a mile down from the farm my grandfather worked. She'd walked the distance every morning and cooked, then returned home to the full day's work of a farmer's wife without one word of complaint.

I covered her hand with mine, wishing for the millionth time that I could make things better for her. When you've only got one person who loves you, you have to wish extra hard.

"Miss Allison Daniels?" a man of about fifty asked as he neared.

I stood and shook his hand. "My friends call me Allie," I said. "And this is my grandmother, Edna Daniels."

"Garrison D. Walker, at your service."

The lawyer smiled and waited for her to offer her hand. But Nana wasn't about to let him see her plastic string, and he was too much a Southern gentlemen to offer his hand first to a lady.

Walker turned back to me. "We've had a hell of a time finding you, Miss Daniels."

"I wasn't aware I was lost." I smiled, thinking Garrison Walker had too many teeth. "I didn't know Uncle Jefferson was dead." I knew I should be concentrating, but the man made me nervous. His grin looked like it belonged on a mouth one size larger.

"Your mother didn't tell you Jefferson died?" Walker asked as he stopped grinning—thank goodness. "We sent her a registered letter the day of his graveside service. He'd listed her phone number and address as the only person to be notified." Walker paused as if expecting me to fill in a blank. When I didn't, he added, "Quite frankly, I was surprised when Mr. Platt named you his only heir. I told your mother to let you know of his passing since we had no address on you."

"Maybe my mother had trouble reaching me. She's out of the country a great deal," I managed to mumble as I remembered the string of men who always stood beside her in pictures. She'd send us snapshots from all over the world with little notes on the back like, "Walter and I in Rome," or "Me and Charles—Paris." I'd decided years ago that in her odd way she thought she was sharing with us by sending photos. No gifts or calls, just pictures of her and strangers.

"How long ago did he die?" I'd made a point that every time we moved I called and left a message on my mother's machine. She could have found me, but I didn't feel like going into family problems with Garrison Walker.

"Almost two months." Walker lowered his head and sighed. "He had a long life though, dying at the age of eighty-three."

I couldn't shake the feeling that Walker was pretending to care. But the information was helpful. His age eliminated any possibility of Jefferson being my father, unless he played football in high school during his fifties.

Walker continued, "Your mother said to send all information to her, and she'd forward it to you, but I've been in family law long enough to know to deal directly with the source. Since you are not a minor, I had to locate you."

Nana found her voice. "Did you hire a P.I. to find

Allie?" She loved detective shows. She even told me once that she'd leave my grandpa if McGyver ever came by the farm.

Walker smiled as if talking to a child. "No. When I realized weeks had passed, I went online. I had your legal name and county in which you were born. Within fifteen minutes I'd located your current place of employment."

"Former employment," I corrected without explanation. The man could probably piece together my whole life from what he'd learned on the Internet. Places of employment, changes in addresses. Going-nowhere jobs.

To my surprise, Walker looked embarrassed. "Oh, sorry. I didn't mean to leave you standing. If you'll step into my office, I'll need you to sign a few papers, and then the keys are yours. I'm afraid the only money he left was to cover our fees and for your traveling expenses."

He paused as if expecting me to question him.

I shrugged. I hadn't expected anything, so Walker's news wasn't disappointing. The idea that I had the keys to something I owned, other than my van, was a foreign concept to me.

The lawyer glanced around the empty waiting area as if wishing for clients to appear. "Would you like me to drive you out? I could work it into my schedule."

"No thanks. I've got a map." Something in the way Walker stared at me gave me the creeps. Mixed signals were bouncing off him. I found myself thinking a little less of Uncle Jefferson for picking him to handle the will. If it's possible to think less of someone you don't know.

Walking to the van a few minutes later, I tried to forget about the lawyer. I had the keys. I could leave his problems in his office. They weren't in my bag of worries.

"Did you notice?" Nana whispered. "That lawyer had wobble eyes."

Laughing, I had to ask, "What are wobble eyes?" Nana thought she could tell anything from a person's eyes and most of the time she was right. She told me once that she had Gypsy blood on her mother's side and Gypsies are all born with a gift for something.

"The lawyer's eyes wobbled between caring and disliking, maybe even hating. I've seen it before a few times in salesmen who used to come around. They'd do their talking, swearing they had one hand on the Bible, but the other would be trying to get into your pocket." She sat back and crossed her arms. "I don't like him."

And that was it, I knew. Nana wouldn't be changing her mind. "Well," I consoled, "we'll probably never see him again." Cross my heart, I almost added out loud. "We got the keys."

We drove out of Lubbock, Texas, giggling. Keys! I had keys to my very own place. Some man I never knew, in a place where I'd never been, had left me a house I never even knew existed. Maybe he got my name mixed up with someone else. Maybe he met my mother and figured I was overdue for a break. Maybe he picked me out of the phone book.

It didn't matter. I didn't care. If the place was run down and in need of paint, we could fix it up, and what was left of the five thousand would keep us going until I found a job. I had half a degree and a ton of experience doing everything from retail to bookkeeping. I'd find something to keep food on the table. After all, we already had a roof.

We changed into our comfortable clothes at a truck stop on the edge of town. I found a county map plastered to the wall and studied it as I braided my hair. A pinpoint dot marked the forgotten lake community where my place was located. The middle of nowhere, I thought.

When I got back to the van, Nana was staring out at the

dry, flat land with an acre of topsoil blowing across our hood. She whispered, "You sure there's a lake in this country?"

"The man inside said it was about thirty miles from here in a little canyon. He said he thinks it's an old private community made up of mostly rich folks who want to get out of the city."

Nana stared at the skyline of Lubbock. "I can see why," she said. "I was through here a few times when I was young. Nice people, as I remember, but you'd have to have roots growing out of your toes to want to live in this wind."

Before I could leave the city limits, Nana saw a dollar store and yelled, "Stop."

I pulled into the parking lot without argument. I had long ago given up trying to understand her fascination with stores where everything cost a buck, but twenty-seven dollars lighter we were back in the car with enough snacks to last a week. Nana still had pioneer blood in her. She believed that wherever we traveled, there might not be food and she needed to be prepared.

Almost an hour later, after two wrong turns, we pulled past the broken-down main entrance to Twisted Creek Community. The gate had been propped up by the side of the road so long ago that morning glory vines almost covered it. From the entrance, the road wound down into a canyon, twisting between brown sagebrush and foot-high spikes of faded buffalo grass.

"Walker said the road makes a circle, so it really doesn't matter much which way we turn at the gate." I looked for any sign of life. The place reminded me of a forgotten movie set left to decay in the sun and wind. Everything in the canyon seemed to have turned brown with the fall. The monochromatic landscape might have seemed dull to most people, but I found it a grand study in hues. The wonder of a world painted in browns reminded me of the Civil War photographs by George S. Cook. Dark, haunting, beautiful.

Nana watched as views of the water flashed between the weeds. "Look. I see the creek."

I slowed, noticing a winding, muddy stream of water with reddish-brown banks on either side. At the base of the canyon, the creek pooled into a lake.

"I remember living near a creek when I was a kid." Nana rolled down her window. "We used to carry our laundry down beside it every Monday morning. My momma would have my two brothers build a fire while my sister and I filled the wash pot with water and lye soap so strong I could smell it in my nose until Wednesday. Then, while we all played in the stream, she'd wash the clothes and hang them on branches to dry."

I looked for a mailbox with 6112 on it as I asked the same question I'd asked every time I heard this story. "Why didn't your mother make all you kids help?"

Nana smiled and repeated what she always said. "Your grandmother liked to do laundry."

I didn't correct her that the story was about my great-grandmother. I just nodded, knowing she'd confirmed that craziness runs in the women of my family. The men, it appears, just run, for not one of Nana's stories ever mentioned her father.

My grandfather, Nana's Henry, had stayed around. If you can call staying around working from dawn till dusk. Every night he'd stomp in and fall asleep as soon as he ate supper. Same routine every day, seven days a week, until a heart attack took him in the middle of a half-plowed field. He would have hated that.

It seemed strange, but the only memory I have of Henry is him in his recliner with his eyes closed. Maybe that's why he looked so natural at the funeral. Nana always said he was a good man, but I remembered no good or bad about the man. Except maybe how he liked order in his world. He wanted the same seven meals served at the same time and on the same night of the week. Growing up I always knew what day it was by the smell of supper. I never saw him hit Nana, or kiss her. Their life was vanilla.

"I'm glad we had those days by the creek," Nana said, interrupting my thoughts. Her short gray hair blew in the wind. "With Frank and Charlie dying in the war, they didn't have much time for fun in this life. We used to laugh so hard when we swam that Momma would make us get out and rest. There's no better sleeping than lying in damp clothes on a hot day by the creek. I'd feel so relaxed and lazy I wouldn't even bother to swat at flies buzzing by."

Nana stretched as if feeling her memory before continuing, "We were always careful though with Poor Flo. I thought she'd grow out of being frail, but she didn't even live long enough to marry." Nana leaned back in her seat. "She had the flu back when she was little, and it left scars on her heart."

I felt sorry for Poor Flo even though I never met her. She'd been dead more than sixty years, and Nana still mourned her. Nana told me once that some memories stick to your soul. I think Flo was like that with my grandmother.

As we moved around the circle of homes and barns huddled close to the water, I noticed how every house looked overgrown with weeds, and all were in need of paint. This may have been where the rich folks lived fifty years ago, but now the neighborhood had fallen on hard times. I saw a few gardens, a few fishing boats, a few signs of life.

We passed a junkyard of broken-down boats and old rusty butane tanks with worthless cars parked in between. The mess made me think of those wild salads at fancy restaurants where it looked like they mowed the alley and washed it up to serve.

Nana patted my knee three times as she always did. Three pats for three words she used to say.

She didn't say the words now, she didn't have to.

"I know," I said as the van rattled across a bridge. "I love you, too."

Chapter 3

September 17, 2006
1100 hours
Twisted Creek

Luke Morgan swore as he stomped through the bush toward Jefferson Platt's property.

He didn't have much time. He'd been here two days, talking to residents, checking out the area for trouble, but he had put off going to Platt's home.

Until now.

Much as he hated to acknowledge it, once he went inside, he'd have to admit the old man was dead.

Jefferson Platt had been a fixture in his life for as long as Luke could remember. Platt had taught him to fish when he'd been five. He had been his grandfather's friend for forty years and in so doing Jefferson had watched first Luke's father and then Luke grow up. Jefferson had been Luke's safe house when a bullet almost ended his career five years ago. The smells of the lake ran as thick in Luke's blood as his Navajo heritage.

Going into Jefferson Platt's apartment would be like

closing a door, and Luke had closed enough doors in his life lately. This was the one place on the planet Luke thought never changed . . . and now it had.

He circled near the lake, deciding it would be faster to plow through the muddy bank than try to fight the willows and pines that stood fortress-thick between his land and Platt's. If he'd had time, he would have gone around to the road and walked over, but he could feel trouble coming as clearly as his Navajo grandfather used to say he felt storms brewing all the way to the edge of creation.

Reaching the lake's shoreline, Luke stopped a foot before he stepped out in the open and pulled his Glock 9mm from his boot. He wasn't in the mood to clean lake water out of the weapon again.

Pressing the gun in his vest pocket, he jogged down the shore to a long dock everyone called Jefferson's Crossing. With a jump, he grabbed the side of the muddy dock and pulled himself up. From here on he would be in easy sight of any fisherman passing, so he walked slow, hoping they'd notice no more than they'd seen the past few days—a drifter circling the lake. With a week's worth of growth across his face, he was a far cry from the efficient ATF agent who'd left his post in Austin for a leave he'd listed as "personal business."

Within minutes he had slipped inside the kitchen window and climbed the stairs. Boarded up, the place he'd visited a hundred times seemed unfamiliar. Glancing down, he could barely make out the outline of the old potbellied stove in the center of the wide, empty room or the small safe no one had remembered how to open in so many years it had become simply a stool huddled beside the stove. The mismatched pair stood alone in the room that had been Jefferson's store.

Luke smiled, remembering one summer when Jefferson

had told him that the safe's combination was someone's birthday. Luke had spent hours trying every set of numbers he could put together. Jefferson had laughed at him, along with everyone else who wandered in.

Luke turned away, forcing his mind to present problems. He took the last half of the stairs two at a time and wasn't surprised to find the second floor a mess. Jefferson's no-doors apartment hadn't changed since he'd been here years ago. His trained eyes missed little. He'd read the police report and knew Jefferson Platt had died in the water a few feet from the dock, but someone had walked across the dusty floor of his bedroom recently. Maybe someone looking for the same clues.

The sound of a car drew Luke to the window. From behind the curtain's shadow, he watched as an old blue van with Tennessee tags rattled down the drive. It was time to move, and fast, but he hesitated. The blonde driving held his attention.

When she jumped out of the car, he thought her little more than a kid until she stepped into the sunshine and stared up at the house. Her hair might be in braids and her shorts barely covering her bottom, but her petite body was definitely all grown up.

"Hell," he mumbled. The new owner had arrived and he was wasting time staring.

Luke smiled as he took another look. It had been a long time since he'd admired a woman without wondering if she had a rap sheet.

Too bad he had to disappear.

Chapter 4

The numbers 6112 flashed past on a post just outside Nana's window. I didn't slow. Something in the back of my mind said if I acted as if I hadn't seen the place maybe it wouldn't be real.

But for once, Nana was paying attention and yelled, "Bingo!"

I backed up and turned into the drive. Forty feet down the gravel road, the left front tire hit a hole, almost knocking us out of our seats, but I managed to keep the van from tipping as we rattled toward the largest of several buildings scattered on the property. My property. At least until Garrison D. Walker figured out he'd made a mistake and found the wrong Allie Daniels.

A hundred feet behind the buildings the lake lapped against dingy sand. Barbed-wire fencing framed the boundaries on the other three sides of the wide lot. The land to the left looked wooded and unclaimed from nature. The acreage to my right appeared too hilly to even get a road through, making my property seem lonely on the space between the road and the water. Cluttered driftwood scattered like bones along the shore and beneath the dock.

Nana leaned forward and stared at the building twinkling in the morning sun. "It's a store, I think."

Tin signs advertising everything from Camel cigarettes to Coors beer looked like they held together the front wall. The steep tin roof had two windows, and with the long wooden porch running the length of the front, the building seemed to smile at us. The downstairs windows were boarded up. Broken wicker furniture littered one end of the porch while metal lawn chairs lined up on the other end as if at attention—old and rusty, but too tough to die.

I let the van roll into the shade of the shack and noticed a long, covered walk out back that led to a dock on the water. It looked in better shape than the building so I guessed it must have been added.

"This is it, Nana." I fought to swallow. "Our new home." We'd lived in some pretty rough houses on land hardly worth plowing, but none looked as bad as this.

Nana smiled and was out of the van before I could throw it into park. She might be in her eighties, but my grandmother was a ball of energy. By the time I caught up with her, she'd already tried the front door.

I pulled out the keys Walker gave me and on the third attempt we were in. Cold, stale air rushed passed us, fighting for freedom and leaving my skin chilled. My body parts were voting on whether to run or stay when Nana flipped on the lights. Bare bulbs above us flickered, then came on along with ceiling fans.

"Would you look at this," Nana whispered as hundreds of tiny lights along one wall blinked to life. "It's like a party in here."

I wondered how much I could get for Christmas lights at a garage sale as I studied a room divided in half by wide stairs.

Fifteen feet of bare shelves lined the north wall, with a high glassed-in counter in front. The oldest cash register I'd ever seen sat on a long table along with several empty wire racks. River rocks the size of footballs formed the wall facing the road. The back wall had two huge bay windows that looked out over the lake. Dark wood framed each view like a homemade picture frame.

The south side of the room must have been a café at one time. There were tiny round tables and a pass-through with a drink chest beneath it. A low counter ran parallel to the pass-through with half a dozen stools anchored in front. The vinyl was so worn the seats looked silver in spots. Any wall space not claimed by shelving had a dead animal head or a mounted fish on it.

In the center of the room, separating the store from the café, stood a staircase that appeared more solid than the entire building. The air smelled damp, but dust wasn't as thick as I'd expected.

I pointed with my head, silently asking Nana to choose either the swinging door in the back or the stairs.

Nana smiled and raised her eyes.

Without a word, we climbed the stairs. With each step I thought of all the horrible things I might find on the second floor. Wild animals, spiders, Uncle Jefferson's body.

I glanced over at Nana and, to my surprise, she laughed. For her, this was Christmas morning. For me, it was more like Halloween night.

The second-floor door stood open at the top of the stairs. We walked into an apartment that was about half the size of the downstairs and twice as dusty. Old papers cluttered the main room's floor, and two of the three lightbulbs above us were burned out. A doorless bathroom seemed wedged in the corner across from the door. Medicine bottles filled the counter and the back of the commode as if they'd been poured there instead of set. A few of the bottles were even floating in the toilet water.

I didn't want to think about when the porcelain had last been cleaned.

Concentrating on the main area, I ventured forward, noticing a few pieces of furniture that looked solid beneath the layers of dust.

From the center I took inventory. Two rooms with an open bathroom in between. No kitchen. I guessed that would be downstairs on the other side of the pass-through. First room contained one desk by the window and a pair of wingback chairs. One wrought-iron bed, unmade. In the smaller room I counted one twin bed covered with clothes, a dresser decorated with more medicine bottles, and a recliner surrounded by fishing magazines.

I lifted one of the bottles of pills, then another, both full.

When I tried the old phone by the bed, it was dead. "No nine-one-one to call if Jefferson ran into trouble."

"Maybe he had no one to call?" Nana reminded me of a bloodhound on a hunt as she circled the rooms. She was cleaning, rearranging, organizing in her mind just like she did everywhere we lived. No place was ever bad to her; some just needed more work than others.

"True," I agreed. "If he'd known anyone, he wouldn't have left the place to me." Looking for loose boards, I watched my step as I moved around the bed.

Nana flushed the toilet. "We got lights and water," she cheered. "Life is good."

I caught a glimpse of a dirty hand sliding slowly beneath the bed and realized that wasn't all we had.

We had company.

Chapter 5

Backing toward the door, I tried to keep my voice calm. "Nana, maybe we should bring in the food we got at the store."

Nana looked over from the window she'd pried open. "You can handle it, dear. I'll start airing this place out."

I'd made it to the top of the stairs without taking my gaze off the space between the bed's mattress and the floor. If someone crawled out now, I could make a run for it.

"No," I managed to say without sounding panicked. "I really need your help," I mumbled, knowing I could never leave my grandmother to fight off the under-the-bed monster.

It flashed in my mind that I'd always known he existed even though this was the first sighting of him I'd ever had. When I'd been three or four I'd wet the bed once because I just knew someone would jump from beneath my tiny twin bed and get me if I ran for the bathroom. When I'd been twice as old, I'd refuse to put my hand over the side. I'd known he'd pull me under if I did.

And now I had proof. I'd seen his big, dirty hand. "Nana, I could use your help." He might be a thief or an escaped convict, but I knew for a fact whoever lay beneath that bed was no less than my nightmare come to life.

"Oh, all right, dear," Nana joined me at the door. "I guess we'd better bring everything in and have a look at the kitchen. Looks like we're home."

I followed her down the stairs, trying to decide what to do. "Scream" had been my first plan of action but no one would hear me. We could drive off, but the intruder would just be waiting when we returned, and I had no one to run to for help.

As we walked to the side of the house, I started looking for weapons. A rake, several old fishing poles, a broken paddle propped beside a holey canoe. Not much of an arsenal.

When we reached the van, I whispered, "Nana, get in and lock the doors. I'll be back in a few minutes."

She raised her eyebrow as she always did when questioning my sanity. I didn't give her time to argue. "Spiders." I mumbled the first thing I could think of that my grandmother hated. "I'll take care of them." I pushed her into the seat and closed the door.

Lock it, I mouthed and ran for the broken paddle. I didn't bother looking back at her. I knew she was giving me the eyebrow again.

The canoe paddle felt solid in my hand, even if half the flat part was missing. I might not be able to kill the monster with one hit, but I could do some brain damage.

I gripped it above my head like a mighty batter preparing to swing and stepped back into the store. Slowly, I moved up the stairs, expecting to see the intruder jump from the top any moment. On the Coward Scale, I'd always been a two. Brave enough to plan, but petrified to act. But this time, with Nana's and my life at stake, I intended to move up the scale.

At the landing, I kicked off my open-backed sandals and let them tumble down the stairs. If a fight came, I wanted to be able to move fast without having to worry about falling out of my shoes.

When the sandals settled, the house fell silent. I took the last few steps, a white-knuckled grip on the handle of the paddle. With a yelp that sounded more pitiful than powerful, I jumped into the room and pointed my weapon as if it were a rifle.

Nothing moved.

I swung the paddle at gut level, from side to side.

Silence.

"You might as well come out," I ordered. "I know you're there."

I took a deep breath, preparing for the worst. This might be my Alamo, but I wasn't going down without a fight. Moving to the center of the room, I widened my stance. If he crawled out from under the bed, I figured I could get two, maybe three good whacks before he stood.

Circling to the other side of the bed, I leaned over for a closer examination, but found only clutter. I poked the paddle beneath the bedsprings, but encountered nothing solid. I tried again and again, then straightened, my weapon gripped tightly.

One of the medicine bottles by the open window tumbled off the desk and rolled across the floor. It took a minute for my heart to settle back into my chest. If I'd had a gun, I would have blasted the prescription just for the hell of it.

In the damp, dusty silence I wilted from warrior to wimp. I'd been running on coffee and no sleep since opening Uncle Jefferson's letter; I must have started to imagine things. Maybe all I'd seen was a scrap of faded newspaper moving slightly after Nana opened the window. No hand. No monster under the bed.

I knelt, lifted the bedspread, and checked. Only dust and trash.

Dragging the paddle, I moved through the two upstairs rooms of my new home, checking out closets and looking behind doors. Part of me wished for the monster, for being frightened would have been far more heroic than being crazy.

I sat down on the desk chair and stared out the window. Dried weeds and muddy water. Winter hadn't yet arrived, but any green of summer had already browned. It felt like my insides had also faded to match the land I now owned. I loved color. Sometimes my eyes ached to see bright greens and reds and yellows, but it seemed I'd been imprisoned in a brown world since birth. Like a swimmer trapped in the desert, my whole body longed for something I'd never had.

I rolled the handle of the paddle across my lap and wondered if I'd imagined the intruder under the bed because making up even a monster is better than having no dreams. Lately I'd caught myself forgetting to hope, much less dream. I was twenty-six, too young to give up. I should be partying, running around with friends, running up my credit cards.

But I knew of no parties. I had no friends to run around with. No credit cards to abuse.

This was it, I thought. I'd finally drifted down until I could go no lower. At least when we were traveling I had hopes the next place would be better, brighter. But now I was tied to this ugly lake. Anchored. I felt like I'd acciden- tally stepped through a time door and gone from being young to old age without ever living. The starting point and the finish line were in the same place for me.

Nana would tell me to make the best of it. Or, she'd raise that gray eyebrow and tell me I was swimming in thoughts so deep I'd get a cramp and drown.

"Nana." I jumped up, letting the paddle tumble to the floor. I'd left Nana in the van.

Running down the stairs and out the front door, I was halfway across the dirt to the Dodge when it dawned on me I'd forgotten to put my shoes back on. Stickers were every-where, attaching themselves to my feet with painful little stings.

I danced, picking at them as I continued toward the van. Most of the stickers were out by the time I reached the pas-senger door, but Nana had disappeared.

I hopped my way back to the porch, pulling out stickers with each step. From the top of the porch, I shielded my eyes and tried to see my grandmother.

No sign of her, but a man passing by in a motorboat waved.

I waved back.

He slowed. "You Allie?" he yelled when he was almost to the dock.

I nodded.

He bobbed his head and revved the little outboard en-gine. "I'll tell Mrs. Deals you're here," he called and mo-tored on down the lake as a tiny wave rippled from his boat and flapped against the shore.

"You do that," I mumbled wondering who Mrs. Deals was and how this old-man-in-the-lake knew my name.

Of course, I decided, Uncle Jefferson must have talked about me. The uncle I didn't have had told his friends I didn't know that I was coming.

I limped back into the store and followed the sound of Nana's voice. I should have guessed she'd head straight to the kitchen, her favorite room in every house.

When I opened the swinging door, she was standing in a neat little kitchen with a MoonPie in each hand. The under-the-bed monster sat less than two feet from her, reaching his big, dirty hand for one of the pies.

The noise I made sounded more like the squeak of an untied balloon than a scream, but it was enough to make the intruder twist around to face me.

The bluest eyes in Texas stared at me. For a moment, all I saw was their color. They were the twilight sky during a storm. Dark, rich, and sparked with lightning.

"There's Allie," Nana said as she handed him the MoonPie. "I told you she was around. She's an artist, you know. Does strange things now and then, like tells me to lock the door against spiders, but I love her anyway."

My grandmother had been introducing me like that for as long as I could remember. Telling everyone I was talented, but strange. To my knowledge no teacher from the first grade through college had ever agreed with her, about the talent, anyway. I might love art and try from time to time to paint or draw, but I seemed to be missing one small necessity: skill. I seemed destined to only show at refrigerator-sized galleries.

My grandmother continued, "Luke, I'd like you to meet Allie Daniels."

Grateful the dirty man with the bluest eyes didn't offer his hand, I stared at him for a moment before he turned back to Nana. He could have been anywhere from thirty to forty. His face was too square to be handsome; his dark brown hair needed cutting. His body rounded in the chair as if he tried to take up less space than his big frame required. I thought of asking him why he'd been under the bed but I wasn't sure I was ready for the answer.

"Luke was just telling me he lives next door." Nana pointed toward the wooded area. "He says he can help out around the place if we need anything done."

"We don't need help." More honestly, I couldn't afford to pay anyone. I didn't realize my words might seem unkind until they'd already exited my mouth.

The big man stood to go. His clothes hung around him. He was more tall than thick.

"I'll be going then," he said without looking at me as he slipped out the open back door and vanished.

"We don't need help, Nana," I repeated.

She nodded, understanding more what I hadn't said than what I had. Without a word, she began cleaning the kitchen. The counters were worn, the sink had a chip the size of a quarter out of one side, the refrigerator light blinked on and off while the door was open, but other than that, the place looked better than most where we'd cooked. There was no food, but all the pots, pans, and knives seemed to be there along with a working double oven.

By late afternoon, we had both the kitchen and the two rooms upstairs at least livable. I tossed out all of Uncle Jefferson's medicine bottles along with the fishing magazines. Guessing from the full bottles, it looked like he quit taking his pills about six months ago. My detective brain cells reasoned that a man not taking his medicine wouldn't drive into town to pick up new prescriptions, so someone must have been bringing them to him. Someone who didn't bother to make sure he took them.

Another fact nagged at the back of my mind while I worked. Why would a man who'd stopped taking medicine leave the bottles around?

Nana's take on Uncle Jefferson was slightly different. She noticed that it appeared he didn't leave a clean stitch of clothing. According to her, he hung on to life until everything was dirty, then he kicked the bucket rather than do laundry.

I suggested maybe Blue-Eyed Luke stole the clean

clothes, but after a quick inventory we discovered my uncle Jefferson was a small man. His clothes would almost fit me so he couldn't have stood over five-feet-five and, judging from the piles of dirty things, he owned no underwear or socks.

Once we found an old ringer-washer in a shed out back, Nana wanted to wash his clothes, but I convinced her to burn most of them. The fabric was too worn to even make good rags. I saved back the few flannel shirts in good condition for myself and dropped the rest out the window. We carried them down to a campfire pit close to the water and poured enough gasoline over the pile to get a good fire going.

An hour before sunset, Nana went to the kitchen to fix our supper. She'd had me move the two old wingback chairs down from the apartment. We shoved them into what must have been built as a breakfast nook in the kitchen. She added a table big enough for two and a little black-and-white TV. Then she pulled out her sewing basket that she hadn't unpacked from the van for two moves and placed it in front of one of the chairs as a stool.

I hadn't liked the idea, but once she'd spread a cloth over the table the little space seemed to welcome us, a private little parlor in the corner of the kitchen.

Climbing the stairs, I wished we had enough furniture to make the apartment above as livable. My grandmother might not ever be able to change her environment, but that didn't mean she couldn't rearrange it. I hoped the outbuildings we hadn't gotten to yet contained furniture, otherwise we'd use boxes for nightstands by the beds.

"Allie," she called up from the kitchen. "You want catfish for supper?"

"Sure," I answered, thinking she was kidding.

A few minutes later I smelled fish frying. The aroma

drew me down the stairs. I hadn't had my grandmother's catfish since we'd left the farm.

"Where'd you get fish?" I asked as I came into the kitchen.

"Found it in the sink, so fresh I swear it was still wiggling." Nana giggled. "Maybe it swam up the drain."

I wouldn't have been surprised, but I wasn't about to look a gift fish in the mouth. I carried in the box of cooking supplies and combined them with the few staples Nana discovered stored in the freezer near the back door. We had enough to serve fried potatoes and hush puppies with the fish.

After we were both so full we could eat no more, Nana covered the leftovers with a tea towel and set them in the oven as she'd done every night of my childhood. Grandpa's supper left to warm.

I started to mention her mistake, but a forty-year-old habit must be hard to break. The year after he'd died, many a morning I'd scraped dishes that she'd left in the oven, but since we'd been traveling she'd stopped the practice. Maybe because we usually didn't have leftovers. Or maybe because she never felt at home . . . until now.

She waved good night and headed upstairs without a word.

I cleaned up the kitchen and walked out back to make sure the fire I'd built with old clothes hadn't gotten out of hand. It might not look too good to burn down the property on my first day at the lake.

I was almost to the campfire before I noticed a shadow sitting close to the dying flames, his back to the house, his shoulders rounded forward.

"Luke?" I whispered. If he planned to kill us, he'd had all day to do it.

Blue Eyes turned around and stared at me. In the smoky

firelight I swear I saw an intelligence in his gaze that would miss little. "Allie Daniels," he whispered as if testing his memory.

I moved closer. "Thanks for the fish."

He nodded so slightly I wasn't sure I'd seen it. "I figured Old Jefferson would have wanted you to have fish your first night on the lake."

"You knew him?"

Luke nodded again. "I came out summers to fish as a kid. He served with my granddad in the army. They'd fish all day and tell war stories half the night."

"Know much about him?"

Luke shook his head. "I hadn't been out in years. After my grandfather died, I always planned to drop by, but I only made it once in the past ten years."

He looked out over the lake and I waited him out.

Finally, he added, "I know his mother's relatives founded this place over a hundred years ago. Worked a ferry service across the creek. He was named after them, and this dock has been called Jefferson's Crossing since the first settlers passed by here."

I liked the name. I liked having a place with a name and not just an address. Before I thought to stop, my fears babbled out. "I think he made a mistake leaving it to me."

Luke didn't answer. He just stirred the rags around as the last of Jefferson's old clothes burned. He was as easy to read as a billboard. Plain and simple. A loner who didn't like people. Every inch of his body seemed to be telling me to leave.

"How far do you live from here?" I said, sounding more like an interrogator than a neighbor.

"Not far," he answered, staring at me. "You finished growing?"

I hated comments about my height, or lack of it, but

since I'd asked a personal question I guess he thought he had a right. I raised an eyebrow in challenge. "Which way?"

His blue eyes glanced down at my chest and I felt like I was back in junior high when I'd first developed. Then, I swear, he blushed when he finally met my gaze. A slow smile lifted the corner of his mouth. "Sorry, maybe I should have said, 'How old are you?' With those pigtails you could be fifteen."

"I'm twenty-six."

He nodded and moved away from the fire as if that was all he needed to know about me.

Feeling a chill, I watched the fire glowing in the night and tried to think of something to say. But I didn't really want company and I guess he didn't either. Every bone in my body hurt from cleaning, and a part of my mind was still mourning the "might have been" part of inheriting this place. I'd hoped for a cottage, not a big, old building that looked like it was put together with spare supplies. The store was empty, the café old and useless, and the apartment barely livable.

Trying to think positive, I listed as likes the big windows facing the lake and the huge rock wall that made the place seem like it had been part of this land forever. Also, if I was listing, I'd have to add Nana's joy. She'd been humming gospel songs all day.

The moon came out and the air chilled, but I kept staring at the fire, forgetting Luke. I closed my eyes and listened to the sounds of the lake. A bird called somewhere on the other side. Every few minutes the splash of a fish or frog rippled the water now black in the night. A low buzz of summer's last surviving insects stuttered in the air like a faraway telegraph. I could feel my heart slow to the rhythm.

The creak of wood along the dock ten yards away sounded and I looked up. Luke was gone.

It took a few minutes for my eyes to focus enough to see his form moving slowly along the dock over the water. He walked, removing his clothes fluidly as if he'd done it a thousand times.

His last stitch of clothing fell just before he dove into the water, slicing through with barely a ripple.

I stood, making out powerful arms reflecting in moonlight as he swam in long strokes toward the center of the lake. I could still hear his movements even after I lost sight of him in the inky water.

If it had been a normal day, I might have reacted to a strange man stripping and diving off my dock, but I hadn't had a normal day in so long I wouldn't recognize one if it came along.

I walked back to the house, locked the doors, and went up to bed.

Chapter 6

2300 hours
Twisted Creek

Luke swam the lake trying to clear his mind. The strange woman unnerved him. She had an innocence about her, but at twenty-six, it had to be an act. He'd long ago given up taking people at face value. In his line of work everyone had secrets. Everyone had a past.

She was a rare mix though. A shy honesty about her blended with a body that would haunt his dreams. When he'd met her, he was sure he saw fear in her eyes, but tonight Allie had wandered out to the fire as if she trusted him. She hadn't flirted at all, but she had to have known he was watching her. He decided the safest way to handle Allie Daniels was not to handle her at all . . . friendship, that's what he'd offer, and nothing more until he knew who he was dealing with.

When he returned to the dock, she was gone. He wasn't sure if he was glad or disappointed. The fire had died, leaving the dock so dark that he had to feel for his clothes.

He tugged on his jeans and carried the rest. Dropping off the side of the dock, he walked in the ankle-deep water until he circled onto his property, then crossed into the blackness of the trees. Scolding himself, he decided to be more withdrawn around her, telling her nothing. Despite her innocent act, if Jefferson's death was not from natural causes, she was the most likely suspect.

Forcing his brain to look at only the facts, he reasoned: She had the most to gain from Jefferson's death. For all he knew, the outdated tags on her van were stolen and she lived somewhere around here. Allie could have somehow worked her way into Jefferson's good graces in the five years since Luke had visited the old man and talked him into leaving her the place. Then, she couldn't wait for him to die naturally, so she helped him along. Even if she was small, how hard could it be to push an old man off the dock?

He laughed as he stepped onto the porch of his one-room log cabin. His theory didn't hold water. Nana and Allie didn't fit any profile of any kind of criminals. Allie didn't seem the type to murder and he couldn't imagine Nana driving the getaway van.

But that didn't clear the fact that something was going on out here at the lake. Luke had seen signs. If someone had killed Jefferson, they might have done so because he noticed something he shouldn't have seen. When he'd circled the lake on foot yesterday, Luke swore he smelled meth cooking, even if he couldn't find it. Half the cabins out here, including his own, weren't on any map anywhere.

A chilling thought crossed his mind. If someone killed Jefferson Platt, he might go after Allie and Nana next.

Luke locked his door, then walked past his couch and swung up to a tiny loft in the rafters of his cabin. He'd slept there as a kid and now the space barely accommodated his six-foot height, but if someone came through the door, he'd be wide awake before they could spot him.

In his line of work it paid to be where people did not expect him to be.

Chapter 7

Sometime after dawn, I smelled biscuits baking. Without bothering to open my eyes, I took a deep breath knowing the aroma was just a hangover from my dreams. I wanted to enjoy it as long as possible. Last night I'd planned to stay awake and worry about which bed Uncle Jefferson spent his last night on, but I'd fallen asleep before I could get all my worries organized.

Between no job, little hope of money coming in, and a nude man jumping off my dock to chase the moon across the lake, I felt like I had my quota of problems. The lake house hadn't been what I'd hoped for in Garrison D. Walker's letter, but then nothing in my life ever measured up to the mountain of hope I always managed to come up with. If they gave awards for pointless dreaming, I'd have a room full of trophies.

Opening one eye, I noticed Nana had raised all the windows in our two-room apartment. The morning had a chill to it that the bright sunshine would burn away long before noon. The breeze smelled of the lake. Nothing bad. Just that earthy odor of fish and water.

I stood, pulled on my grandpa's old flannel shirt I'd used as a robe since college, and headed downstairs following the hope of biscuits. The main room at the bottom of the steps smelled cellarlike with the windows still boarded up. To my left were the empty shelves that had once been a tiny store. To my right sat the little café with round tables, wire chairs, and a long bar. I'd passed the rooms too many times yesterday for them not to feel familiar to me.

Tiptoeing across the floor, I forced myself not to look at the dead animal heads on the wall, but their shadows crossed my path. Deer, antelope, wild sheep, and some kind of ugly pig I'd glanced at yesterday and been afraid to face again. When I pushed open the swinging door to the kitchen, I let out a breath as if I'd just run the gauntlet.

Nana swayed as she hummed "Amazing Grace." I slipped into the sunny little room that already looked like it belonged to her. My grandmother must have been up for hours, for she'd removed the burlap curtains and polished the two windows over the sink. She'd stacked her rooster-painted tins of staples along the sill. She'd also opened the back door, letting in long beams of sunlight to dance over a worn brick floor. Her gray hair bounced slightly as she kept time to her humming with little nods of her head.

A cookie sheet of fresh biscuits cooled on the table. "Where?" was all I managed to mumble. I raked one hand through my tangled hair and tried again. "Where did these biscuits come from?"

Nana turned and winked at me. "A nice man in a white truck stopped by about an hour ago. He said he always delivered dairy to Jefferson and wondered if I wanted any. I told him I needed pretty near one of everything."

I opened the old refrigerator. Milk, butter, cheese, and eggs filled the top shelves.

"I got you something in the freezer." She turned back to the gravy she'd been stirring.

"Cherry Popsicles." I laughed and pulled one out. Slamming the middle of the treat on the edge of the counter, I broke it in half and slid an icicle into my mouth.

I hadn't had a Popsicle since I'd been in grade school and was surprised my grandmother remembered how dearly I once loved them. I curled into one of the wingback chairs and let the icy treat freeze my tongue while I waited for the frozen juice to melt just enough to bite into.

Pulling my feet up to the seat of the chair, I hugged my legs, trying to keep warm as I ate. The sweet flavor sliding down my throat was worth every shiver.

Finally, I asked, "How'd you pay the man in the white truck?" I'd stashed my purse, with the last of the traveling money, under my bed, but I knew Nana wouldn't have opened it even if I'd left it in the kitchen.

Nana shrugged. "He said he'd put it on the account and that he'd see me next week." She never worried about money, probably because she'd never had any.

Shoving the warm pan toward me, she laughed. "I put a little cheese in the biscuits just like we used to do when I cooked at the grade school. Those kids always loved my recipes. I had one boy ask if his mother could come up and watch me cook. Another wanted to take me home for show-and-tell."

Picking at one biscuit, I worried. We had enough to pay for the groceries and the bills on this place for a few months, but the money would run out soon. The money always ran out. I thought of telling Nana to be careful, but she was having so much fun cooking with real supplies and remembering and, I didn't want to spoil it. Besides, there was a good chance I'd find a job before we got down to zero.

The problem was, any work would be back in Lubbock and that would mean leaving Nana out here alone for long hours.

She handed me a cup of coffee and I pushed aside problems with a smile. "What do you think we should do first?"

Nana frowned. "I'd like to get rid of all those heads in the front room. I think one of them winked at me."

I couldn't agree more. An hour later, we'd managed to take them down and line all the animal heads and stuffed fish up on the fence by the road. Nana wanted to put a FOR SALE sign out, but I just hoped someone would take them.

She shrugged her thin shoulders almost to her ears. "Maybe someone will steal them if we don't watch too close."

"That's about as likely as one of these critters running off. But we can always hope."

We went back to the house and started cleaning the area that had been a store. To my surprise, beneath the cash register I found a wide ledger filled with neat entries, each dated and balanced to the right. The totals showed Uncle Jefferson made a small profit most days. If so, what did he spend his money on? The lawyer said he had none at the time of his death except for what he wanted mailed to me for traveling expenses and lawyer's fees. There was no sign he'd bought anything, from clothes to furnishings, for thirty years. But if there was income, somewhere there had to be money going out. The only thing on the place that looked younger than me was the final ten feet of dock planks.

I shoved the ledger back under the register and pushed the "no sale" button. The drawer sprang open. Empty except for ten pennies and two nickels. I returned to dusting, plugging in the twinkle lights along the back wall.

Next to a potbelly stove old enough for Ben Franklin himself to have delivered, I found a small safe covered in dust. Most of the lettering on the two-by-two door had worn off and mud was caked to the sides. I rattled the handle, but it didn't open. If I strained, I could push it a few inches, but after a few minutes of effort I decided the safe would make a fine footstool to sit on when winter came and I lit the stove.

In a closet behind the twinkle lights, I found a bucket of cane fishing poles and a stack of dusty, but never used, blankets. I spread the blankets inside the display case and put the bucket in a corner. The place still didn't look like much of a store, but it was a start.

An hour later, the old fisherman I'd seen in the boat the day before stepped up on my porch as I was testing out one of the wicker chairs. "Morning," he muttered around a wad of tobacco, sticking out his hand. "I'm Willie Dowman. Got a fishing shack on the other end, close to the dam." He pointed with his head. "I was admiring that bass you got out by the road."

I fought down the need to question his taste. "Good morning, I'm Allie." I put my hand out to shake his.

He nodded, small little nods in rapid succession like his head was loose and we'd just hit a bump in the road. "I know. Jefferson told us you'd be coming."

Tugging my hand out of his sandpaper grip, I took a step backward, disturbed by the fact he must have known I was coming long before I did.

Nothing about Willie was the least bit threatening, but the short, square-built man smelled like a neglected aquarium. I wouldn't have been surprised to see algae growing out his ears.

"I used to come out on weekends to get away from my wife." His bushy eyebrows wiggled, doing the wave across his forehead. "Since I retired, I come out most every day."

"Why don't you leave her and move out here?" I asked just to see what he'd say.

Willie looked like he thought about it for a minute, then shook his head. "Who'd cook all the fish I catch if I left her?"

I asked him who Mrs. Deals was since he'd yelled that he planned to tell her I had arrived. But talking to Willie wasn't easy. We might be standing eye to eye, but somehow I got the feeling he was having a different conversation than I was. He never answered the questions I asked, but rambled on about people I didn't know as if they were family. Talking to Willie made my head hurt.

I moved inside out of the sun and he followed, taking the third stool at the bar as if it were his assigned seat. I introduced him to Nana and they both nodded at each other in greeting.

After haggling for a while, he finally agreed to pay me three dollars and a bushel of apples for the mounted fish. The money smelled of bait and the apples he brought in looked like he'd picked them off the ground by a wild apple tree. I wondered if I'd been had, but he was hauling off a stuffed bass so the deal couldn't be all bad. We shook on it.

"What did you do for a living before you retired?" I asked just out of curiosity.

He grinned. "As little as possible."

Then, without a hint of barter, he offered a buck for two of Nana's biscuits. She wrapped them in waxed paper and handed them to him across the pass-through.

Ten minutes later, the mailman drove up in a battered, blue hatchback and delivered a sack of mail.

"I've been holding this till you got here," he grumbled as though angry that it took me so long to show up. "All you got to do is put it in order and the folks around will pick it up. You're the one drop I'm allowed in this area."

I peeked in the bag. Most of it looked like catalogues for fishing equipment.

The mailman nodded his good-bye as if he were in a hurry, but stopped at the road to talk to Willie, who was hauling the bass to his truck.

Wondering why the mailman had been so unfriendly, I studied him from the porch. He was a tall, thin guy in his forties with thinning hair and fingers so long they must have had an extra knuckle in there somewhere. Alien hands, I decided, like E.T.

I laughed suddenly. So far all the men I'd met in Texas seemed strange. Luke, my under-the-bed monster, was turning out to be the best of the lot. Though he wasn't exactly handsome, he was a lot easier on the eyes and nose than the other two.

Almost as if he heard me thinking of him, Luke stepped from the side of the house.

"Morning," he managed.

"Morning," I answered.

When the mailman crunched back across the gravel in front of the porch, Luke slipped into the shadows.

"Sorry, miss," the mailman began. "But I have to have the bag back. It's U.S. Postal property." The spider of a man looked as if he thought I might make a run for it with his official bag.

I dumped the rest of the mail out on the porch.

As the mailman watched me, I asked, "Want to buy one of the heads out by the fence?"

"Nope," he answered, "but you got any more of those biscuits? Willie said you were selling them. Jefferson never had anything worth eating to sell with his coffee."

I led him to the pass-through window.

Nana wrapped two more biscuits and passed them along with a small paper cup of coffee. "The coffee's free to uniformed men," she said, "but the biscuits will cost you."

While the mailman folded back into his hatchback, a dented Mustang rattled down my road, pulling a flatbed trailer with two canoes. Boys, so young they must have been skipping school, asked if they could set their boats off from the dock.

I couldn't think of a reason to say no. While Nana wrapped more biscuits, I helped them unload.

When I walked back from the dock, I noticed Luke standing by the side of the house watching. "Did you mean it about helping out?" I yelled.

"Yep," he answered without looking overly interested.

I decided to spend a few more dollars of my traveling money. "I could pay you ten bucks an hour, plus meals, if you'd help me get this place in shape."

He nodded once. "What'll we do first?"

I looked around. The list was endless. "How about we clean out the rest of Jefferson's things from upstairs?"

He followed me up and we worked without talking.

By noon, Nana had made twelve dollars in biscuit sales and I'd made another three off a deer head.

After a lunch of soup and sugar cookies—left over from our dollar-store raid—Nana decided to cut the good parts out of the pitiful apples I'd traded with Willie and make fried apple pies. While she baked, I tackled the boards covering the front windows.

I didn't think it would be hard. I'd seen men put the hook of a hammer between a board and a wall, then pop it off. Only problem was whoever nailed the planks over the windows forgot to leave any room for the hook. After five minutes of struggling, I had splinters in my palm and had managed to hit myself in the knee with the hammer. All the boards were still in place.

Manual labor had never been my strong suit, but you'd think with two years of college I could manage to get a few boards down. I'd even tried using a few carpenter swear words Nana wouldn't notice, like "screw you, you knotholed plank."

It didn't work.

I wasn't surprised when Luke stepped onto the porch and took the hammer away from me. I must have looked like an idiot. His big hand wrapped around the first board and with a tug he loosened it.

In the sunlight I could see that he wasn't near as dirty as I thought. His clothes were worn, but relatively clean. He wore a pair of hiking boots and an old fishing jacket. He didn't look directly at me. I caught myself wishing he would, just so I could see his blue eyes.

I shook my head, disgusted with myself. I wasn't nearly as starved for a man as I was for color. It was pathetic.

While Luke worked, I sat on the porch and sorted the mail, tossing most of it in a plastic laundry basket with my uninjured hand.

He made easy work of the boards, then lifted them over his shoulder and carried them to one of the sheds. I'd waited for him to say something when he returned. He didn't. I couldn't think of any way to open a conversation.

To my surprise, he lowered on one knee beside my chair and pulled a knife from his pocket. It was one of those expensive kinds that could do anything. Pulling the tweezers from the end, he took my hand and began pulling out splinters with no regard to my yelps.

I tried to pull away several times, but he held my hand firmly against his bent knee until he was finished.

The nearness of him made me nervous. He wasn't flirting; in fact, he wasn't even friendly.

When he finally let go and folded up his knife, I cradled my hand and said, "Great bedside manner, Doc."

He shrugged as if he could care less what I thought. "Get some antiseptic on that. Jefferson used to keep it in his desk drawer."

After picking up the hammer, he was halfway to the shed when I yelled, "Thank you."

He didn't even turn around.

Wandering back inside, I opened a few bills addressed to Jefferson Platt. None were overdue, telling me that for some reason Uncle Jefferson paid his bills in advance.

Tucked between two shelves, I found a neat little office space complete with an old Hunter desk and a lamp. The half-moon desk had nothing on it but a dented juice can full of pencils, another ledger like the one I'd found beneath the cash register, and a half-used tube of antiseptic. The top of each shelf was lined with file boxes, dusty from years of storage. I made a mental note to check in them when I had the time. Anything that dusty couldn't be too important and the reading would be no more interesting than the other ledger.

As I rubbed a few drops of the antiseptic on my palm, I searched the tiny office for any clue as to who Jefferson Platt had been. There were no personal documents. No pictures. Not even an old calendar with dates marked out. I opened the one file box I could reach to find receipts dated in the eighties.

I had the strange feeling Uncle Jefferson cleaned up everything in his office before he died. Or someone else had. How could he be so neat about some things and leave his rooms upstairs such a mess? I wasn't surprised to find the second ledger empty. I almost felt like he'd counted his days off in the old ledger, then left the new one for me. But how could he have? I didn't even know the man.

But Luke had. He'd even known where Jefferson kept the medicine. I decided I needed to have a long talk with Mr. Blue Eyes.

"Company coming up the road," Nana yelled even before I heard a car.

I didn't make it to the front door before someone pounded on it full force.

I thought of darting up the stairs and yelling that I'd seen enough strangers for one day, but whoever it was didn't sound like he had much patience.

Reluctantly, I opened the door.

The uniformed man before me eclipsed the late-afternoon sun. He had to be close to six-six and wore a hat that added another three or four inches. The gun belt around his ample waist held enough ammo to wage war. Though he didn't look much over forty, his sideburns were the same silver of his Colt.

"Miss Daniels?" He smiled down at me as if he were talking to a child. "Allie Daniels?"

"Yes." I straightened to all five-feet-one of me and stared at the lawman. "May I help you?" The only reason I could imagine that he'd be here was that he'd figured out I wasn't supposed to have this place and he'd come to evict me.

The huge man laughed. "You ain't much bigger than a chigger, darlin'."

I stepped back and waved him in as anger settled over nervousness. Why was it some people think it is fine to comment on my stature yet I can't return the insult?

I mentally continued to add up the lawman's crimes when he used an endearment. I swear, I'd been born hating men who call all women "dear" or "honey" or "darling." It always made me feel more like a product than a person.

"Hot out there for September." He walked into the store part of the main room and looked around as if he had a right to inspect the premises. "You've done a good job of cleaning up the place. Last time I was in here, Jefferson was closing it down and there was trash everywhere."

He glanced back at me and straightened as he added, "I'm Sheriff Raymond Fletcher. Just dropped in to meet you and let you know I'm around if you have any problems."

"I'm—"

He didn't give me time to finish. Strike three.

"Oh, I know all about you. Jefferson told me you'd be coming." The sheriff propped his foot on one of the stools running alongside the bar.

I was getting a little tired of hearing that everyone knew I was coming, but I didn't comment. The giant seemed more interested in talking to himself than anyone else, so I saw no need in interrupting.

"That old man said he made a good living out of this place, but I don't see how. After September there's no one out here during the week but what I call the Nesters. I come out and check on them regular just to make sure one of them hasn't died or started up some other kind of trouble in my county. No matter how much of a nothing this little lake settlement is, it's part of my jurisdiction. I make a point of knowing what's going on in my county."

"Nesters," I squeaked like the chorus in a doo-wop band.

Sheriff Fletcher grinned. "That's what I call the people who live out here year-round. Misfits mostly. Folks people in town wouldn't put up with." He walked toward the passthrough and continued his lecture. "Now on the weekends you'll find lots of fishermen and a few of them mountain-bike riders showing up if it's not raining." He winked. "I don't allow any of them four-wheeling trash. Cut up the trails, you know, and make all kinds of noise."

He lifted his chin and narrowed his eyes just a fraction as though it occurred to him that I might be one of them.

Luke backed through the swinging door with a tray of fresh, hot pies. He took one look at the sheriff's back and returned to the kitchen. With the next swing of the door, Nana came out carrying the same tray. They'd switched so fast it reminded me of the little doors on a cuckoo clock.

"Sheriff Fletcher, I'd like you to meet my grandmother," I said, wondering why Luke hid in the kitchen and wishing I'd been smart enough to join him when I'd heard the sheriff's knock.

Nana set the tray down on the counter.

The lawman turned slowly, not taking his gaze off me until politeness forced him to acknowledge Nana.

"Afternoon, Sheriff," Nana said. "I'm glad you dropped by. I was hoping to get someone to try my pies. I haven't made them in years, but I think I remembered my momma's recipe."

Removing his hat, he nodded toward her. "Pleased to meet you, ma'am."

I was "darling' " and my grandmother was "ma'am." I couldn't help but wonder if it was age, or the pies, that garnered respect from the sheriff.

He walked over and picked up one of the miniature pastries. "I'd be glad to test them for you."

Five minutes and four pies later, Sheriff Fletcher and Nana were talking as if they'd been friends for years. Neither seemed to notice when I picked up the broom and stepped out onto the porch.

I could still hear their conversation. Nana asked if he

had kids and Fletcher listed all the grand points of his sixteen-year-old son, Dillon, before adding, "I got a daughter who married right out of high school, but my boy is going to go all the way through college. Criminal Justice, you know. I'll bet in ten years he'll be in the FBI. I taught him to shoot when he was five and he knows the law as well as I do. He's been begging to go with me in the squad car since he could talk."

Nana packed a few pies for the sheriff and as she walked him to the porch he told them he'd be back on Monday. As he drove away, she whispered, "Luke said he doesn't like that man."

I looked up from sweeping, hating to admit that I agreed with the lake bum I'd found hiding under my bed. "Did Luke say why?"

Nana watched the sheriff's car clear the gate. "Said he thinks he's better than folks around here."

"Luke sure does a lot of talking to you. He never says more than a few words around me." In truth, I could swear he'd been avoiding me as much as possible.

Nana shrugged. "Maybe I listen." She walked back into the house. I didn't have to ask where she was going. I knew it would be the kitchen. Her soap opera was about to come on. She'd fix her one cup of tea for the day and sit in front of the little TV. Then, when it was over, she'd go back to work, fretting about the soap opera stars' problems as if they were her own.

While the TV blared, I found a quart of green paint and spent the hour painting trim around the old shelves. If we got kicked out of here tomorrow, at least I would leave the place better than I found it.

I wasn't surprised Luke had disappeared. A few hours of work was probably more than he wanted to do, otherwise why else would he live at the lake? There was a hardness about him and I wondered if it was a shell, or went all the way to the bone.

Not that it mattered. He wasn't my type.

I laughed suddenly, realizing I didn't have a type. Unless you count losers. I remembered one guy who'd gone four dates before he talked me out of my clothes and then never called again. The loss of him didn't matter as much as the feeling that he thought I must not have been worth the bother. I couldn't even say he was my first love. I was twenty-six and never had a first love. A few one-night stands I regretted. A few boyfriends who left before they had to use the "L" word. A few almost, who never worked out.

No loves.

After supper, I curled into the bay window seat and watched the sun set. The lake seemed so still, so lonely. I leaned back against the windowpane and listened to Nana run her hand across her wind chime. She'd hung it in the kitchen just as she always did. As always, the music it played made me smile and feel at home.

A while later, she passed by and kissed me on the head. "Good night, dear," she said. "I'm turning in. Sleeping is always good on cool, cloudy nights." Her old hand patted my shoulder three times. I love you without words. "Are you heading up?"

I shook my head. "I think I'll stay down here for a while." I lifted the blank ledger as if it contained something inside for me to do.

Nana turned and climbed the stairs.

Just after dark I noticed a fire burning in the pit out by the dock. The day had been endless. We'd cleaned both upstairs and downstairs. While Nana had washed and hung clothes on a line out back, I had explored the outbuildings. One had worthless tools in it, another parts of old boats. Behind the buildings, several old cars had been parked and left to rust. None looked like they would be worth hauling into Lubbock to try to sell.

The only thing I'd found of interest was a fat cat. He stared at me awhile, then decided to follow me inside. Nana called him General and offered him milk. From then on he was more at home in the kitchen than we were.

I grinned. Having a pet made it seem even more like home.

As a fog settled in around Jefferson's Crossing, I went up to bed. The air felt heavy with the smells of the day—paint, baking, and cleaners. Our rooms were stark, almost cell-like now that we'd thrown all of Uncle Jefferson's junk away. I promised myself I'd let Nana buy a few pots of those plastic flowers she liked at the dollar store and maybe some curtains. A few touches would help.

After an hour, Nana was snoring and I hadn't closed my eyes. I decided I'd landed in purgatory. Somehow, we were stuck in a location that wasn't heaven or hell. We had food and a roof, but no dreams. Once I got the place clean, I had no idea what I'd do.

Drive into town and look for a job, I answered myself, then frowned. Part of me didn't want to leave.

I climbed out of bed and walked to the window. In the years of traveling around, I'd somehow forgot to pack my dreams in one of the moves. When I'd been in school, I'd always felt I was waiting to live—that somehow life lay just around the corner ready to take my breath away. I'd be working in a famous art museum somewhere, talking to creative people, jetting off with friends or at worst teaching at a fine private school and saving my money to travel with Nana in the summer months.

Nowhere in those dreams had there been endless, mind-numbing jobs and people who thought becoming floor manager would be the ultimate measure of success. Not one dream had even hinted at an old lake house on a muddy bank in the middle of Texas.

Staring out at the water, black except for the reflections of firelight dancing along its ripples, I longed for the beauty of the masters. As I stared, the tall form of Luke moved against the firelight that seemed muted in the foggy night.

My curiosity rose as he lifted the basket I'd tossed all the useless mail in that morning. Slowly feeding the fire, he let the catalogues and magazines tumble into the flames.

"He'll set the whole north shore on fire," I whispered as I grabbed my flannel shirt and ran for the stairs.

At the edge of the porch, I tugged at a rolled water hose and charged down beside the dock toward the flames dancing almost as high as Luke's shadow. Maybe my under-the-bed monster wasn't going to kill us. Maybe he'd be happy just to burn us out.

Ten feet from the fire, I reached the end of the hose and almost fell backward with the sudden stop. I pointed the drizzle of water at Luke. "What in the hell do you think you're doing?"

He turned and put down the empty basket. Though his face was in shadow, I could tell by the angle of his head that he studied me. "More pointedly," he mumbled, "what are *you* doing?"

The drip from the hose tinkled across my toes and I jumped with the sudden cold. Tossing the worthless water hose aside, I took a step toward him. My foot sank into the puddle I'd just created.

I straightened, trying to ignore the disgusting sensation of cold mud moving between my toes. "We have to put the fire out," I said far more calmly than I felt. "Not build it bigger." I noticed several big chunks of driftwood at the base of the campfire. Luke had planned for a big fire.

He didn't move, just stared at me with that what-kind-of-alien look he had whenever he faced me.

Straightening, I tried not to notice that I was only wearing a thin T-shirt that didn't quite cover my panties. I pulled the flannel shirt around me.

His eyes met mine. Those blue eyes were guarded now, giving away nothing.

I picked up the basket and headed for the lake. "If you're not going to help me, I'll do it myself. I'm not about to go to sleep with this fire blazing a few feet from the dock. If it catches the walkway on fire, it'll burn right up to the house."

Two feet from the water, the bank turned slippery with mud.

I told myself it didn't matter. I was on a mission. This place might not be much, and I might not have it for long, but I had no intention of losing it to fire.

Mud caked my ankles by the time I was close enough to bail water out of the lake. I made it back to the fire, sloshing and leaking more water than I had remaining in the basket.

I could have spit and done more good.

I tried again and again while Luke watched me. If he hadn't been a foot taller than me, I would have given serious consideration to clobbering him.

On my fourth trip to the lake, I heard a splashing sound coming from the water. I stared out into the blackness. The fog had grown so thick I couldn't see more then ten feet.

The sound came again, like someone slapping at the surface with even beats.

At this point, if the Loch Ness monster came up out of the depths, I wouldn't have bothered to scream.

"Hello!" someone yelled. A moment later a pair of long canoes sliced through the darkness toward us.

"Thanks." The boy in the first boat laughed. "We were too far out to see where to dock. If you hadn't lit the fire, we'd have been on the lake all night."

Luke waded into the shallow water and helped the boys tug their boats in.

"You got any more of them biscuits?" one thin kid asked as he warmed by the fire. "We flipped the canoe that carried all our food."

I nodded and invited them in. While they loaded their boats onto the trailer, I duckwalked back trying to fling off as much mud as possible before I tracked it into the house.

Scrambled eggs defined the limit of my cooking skills. That, added to the fried pies, seemed to keep the four teenagers happy. They sat in a line on the stools, inhaling the food and coffee while they talked about their grand adventure.

I had a feeling it would be even more exciting by the time they got home.

"How much?" one finally asked when his plate appeared licked clean.

When I looked confused he added, "For the food."

"Nothing," I said. I would have fed them even if they hadn't a dime.

The boys stood and left, thanking me.

When I turned back to clean the plates, I found a twenty in the tip box.

Chapter 8

Wednesday
September 18, 2006
2200 hours

Luke stayed out on the porch telling himself he needed to keep an eye on the fire, but he knew in truth he needed to keep his eyes off Allie.

She'd almost stopped his heart when she'd stepped from the fog into the firelight wearing nothing but a shirt he could almost see through and pink underwear.

Pink panties. Dear God. Didn't she know that women out of their teens wore black, or red, or even white, not pink? At least he thought they did. He couldn't really say he'd had a great deal of experience researching the matter.

But there she stood, her hair reflecting in the firelight, her breasts high and pointed, and her pink panties showing—her eyes blazing at him like she wanted to throttle him.

Luke thought of explaining, but he was having far too much fun watching her storm around.

Then, when she'd realized why he'd built the fire, she didn't even look in his direction. No thank-you. Nothing.

Luke leaned against the porch railing and stared into the night. Allie Daniels was messing with his mind. Hell, the sight of her was messing with his body. He was a man who prided himself on always being in control. He liked his job, it challenged him. And he liked having no complications in his private life.

Shifting his weight, he realized he had no private life. The only reason he'd taken time off from work was to investigate Jefferson's death. He didn't just work for the ATF in drug enforcement, he *was* the badge he carried. Most nights he left the office, stopped off for fast food, then did paperwork until he couldn't keep his eyes open. He kept his life and the people he met in neat little files.

She might not be a suspect, but she was definitely a person of interest in this investigation.

He shook his head as the sound of her laughter drifted onto the porch.

It was late. Luke needed to bank the fire and get some sleep. He had predawn plans at a few of the houses he'd found on the west shore. The more he walked the land of this lake, the more the place smelled of trouble.

But as he stepped off the porch, all he could think about was pink panties.

Chapter 9

After I did the dishes, I walked back out to the porch and noticed Luke had let the fire burn low. Sitting on the first step, I watched him move onto the dock. The one yard light still burning appeared fuzzy now that the fog had turned into a slow rain.

Tomorrow I'd say I was sorry for acting like an idiot. If he hadn't built the fire, the teenagers would have spent a miserable night on the lake at the least. I felt bad for not even remembering their old car parked over beside the junkers. The day had been so long it seemed like a week had passed since they'd asked to shove off from my dock.

A thin smugglers' moon rose, offering just enough light for me to make out Luke. He walked down the long dock toward the water as he had the night before. In fluid movements, he removed his clothes without slowing his stride, dropping them carelessly. The outline of his form was long and lean, powerful with movement and as natural as an animal in his element.

He dove into the water, his hands over his head, and sliced the midnight lake as soundlessly as a shadow's passing. I sat motionless, listening to the whisper of his long strokes cutting into the water.

When I stepped back inside, the twinkle lights along the back wall greeted me and I was glad I'd left them up. I walked to the small office area tucked almost invisibly between tall shelves. I'd intended to turn off the desk lamp, but reached for a pencil from the can and opened the empty ledger instead. On the back of the first page, without lines to hamper me, I sketched what I'd seen in long bold strokes.

An hour later, I went to bed still thinking of the slim form stretched between land and lake. It might be Luke's body I drew, but somehow my feelings had poured across the paper.

In what seemed like minutes, I awoke to the sound of Nana talking to someone. It took me a few seconds to get my bearings. Sitting up, I decided Uncle Jefferson never put up doors on this apartment so he could hear anything going on downstairs. The stairwell acted like a megaphone to the second floor.

Bumps and scrapes rattled as if someone were moving bricks downstairs.

My first thought was that we were being robbed. But that seemed unlikely. Who would want anything on the ground level, or upstairs for that matter? Even the old safe was just a joke around the place. It seems Jefferson spent years trying to give the thing away but no one had the strength to carry it off.

I shoved my legs into jeans as I hopped toward the landing. I managed to pull on my shirt by the time I reached the stairs.

Now the voices were clear. I slowed, listening.

"I'll put the chips over here and the drinks here," a woman announced. "Where do you want the candy and bait?"

I reached the bottom of the steps to find a dozen boxes stacked in front of the shelves. "What's going on?" I asked to no one in particular.

A large woman, dressed like a man down to her black, round-toed shoes, faced me. She had short, curly hair that reminded me of Neapolitan ice cream. Her roots were white, then two inches of dark red. The tips were chocolate brown. "Howdy." She grinned and her clean-scrubbed face crinkled like twisted plastic wrap. "I'm Micki. Mrs. Deals called and told me you guys were moving in so I figured it was time for me to make a delivery."

Shaking my head, I tried to settle on which question to ask first. The smell of dead fish distracted me for a moment, then Willie Dowman wandered into my line of vision with a cup of coffee in his hand. He sat on the safe by the cold stove, propped his elbows on his knees, and watched.

Nana handed me a cup of coffee, then offered one to Micki, giving me a moment to think.

"Nice to meet you," I managed. "There must be some mistake. We didn't order a delivery, and I don't know a Mrs. Deals."

The woman lifted a clipboard. "Your uncle ordered this over two months ago. Said for me to deliver it when you arrived." Micki's smile sparked across her face and then was gone, replaced by an all-business stare. "I guess he figured you'd never know what was needed."

"I guess," I agreed.

Micki continued, "And Mrs. Deals is the old lady who lives down the road in that big house that reminds me of the Alamo. She's got more rooms in that thing than she can count. She also has the only dependable phone. Cells don't work out here half the time and most folks don't bother putting a line in at their cabins." She gave me the "duh" look middle school girls always seem to know. "Mrs. Deals keeps up with everything."

She pointed to a box marked "cookies." "My guess is she's missing her Milano cookies. Jefferson always stocked them for her. Said she never bought but one bag at a time like no one would notice that way."

I glanced at all the boxes marked with brand names for snacks, drinks, and candy. I decided on a more direct approach. "We can't pay for all this."

Micki shrugged. "Jefferson has an account and it's well in the black. All this stuff has already been paid for in full, plus the next couple of loads. He said he wanted you stocked for the fall. I left you our listing, but if you need something not on it we'll try to get it for you. I make my rounds once a week."

Willie and I watched as Micki unloaded another four boxes from her delivery van while Nana went back to the kitchen.

As the air filled with the smell of cinnamon rolls, the shelves behind the cash register filled with basic first-aid supplies, batteries, and cleaning supplies. The wire racks were loaded with candy and gum. Milanos and Oreos shared a spot right next to the door.

Micki stacked a few cans of soup and beans on the long wall shelves. "Your uncle usually kept the bait in his fridge in the kitchen, but I always thought he could have slid that old drink chest over here by the wall and plugged it in. The chest would keep the bait cool and be far away from any food. It made more sense, but Jefferson wasn't one to change."

I nodded in agreement and she relaxed as if she'd been saying the same thing for years and finally someone listened.

When I signed her clipboard, she snapped it shut and offered a friendly smile. "I'll help you move the chest." Then with a glance at her Timex, added, "I'm officially on my break now."

"Thanks, but does bait need to be cold?"

Micki winked. "So I've heard. I never caught anything but husbands. And some of them ended up smelling worse than warm worms." She wiggled her body. "In those days the bait I used for that kind of fishing was plenty hot, I can tell you."

We shoved the old drink chest across the floor.

Laughing, I asked, "Did you catch your limit?" I decided I liked the break-time Micki.

"I think that last one was over my limit. I should have stopped with three." She ripped a piece of paper from her clipboard. "I'll be back next week, but if you need anything, just tell Willie to tell Mrs. Deals and she'll call. I'll bring it out for no charge as long as the order's over a hundred."

I folded the paper and invited her to breakfast. Willie and Nana were already at the counter testing the cinnamon rolls.

She shook her head and moved her empty dolly toward the door. "No time today. This is Thursday and every little store from here to Lubbock needs supplies for the weekend." She waved. "Maybe next time."

Walking her to her delivery van, I wondered what might happen when the weekend hit. It seemed like we'd had company since we pulled up.

Before she started the engine, she rolled down her window and motioned me over. "Watch that old man," she whispered. "The Landry brothers who fish out here are fine, but that one." She raised an eyebrow.

"Willie?" He was the only man I could see.

She nodded. "Far as I know, he's never done anything more than brush against a few women, but I wanted to warn you anyway."

Great, I thought, I'd left Nana in the café with the lake pervert.

Micki started her engine and I hurried back inside.

I watched Willie Dowman while he ate, but saw no sign. I decided to make sure all the doors were locked at night.

To my shock, Nana stood up and hugged him good-bye. I was speechless. My Nana was a hugger, always had been, but if she knew . . . knew what, I reasoned. If I told her what Micki said she'd just tell me that she looked into his eyes and saw a good man. Nana was the one person in the world who had never listened to gossip and she wasn't likely to start now.

Willie paid for his roll and coffee and wished me a good day while I studied him. I decided if he ever did anything fresh I could probably knock him over with one blow. I also decided not to say anything, but to watch him until I knew for sure. If he showed one sign, I'd be calling the sheriff. I had a feeling Sheriff Fletcher would straighten him out.

After breakfast, I talked Nana into going to town. Since she'd already made more money than I had, maybe we should stock up on flour and sugar and make a few things the fishermen might eat.

About an hour later, I left Nana at United and drove over to the mall. Like a speed shopper, I bought sheets, pillows, curtains, and bath rugs. I might have to sleep on the bed

Uncle Jefferson left, but at least I'd do it on clean linen. I'd managed to catch everything but the pillows on sale. Walking to the car with all the bags, I felt rich for once.

When I got back to the grocery, Nana waited with two buggies full of supplies. I told myself we'd have to spend a little money to make money and didn't say a word as I paid the two-hundred-dollar bill.

We stopped for tacos on the way out of town and laughed as we ate them on the drive back.

As we pulled onto the lake road, Nana told the same story about Poor Flo and her mother washing in the creek. She'd often told stories again and again, but usually not this close together. I didn't want to hurt her feelings by mentioning it. Maybe it was just this place, or being back in Texas, but the past drifted thick across her mind.

"I loved Flo so much," she said after a few silent minutes. "I made her promise to never, ever leave me. I made her swear. I didn't want to grow up and old without her. I told her I needed her all my life, but she must not have been listening."

I reached over and took Nana's hand. Her memories were like her life, a mixture of happy and sad. She could no more have one without the other than she could have lived in days without the nights.

Once home, Luke showed up to help me carry in all the groceries. He didn't say anything, but I guessed he was waiting for an apology. I touched his shoulder once as he passed me with a load, but he didn't stop. I felt the solid muscle beneath his shirt, but short of tackling him I didn't know how to make him turn and give me time to say I was sorry.

When Nana offered him supper, he refused and disappeared without even glancing in my direction.

Before Nana's stew was ready, I sat in the wingback

chair in the corner of the kitchen and tried to figure out what I should charge for the goods that were stocked on our little store's shelves.

The wind chime rattled, telling me that someone had opened the front door. I jumped, feeling like we had our first real customer. I'd dusted everything and turned the labels out. I was ready.

When I entered the store, an old woman in a wool coat a size too large nodded at me, then raised one eyebrow and looked me over.

I nodded back, feeling like a shoplifter in my own store.

She picked up a two-pound bag of flour and a box of Milano cookies, but made no effort to speak to me.

"I'm not sure what to charge," I mumbled, embarrassed that I hadn't figured it all out before putting the OPEN sign on the front door.

The woman straightened even more and leveled me with her stare. "I know how much they are." She fished in her purse and pulled out three dollars and a quarter. "I'll need two cents in change, Allie."

I opened the cash register and handed her two pennies. "I'll get you a bag."

Running to the office, I found the sacks in the third box I tried. When I looked up, the old lady was gone.

I smiled all the way back to my seat in the kitchen. Once settled, I said simply, "I just met Mrs. Deals."

"Was she nice?" Nana asked.

"Very." I laughed. "And helpful." I figured Mrs. Deals was about as nice as she gets, and I didn't mind keeping the cookies in stock if there was any chance of sweetening her up.

"Willie said her son disappeared years ago. Most think he ran away from home." Nana talked as she worked. "Mrs. Deals moved out here thinking that if he ever did come back, he'd come here where he was happy. Willie said she paid a fortune to get that line put in so he could call."

"Willie knows a lot."

Nana shrugged. "I had to ask him, then he said he only gives out the facts, no extras."

I went back to my pricing and finished off the cup of coffee. Nana sat next to me without another word.

When I looked up, the shadows had stretched across the windows. Another day gone and I was still here.

I watched Nana's old hands knead pastry to make more pies. She'd been old all my life, I thought. I could never remember her hands manicured or polished, but to me they'd always been beautiful—strong and solid.

She didn't look up, but I could see her smiling. She loved to cook and she loved me. In her world, that was enough.

At dusk, she went up for her bath and I walked down to where the road turned onto Uncle Jefferson's land. Funny, I was starting to think of him as Uncle Jefferson even in my mind—this man I'd never met.

When I reached the fence, I said, "Would you look at that, Uncle J, someone stole that ugly pig."

Tacking a sign on the post that said OPEN FOR BUSINESS I wondered if there was anyone who ever came down this road who didn't already know we'd moved in.

In the twilight, I saw Luke coming toward me. He had that slow, easy walk of a man who'd spent years knowing where he was going.

"You planning to light the fire? It looks like it might rain."

He nodded.

"Mind if I help?"

He shook his head as we strolled back to the lake, gathering firewood as we walked.

"You know Willie Dowman?" I asked.

"Yes," Luke answered.

I waited for more; then, frustrated, asked, "What do you know about him?"

"He's been coming out here fishing for years."

"Anything else?"

Luke was silent for so long I gave up on him answering. When he finally spoke, I jumped at the sound.

"I've heard he gives away most of the fish he catches."

"He doesn't take them home to his wife?"

Luke shook his head. "His wife died about ten years back."

Great, I thought, *now I feel sorry for the pervert.* It occurred to me that Micki, my friendly delivery woman, didn't look all that normal either. All business one second, all friendly the next. I added another person to my list to watch as we built a fire.

It was full dark by the time we'd dragged enough dead wood over to the pit. Luke struck a match. I sat on one of the rocks that had been pulled around the circle and watched the flames take.

"You learn this as a Boy Scout?" I asked just to break the silence.

"Something like that," he said as he moved to the other side of the fire and propped against another rock.

"I've given up worrying about when you're going to kill me," I said, promising myself this was the last time I'd even bother to try to talk to him.

Laughing suddenly, I decided that if we'd been in a bar that was probably the worst pickup line ever. No wonder I hadn't had a date in two years.

I could see his intelligent blue eyes tonight. He was studying me as if he were Jacques Cousteau encountering a new species of backward-swimming fish. "I'm glad you're not afraid of me anymore," he finally said and flashed a smile.

He took a minute, then added, "I light the fire because Jefferson did." He looked out over the water. "Some nights he wanted to help late boats, but most of the time I think he was just trying to get rid of all the driftwood that piles up along this beach. Every time there's a storm or a branch falls in the water it seems to circle around and land on this little stretch of beach."

"He swam the lake, too? That's why you do?"

Luke laughed again. "No. I've done that since I was a boy. I'm surprised you saw me. Maybe I should knock out that last dock light."

I needed to talk, and it didn't matter that he was one of the inmates in this nuthouse. "I've got other things to worry about besides you. I can't sleep for worrying and that's not like me. Usually I sleep like a rock. Nana said once I slept through a tornado in Kansas. On the farm, I used to fall asleep watching the stars at night. My grandpa probably carried me to bed until I was ten. Nana always said he didn't want to wake me because if the last thing I saw was stars, I'd have good dreams."

Luke stared across the fire at me and I knew he was probably reading "chatterbox" written on my forehead, but I didn't care. There were things I needed to say and he seemed to be my unlucky victim. "Worries keep me up now. First, I think it must have been a mistake for me to inherit this place, but it's growing on me and I haven't seen Nana so happy since we left the farm. Every day we stay will make it harder for us to leave when that lawyer in Lubbock figures out he handed over the keys to the wrong Allie Daniels."

Pressing the heels of my hands against my eyes, I swore I wouldn't let myself cry, not in front of a stranger. "I don't know where I belong, but this can't be it. I'm just so tired of looking." I wanted to add that I was so homesick for a place to belong, but he probably already thought I was crazy. Homesick for something I'd never had. Growing up, I'd been the poor tenant farmer's grandchild whose mother didn't want her. At college, I'd worked two part-time jobs and hadn't had time for socials and sororities.

I straightened suddenly, hating myself for being so pathetic. I should do like that song Nana always sang and count my blessings. But when blessings include live bait in the cooler, deer heads on the fence, and a bum who lights fires in my yard every night, it was a chore just to keep counting.

I closed my eyes and let the warmth of the fire soak into my bones. For a long while, I listened to the sounds of the lake. Then I heard a splash on the water and looked up at the cloudy sky.

Luke was gone, racing the moon once more. His nightly ritual made as much sense as my life. I stood and walked slowly back to the house. I felt like an aging warrior afraid of tomorrow's battle, but determined to face head-on whatever came at sunrise.

Chapter 10

Thursday
September 19, 2006
2230 hours

Luke stood on the dock and let the cold air dry his body. He'd swum far longer than usual but he needed to use up as much of the energy trapped inside him as possible. Watching Allie pour out her fears to him had been torture.

If he'd stayed there a minute longer, he would have pulled her into his arms. Even now, he could almost feel her against him. She was a beautiful, bright young woman. She didn't need to think the weight of the world rested on her.

Dressing slowly in the dying campfire light, he heard a boat bumping against the end of the dock.

"Hello," Luke said more to let the fisherman know that he was near than to be friendly.

"Evening." A young man stepped out of his boat. "Mind if I tie up here for the night?"

"It's not my place." Luke moved closer, trying to see the man's face. "But I don't think they'll mind."

"Good." The stranger offered his hand. "I'm Timothy Andrews. I'm staying at my dad's company cabin a few hundred yards north. Our docking ramp was damaged last week in that wind, and I'm afraid I might gut the bottom of the boat trying to pull up during this fog."

Luke guessed the guy to be twenty-two, maybe a year older or younger. He had a friendly smile, but shadows under his eyes as if he were ill, or unhappy, or on drugs. "Luke Morgan." He offered Timothy his hand.

Timothy's grip seemed slight, but he said, "I heard old Jefferson talk about an old friend he once had named Morgan. He was Navajo."

"That would be my granddad. He was a code talker during the war. Met Jefferson in Germany and they became solid friends." Luke knew he was giving out too much information, but he hoped it would encourage Timothy to talk. A man stepping out of a fishing boat at night with no catch swinging from a line might have business on the lake other than fishing.

Timothy fell into step with Luke. They followed the path lit by the dim glow from the store windows. "I read a book about what the code talkers did during the war. Very interesting." Timothy also seemed to be making an effort at conversation. Maybe it was the night. Maybe something about the fog made people want to connect. "World War II is kind of my hobby. I read everything I can find on it. You got some of your grandfather's stuff from that time?"

"Not a thing," Luke answered as they headed up the drive to the main road.

"Too bad." Timothy shrugged.

They talked about the fog and winter coming on as they walked. When Timothy reached the gate, he tapped the OPEN sign. "Glad this place is back in business. Good night, Luke Morgan."

Luke waved as the kid disappeared into the mist. Timothy had seemed excited about the war, but little else. Luke couldn't help but wonder what a young man his age was doing besides reading. Maybe just taking some time off? Maybe hiding out?

He added the Andrews place to his list to check out later tonight as he walked back to Jefferson's Crossing. Between the fog and the rain, the store looked as if it were the only spot of life in the world. Luke had spent so much time in cities, it always took him a few nights to get used to how dark the country was.

As he rounded the corner of the store, he saw Allie asleep on the porch. The warm glow of the tiny lights left on inside sparkled in her hair. She was curled up looking cold and very much alone. A ledger book lay across one knee. A pencil still rested in her fingers and a fat old cat curled inches from her feet.

Luke debated. He couldn't leave her here. The night was too cold. And, if he woke her up she'd probably start talking again. If she cried, he wasn't sure what he'd do.

Studying her face, he noticed she wore little or no makeup, unlike most of the women her age.

He tugged the pencil from her hand, but she didn't stir.

Lifting the book, he noticed a drawing of old hands working a mound of bread. Nana, he decided. Allie's work wasn't half-bad. Luke shifted, almost touching her.

She still didn't move. It would be a crime to wake her.

Carefully, he tugged her legs over one arm and circled her shoulders with the other. When he moved her, she shifted against his chest like a baby kitten seeking warmth.

He carried her into the store and up the stairs as silently as he could. The glow of a night-light made it possible for him to see the half-bed turned down near the window.

Lowering her gently, he tugged off her shoes and covered her with the blanket.

She wiggled into the pillow.

Luke backed out of the room, not wanting to take his eyes off of her until he had to. He decided listening to her talk was definitely easier than watching her sleep.

Chapter 11

On Friday, business hit us before Nana and I finished breakfast. The first customer was a shy lady, from directly across the lake, who wanted to know if we had any tulip bulbs. I promised to put in a special order with Micki for next Thursday and she seemed tickled.

Next came a couple dressed in business suits. Paul and Lillian Madison. She looked bored, but he seemed friendly enough. He bought fishing magazines and canned soup; she asked if we carried wine. I didn't have time to talk to them, but I got the feeling they were part of the weekend trade. Both looked like their hands fit briefcase handles far more comfortably than fishing poles.

I'd sold bait, drinks, and several bags of chips by nine and Nana made twenty bucks with her biscuits and fried pies. By eleven, people began asking if we sold sack lunches. Nana enlisted Luke to help her make ham sandwiches, and I watched a dozen lunches go out the door within an hour.

Mid-afternoon Willie Dowman dropped by to tell us Mrs. Eleanora Deals planned to come to the café for dinner Sunday night if we were serving.

"A meal?" I asked, startled that anyone would even ask.

Willie nodded. "Jefferson tried to serve Sunday dinner a few times a month in the winter. Course, the last few years it was little more than tomato soup and crackers, but we all came if we could."

I glanced at Nana and she smiled. "I'm making catfish gumbo and cornbread. Tell her she's welcome."

Willie picked up his order. The last two fried pies. "I'll be coming about the same time Sunday night. She'll want me to pick her up in the boat and cross over the water, but Mrs. Deals likes to eat alone, so we'll be needing separate tables."

I followed him out to his boat. "Did Jefferson really serve dinner in the café?"

Willie shook his head. "In truth, not often, but he must have planned to at one time or he wouldn't have ordered the chairs and tables. I don't think he ever served anything but drinks and ice cream in the summer, but he had this idea a Sunday meal would be nice in the winter. It would get us together to check on each other and I think he thought the profit would help carry him through the winter." Willie climbed into his boat, then turned and reached his hand out to catch my arm. For a moment he just held it, then he patted lightly. "Jefferson told us all that you might make it a weekly event."

"He did?" I tried not to pull away or act relieved when he finally let go of me.

"Yep. Said you were talented in everything you tried. He was sure proud of your art. Told me once you won a contest in school."

In high school, I thought. How could Jefferson Platt know about that?

Willie motored off with me standing, openmouthed. All I'd have had to do was flop around a little to look like a docked fish.

Up until now, I'd thought Jefferson Platt had made a mistake and named the wrong person. I'd thought our days at the lake were numbered and we'd be packing the van soon.

But he *knew* me. A man I'd never even heard of had somehow kept up with me enough to know I had won a drawing contest once.

Before I had time to reason out my inheritance, I noticed Luke sitting at the end of the dock. He stared at a man in a rowboat a few hundred yards away.

I walked up beside Luke and took a seat. In a strange way, this lake bum and I were becoming friends. For a while I just dangled my legs in the water and we watched the young man in the boat. I thought of the way Willie touched me, patting my arm. It didn't seem at all perverted, but I guess he had to start somewhere. In truth, I wouldn't have thought a thing about the touch if Micki hadn't said what she did about Willie.

I relaxed, enjoying the first break I'd had all morning. I joined Luke in his pursuit of staring.

"He's not fishing," I finally said, pointing to the man in the row boat. "I don't see a pole."

Luke looked at me as if he hadn't realized I was there.

I quickly turned away from his blue eyes. I could so get lost in those eyes if he were normal. He had a great body and thick brown hair, but something about a man who races the moon every night made him not my type.

I turned back to the guy in the boat, needing to redirect my thoughts. From this distance he looked young, early twenties, I'd guess, and thin as he huddled in the center of the boat. He would have noticed us if he'd looked up, but he just stared down at the water.

"What do you think he's doing out there?" I didn't expect an answer. I was just voicing my thoughts. "He has no pole, no coat or hat against the sun and weather. His oars aren't even in the water so he doesn't seem to have any plan other than to drift." I almost added that he was a strange duck, but I seemed to be in the middle of the flock.

Luke stood. As he turned to go, he said in a low, sad voice, "He's trying to decide whether to fall in or not."

I looked back at the young man without asking Luke what he meant. I knew.

That night when the house was quiet, I reached for the ledger and drew my next sketch. A thin man huddled against the wind off the water. A man drifting between life and death.

Chapter 12

Early Saturday
September 21, 2006
0100 hours

The wind whirled as if shoving winter across the chilling lake. Trees, already dry and brown, rattled like paper bags as Luke Morgan moved through the late-night shadows.

No hint of the easygoing bum who'd walked the shores for the past week remained. Now, a trained soldier moved stealthily through the night, measuring his steps, evaluating his surroundings.

Luke had done this kind of surveillance more times than he could remember. Drug dealers, thieves, and murderers moved in shadow. If he planned to catch them, he had to do the same.

Half a mile inland from the far north shore of the lake, he found what he'd been looking for—a burned-out hull of a cabin. Kicking the ashes, he shined his flashlight on wood still smoldering. The place could have easily burned two nights ago when the fog had been so thick no one would have noticed the smoke. The rain that had followed that night would have erased most of the clues, but not all. Luke would come back at dawn and piece together what had happened. He might be able to reason out how long the meth lab had been operating and how many people probably worked there. The criminals who set up labs were like fire ants. They get burned out of one place, they just move to another.

He'd already called headquarters and informed them of the facts. This was the third cabin he'd found. All had been burned. The first looked to have been set six months ago, a second two months ago, and now this. All the facts told him two things he didn't want to admit. One, a meth lab was in full operation at Twisted Creek, and two, it was growing in production. If they had already wasted three cabins he'd be willing to bet they were now setting up shop in the fourth. Eventually they'd run out of the most isolated spots and move in closer to where people lived.

And when they did, someone would get hurt.

He had to admit these guys were good at covering their tracks. He'd found no tire tracks on roads into the labs so they must have reached them by boat. Then, when they cleared out, they left nothing but ashes.

As he walked back toward home, Luke circled close to the cabins near Jefferson's Crossing. The Andrews Company cabin came into view first. It had half the lights inside burning. Luke had no trouble standing in the trees and looking into the house.

Timothy Andrews sat in a recliner with a book almost touching his nose.

Luke took the time to survey the place. Leather furniture, a big fireplace, books stacked in little piles everywhere, and one huge wall covered with rifles.

He moved closer until he stood a few feet from the light and studied the rifles. He'd seen a collection like this

before. Remingtons. Numbered replicas as fine as the orig-
inals made for every year of production.

Luke glanced back at Timothy. Why would a young
man think about drowning when he had twenty or more
guns available?

Luke laughed. He was thinking like a cop, not a book-
worm. He'd worked two years in Houston as a policeman
before he'd got on with the ATF. During those two years,
three of the men from his training class had been shot, two
had committed suicide with their service weapons, one was
run over by a drunk while he directed traffic, and none died
by drowning. It wasn't a way he thought about dying.
Maybe that was why Jefferson's death bothered Luke.

Moving back into the night, Luke crossed Allie's property. He wanted to circle round and see if she'd fallen
asleep on the porch again, but he didn't dare in his black
clothes. He'd probably scare her to death if she heard as
much as a twig snap.

This morning she'd caught him sleeping on the dock
with a pole in his hand. By the time she sat down near
him, Luke was awake, but he didn't move. She waited a
few minutes and then began flipping water on him. When
he finally looked at her, she tried to tell him it must be
raining.

He'd thought of tossing her into the lake. It took all his
control to remind himself to keep his distance. Friendship
was all he'd offer her. He didn't have time in his life for
more, even if she were interested.

She'd done the strangest thing an hour later. She'd bor-
rowed his old canoe and paddled out to Timothy. Luke
couldn't hear what she'd said to the boy, but Timothy had
nodded several times.

Then she'd paddled back and thanked him for the use of
his boat.

When she started to walk away, he had to ask what she'd been up to and all she said was that she asked the kid to dinner Sunday night.

The rest of the day she'd done her best to ignore Luke and he'd returned the favor.

Chapter 13

On Sunday it began to rain around noon. No one came by the store after that. Nana cooked and I tried to catch up with the books. Friday and Saturday we'd made twice as much as I thought we would. My dream of saving enough money for a rainy day began to form. People came in for Nana's breakfasts and stayed to buy.

With thunder rumbling outside, I checked the old ledger book and confirmed that business was great for this time of the year. After noon, I helped Nana put up beans and black-eyed peas. We'd done apple jelly Friday night and sold several jars already. The homemade jars lining one shelf gave the store a fresh look.

Willie had dropped by Saturday with a bushel of green beans and said he'd give them to us if Nana would can them and give him two jars. She bartered with him saying she'd give him four if he'd buy the jars. It was not a fair deal, but Willie fell for it anyway.

They sat on the porch and snapped peas for two hours. Both rocked as they worked. Nana hummed gospel tunes. Willie swore now and then when his arthritic fingers wouldn't seem to work. It made for an interesting melody.

I thought of asking him how his dead wife was doing, but I'd worked out in my mind why he'd lied. An old man complaining about his wife was normal. A man saying she'd died was sad. Maybe he'd had his bucketful of sadness.

By five-thirty Sunday afternoon, I'd reorganized the supplies in the store and arranged the tables in the café area. Nana arranged old bandana napkins in the center of the little tables and set a candle in the middle of each. If I counted that and the twinkle lights, we almost had atmosphere.

We had no idea who would come to our dinner, but I'd left signs at both the dock and the road: SUNDAY SUPPER— SIX BUCKS.

"We'll be eating the gumbo all week if no one shows up," Nana mumbled as she lined pies along the bar.

"Willie said he and Mrs. Deals are coming." I tried to remember if he'd said they would come or would try to come.

Nana cut the pies. "I invited Luke, but he didn't promise he could make it."

I couldn't imagine what would keep him away. Near as I could tell, he did nothing except magically appear now and then. He worked when I asked him to do something and claimed all he wanted was a meal for his efforts. And he slept on the dock every morning as if he'd been out all night dancing at some bar. I'd touched him enough times to realize his muscles were hard as rocks, but the man seemed a bit lazy to me.

"The rain might keep everyone away," I offered, not wanting to get Nana's hopes too high.

"Might," Nana answered, spreading a towel out by the door. "But if they do make it, you tell them to wipe their feet when they come in."

I nodded, wondering if any café in the history of the world had ever had a towel at the door.

I jumped a few minutes later when one of the Landry brothers opened the door. Near as I could find out no one knew either of the brother's first names. They kept to themselves and only stopped by for bait.

"May I help you?" I asked, knowing that if he took a seat I'd be mopping up a puddle of rain. He couldn't have been any wetter if he'd swam over.

He stood on the towel and said in a voice that sounded like it had aged with lack of use, "Two orders to go for dinner."

I stared openmouthed. This wasn't McDonald's and what person in his right mind would fight this storm for two take-out orders of stew that would be cold before he could get them home?

"All right," I said as I shook my head and walked over to the pass-through. "Two dinners to go," I yelled.

By the time I walked back to the store and rang up two meals, the Landry brother had fished enough money from his pocket to pay me. The money was wet and crumpled, but I took it.

Nana came through the swing door with a collection of plastic storage bowls. She handed them to the dripping man standing on her towel. "I packed extra corn bread 'cause you'd order it if you were eating in. I also gave each order two pieces of pie, one apple and one buttermilk." She smiled up at him. "You'll like the buttermilk better."

He just stared at her as if she were speaking a language he'd never encountered.

I found a plastic bag to put all the bowls inside.

He thanked us both with a slight bow.

"Now you bring my bowls back, you hear," Nana said as she held the door open for him. "And I don't want any of them smelling like you stored bait in them."

A few minutes later I heard the sputter of an old engine moving away from the dock and wondered if the other Landry brother waited in the boat.

At straight-up six Mrs. Eleanora Deals arrived, complete with raincoat, umbrella, and galoshes. She didn't bother to introduce herself, just asked if we were open for business, but I had no doubt who she was. I could almost smell the Milano cookies on her breath. When I nodded, she said she'd like a table for one.

She removed her coat to reveal a navy dress that had to have been at least twenty years old. The white lace at the collar looked frayed slightly. Everything about her spoke of old money—mildewed old money.

Willie followed her in and also asked for a table for one. He was friendly, but seemed to want to be alone.

Next, Luke stepped from the kitchen and took one of the stools, keeping his back to the others.

When I passed him, I put my hand on his shoulder. Luke's muscles tightened beneath my touch. He couldn't have made it plainer that he wasn't interested in talking to me than if he'd screamed rape. Whenever I got within three feet of the man, I swear he acted as if I were contagious.

"Sorry." I brushed his shoulder as if I could brush away my touch. "I just wanted to see how wet it is out there."

Blue eyes studied me. "It's wet," he mumbled.

While Nana served them soup, I answered a light tap on the door.

The thin young man from the boat stood before me. He had dark circles under his eyes and a book in his hand. "Do you have a table where I can read while I eat?"

"I do," I answered. "Welcome, Timothy. I'm glad you could make it."

Before I could close the door, a chubby, middle-aged woman rushed up the steps. "Am I too late?" she asked a little breathlessly.

I held the door and smiled. "No, come in." I recognized her as the woman who wanted to know if we had any tulip bulbs. "I'm Allie."

"I'm Mary Lynn O'Reilly from directly across the lake. I saw your sign when I dropped by while you were busy Friday. I was so pleased to see that you're serving a real meal. It's been ages since I've been out to dinner." She lifted a large purse. "Is it okay if Poseidon comes in? We always eat together, and on a stormy night like this I couldn't leave him at home. He'll be quiet. No one will even notice he's with me."

I looked down at a tiny white poodle with a bow set lopsided on his head. I knew I was probably breaking every health rule in the state, but I decided any place that until three days ago had animal heads on the wall could allow this mutt in the door. "Sure."

Mary Lynn smiled, obviously warmed by my kindness. I couldn't help but wonder how many places she'd been asked to leave.

"Do you have a table for one?"

I almost said that a table for one was all we seemed to have, but I only replied, "Follow me."

The last guest, Paul Madison, was the city fellow I'd seen a few days ago. His "do you have wine" wife was missing. He took the table near the kitchen door. He still wore a dress shirt beneath a thin Windbreaker, but unshaven he looked a little more like he belonged out here. I'd guess him as a banker or a stockbroker.

I started to ask why he was still here—weekenders were

long gone by now—but he didn't look like he wanted to talk. So I just smiled and nodded at him. He returned the greeting, minus the smile.

Nana and I served the soup and corn bread. The storm seemed to grow worse, but no one said anything. Mary Lynn whispered to her dog, calling him Posey. Willie complimented Nana several times. Timothy read as he ate his meal without looking up from the book. Mrs. Deals picked at her food and Luke leaned over his bowl as if he could make his big frame disappear.

When Posey barked as the fat cat crossed the store, I knew I had to step in. "I'm sorry to bother everyone," I said, noticing Mary Lynn looked frightened. "Does anyone mind if Miss O'Reilly's dog joins us this evening?"

I wasn't at all surprised when everyone spoke at once.

Mrs. Deals said some of her best friends had been dogs.

Willie swore the dog smelled better than he did, and to my surprise everyone else nodded.

Timothy got up and went over to Mary Lynn's table. He asked if he could pet Posey.

Mary Lynn nodded shyly.

Then everyone settled back in their chairs at their tables for one and finished their meals. I smiled and looked around, catching blue eyes staring at me. To my shock, Luke winked.

While Nana offered everyone dessert, I moved to the shadows and reached for my ledger book. I knew I didn't have time to draw, so I gripped the book as I studied the guests, each alone like a castaway on an island. Five strangers together in their solitude.

Except for Luke, they took their time eating. Mrs. Deals sliced off small birdlike bites of her pie. Mary Lynn stopped often to cuddle her dog and remind him to be good because he was a guest. The sad young man only ate when he turned a page. Willie watched the storm.

When Luke stood, he left a ten-dollar bill beside his plate and went out on the porch. The others took their time and paid at the cash register. I thanked each one, but didn't try to make useless conversation.

Paul Madison asked if he could buy a few groceries. I turned on the lights in the grocery area so he could shop.

When Nana brought a small to-go bag for Mary Lynn's dog I thought the woman might cry. Everything about her told me that she was a proper old maid, living alone, probably gardening and quilting. Everything, except her eyes. They darted as if from fear. She reminded me of a child who'd been struck by so many people she feared a blow from everyone she met.

"Next Sunday?" Mary Lynn asked as she hugged her dog tightly. "You'll be open again for dinner?"

"I'm planning on it," I said.

Mrs. Deals, who was putting on her galoshes, snapped, "I'd like the same table."

"You'll have it," I smiled, knowing that was probably as close to a compliment from her as I could hope for.

The melancholy young man lifted one finger, silently making his reservation.

I raised my voice so everyone could hear. "All your tables will be waiting."

They filed out with only a nod toward one another. Willie turned his flashlight on the path for Mary Lynn so she could make it to her car and Timothy stopped to talk to Luke.

I saw him pass something to Luke, but I couldn't tell what it was.

I helped Nana with the dishes, then curled up beside the window and sketched the dinner party. The sounds of the lake blended with the soft rain, making this place seem a million miles from anywhere.

Timothy's outline covered one page. Luke, eating alone at the counter, covered another. Mrs. Deals, with her very proper stance, another. Mary Lynn, hugging her dog as if he were her only friend, another. And the last sketch I drew before I closed the ledger was Nana leaning back in the porch chair snapping peas. The strength of her hands showed through in the lines; peace brushed her face.

About midnight, I moved to the huge bay window that overlooked the lake. I stared out into a world that seemed washed clean by the rain. The moon was high, but I could see a tiny twinkle of light from across the lake. Mary Lynn's place, I thought. And the circle of security lights up on the rise—that must be Mrs. Deals's big house.

I'd met them, I thought, these odd people the sheriff had called "the Nesters," and I knew, strange as they all were, that they were somehow my people. My destiny.

Chapter 14

Monday
September 23, 2006
Midnight hours

Luke silently paced along the porch in front of Jefferson's old store. He felt restless. It was too rainy to either swim or build a fire. He loved both. Swimming had been his exercise of choice since he'd been in college and he liked watching the fire climb up the night sky. Campfires always reminded him that he was a quarter Indian. He liked the idea that his roots had dug into this land for thousands of years. Sometimes, when he swam in the lake or ran in the woods, he swore a wildness in his blood warmed as if he were home.

Turning over in his hand the patch that Timothy had given him, Luke stared at it once more. The symbol of the code talkers, a special group of men, all with Navajo blood, who had used their language as a code that the Nazis never broke. Luke had heard of the group, he'd even seen a few movies that mentioned them, but he'd never realized how different they must have been. For the first time since his grandfather had died, he wished he'd listened closer to the stories his grandfather and Jefferson had told.

Timothy said he found the old patch among a box of patches he'd collected from World War II. He'd said Luke could have it. That it would mean more to him.

The boy was right. Luke closed his hand around the Marine patch. It meant a great deal.

He was aware someone still moved around in the store and guessed it would be Allie. She usually turned off the twinkle lights when she went up the stairs. He'd watched her a few times, locking the doors, checking the windows as if the tiny locks would protect from everything in life.

He had a feeling she'd make a go of this place, but it could cause problems. As long as this lake was a dying community, the drug dealers would feel safe. If it started to prosper, they'd have to find another place . . . or run her out. He couldn't shake the feeling that they were moving in from the outskirts. He'd found more damage besides the fires. After he'd talked to Timothy, Luke had checked out the Andrews dock. More than the wind had destroyed the landing.

If someone wanted the people out here to leave, it wouldn't be that hard to make life tougher on them. Drug dealers wouldn't worry about the old men, or even people like Mary Lynn and Mrs. Deals, but cabins like the Andrews one brought successful businessmen out to fish.

Luke decided it might be wise to take a few weeks more of his vacation time and hang around.

Someone touched his shoulder and he twisted away, almost reaching for his Glock before he caught her in the corner of his vision.

"Sorry," she muttered. "I always seem to be touching you and I know you don't like it. But it's kind of like trying not to think of the word *elephant* when someone says not to."

She moved a few feet away. "I just came out to say thanks for fixing the old potbellied stove this morning. In another month we may need it to keep the place warm." She dug in her pocket and pulled out a ten. "You don't have to pay for the meal. We traded work for food, remember."

Somewhere she'd gotten the idea that he couldn't afford food and Luke didn't know how to tell her otherwise. He'd been wearing his oldest fishing clothes when he'd met her and she seemed convinced he was broke. If he told her he had a job, she'd ask what it was and then his cover would be in danger of being blown.

"I wanted to pay," he finally said as he stared at her, wishing she'd look up at him and not at the money in her hand.

"Oh, all right," she answered in a tone that said she was trying not to hurt his feelings.

"And another thing." He was just tired enough to let his guard down an inch. "I never said I minded you touching me." He could name every time she had. The accidental brushings of her arm against his. The way she patted him when he was working. The times she'd passed by and let her hand brush his shoulder.

Allie finally looked up at him. "You don't?"

Luke closed all the extra space between them. "No," he whispered, almost touching her lips. "I don't."

Before he thought, he pressed his mouth to hers and kissed her. She was so close he could feel her whole body shake and react, but he didn't pull her to him.

For a few heartbeats she let him kiss her, then slowly she kissed him back. Not a soft, chaste kiss or a hot, passionate one, but a solid kiss of longing that whispered hesitance from the past and promises of the future.

Before he lost what control he had left, Luke stepped away. "Good night," he snapped, and turned into the rain before either of them said or did anything else.

He was halfway back to his cabin before he noticed the rain pounding down on him. "Hell," he mumbled. With the mood he was in, lightning could probably strike him and he wouldn't notice.

He laughed. Maybe it already had.

Chapter 15

After staring at the rain for a while, I walked back inside, turned out most of the lights, then curled into the bay window. The rattle of the storm behind me seemed to echo my thoughts.

I flipped open the ledger and looked at what I'd drawn.

Tall, lanky Paul Madison, who bought groceries for one, had stood at the door, an arm tightly around his sack, the stare of a lost man on his face.

Shy Mary Lynn and her pet. Though her body had settled into a middle-aged plump, she'd looked, frightened, with huge child eyes into the night.

Timothy, his nose buried in a computer book and his hair so long it formed a curtain over his eyes.

Mrs. Deals, her hands birdlike thin, her face as pale as porcelain.

I grinned, knowing I'd captured each one exactly as they were. The only two who looked like they belonged together were old Willie, frowning over the storm, and Luke, frowning over the crowded room.

When I looked at Luke hunched over the counter as if he thought he could shrink enough to be invisible, I thought of how he'd kissed me. I'd been kissed by several boys and a few men gauging my interest, but none had kissed me like Luke had. It hadn't been a game with him. He didn't seem to be asking, or offering more.

The fat cat Nana called General curled up on the cushion beside me and pushed his head against my arm. I rubbed the tabby's fur. "Did you eat all the leftovers?" I asked.

General didn't answer.

"You'll be too lazy to chase mice soon."

General closed his eyes, looking bored with my talk.

I stood and put the book on the highest shelf in the tiny office next to a row of file boxes that I promised myself I'd at least look at tomorrow. The records from years past might prove helpful.

I climbed the stairs, thinking of Luke's kiss and wondering if it was just an impulse or if he planned to do it again. Though it had been nice, I decided I wanted to be an active participant next time and not just a bystander run over by his moment of desire.

Still trying to predict what he might do, I dressed the next morning and hurried down to join Nana. I could smell biscuits and knew I'd overslept again. Which wouldn't have bothered me any day but today. Monday.

The sheriff usually came on Monday. I could hardly wait for his expression when he realized I not only was still here, but I was growing roots.

"Nana," I yelled as I pulled up the blinds. "You'd better make extra biscuits. The sheriff is probably on his way."

"What sheriff?" she yelled back.

I frowned. How could she forget a man so big his casket would probably beep when they backed it into the grave?

Before I could make it to the kitchen to see if she was kidding, a pounding knock hammered on the door.

I opened up. "Morning, Sheriff," I said as sunbeams squeezed in around his bulk.

One big muddy boot stepped over the towel, then another. "I figured you'd already be open. Jefferson always rose early. He'd have a pot of coffee half drank and be waiting for me."

Sheriff Fletcher walked around the store checking out all my new merchandise as if trying to decide what to shoplift. What looked like size fifteen footprints marked his progress.

"I've got coffee," I said, more hopeful than sure. "Would you like a cup?"

He nodded and picked up one of Nana's jars of jelly. "Did you make this here?"

I passed him a cup of coffee. "We did."

"Did you wear hairnets?"

"Of course," I lied, having a feeling all sins were equal in his eyes. "But General had trouble keeping his on."

Fletcher looked at me as if deciding if I was trying to be funny or if I had flipped over into crazy.

Nana pushed her way though the swinging door with a cake plate loaded with apple fritters. She set them down and walked back into the kitchen as if she didn't have time to notice us standing five feet away. She had so much flour on her face she could have tried out for the Ghost of Christmas Past.

I offered the sheriff a fritter, hoping the fried dough would put him in a better mood.

It did. He set the jelly jar down. With coffee in one hand and an apple fritter in the other, he was about as defenseless as he ever got.

"How's that boy of yours doing?" I asked quickly, before he thought of a law we were breaking.

"Dillon." He smiled without stopping his chewing. "He's fine. Going to be quarterback in the first game next week. I won't be surprised if he gets a free ride to college playing ball. That boy is good at everything he tries."

I walked toward the door as he rambled on about his only son. By the time he'd finished his food and coffee, we were on the porch.

"Anything strange going on here that I should know about?" The sheriff handed me the cup and stared out along the dock.

I opened my mouth to say no, but knew it would be a waste of time. The sheriff spotted Luke and lost all interest in me.

I tried to distract the lawman. "Do you know a sweet lady who lives out here by the name of Mary Lynn O'Reilly?"

Fletcher didn't turn away from watching Luke but answered, "Harmless nutcase." He shrugged. "Sad, really. No backbone. People have worse things happen to their family and don't run away and hide like the last roach in the basement."

He had my interest. "What things?"

Fletcher glanced at me as if I were a bother, but answered, "Her daddy was a big-time preacher in Lubbock. Folks came all the way from Snyder to hear him." He let out a long breath, telling me he was probably tired of telling the story. "Police found him and some hooker shot to death at the motel one night. Never knew who fired the shotgun, but it did make a mess. Did you ever see what brains do when they fly into a fan?"

I was too busy trying to swallow to answer.

"Drove Mary Lynn's mother crazy and she killed herself a month later. Mary Lynn, their only child, had been sheltered and homeschooled through high school. She was in her first year of nursing school at Texas Tech when she buried both her parents. She was left alone to face the gawkers and the lawyers. Some said she would follow her mother, but she didn't, she ran out here to hide. Closes herself up in their summer cabin and never goes to town." He straightened his gun belt. "I check in on her now and then to see if she's cracked up completely. Comes from weak blood."

"That's nice of you to check on her," I managed to say, thinking it was no wonder Mary Lynn hid out here if there were many like Fletcher around.

Fletcher didn't catch my sarcasm. He watched Luke walking toward the store.

Luke was halfway up the dock when he glanced over and saw the sheriff. For a moment, he hesitated as if debating making a run for it.

I couldn't breathe.

The sheriff frowned and started toward Luke.

I could only stand frozen and watch as the big lawman got right in Luke's face and pointed his finger. They were too far away for me to hear everything, but the sheriff seemed to be asking rapid-fire questions and Luke didn't look like he was answering many.

Luke's hands were open at his sides and he stood his ground.

Finally, without even a wave, the sheriff stormed off and headed to his car. I could hear him shouting orders into the radio as he pulled away.

Luke walked slowly to the porch as if nothing had happened.

"What was that all about?" I asked.

He shrugged. "He's looking for a reason to arrest me."

"You got one?"

Blue eyes looked directly into mine for once and he answered, "Nope. How about you?"

I laughed. "Nana and I are guilty of not wearing hairnets when we cook. Will you bust us out if he takes us in?"

He winked. "You bet."

I studied him with his old clothes and worn boots. For all I knew he was just like Mary Lynn, hiding out from the real world. He could be a drifter or an outlaw, but one thing for sure, he wasn't afraid of the cops. I didn't know whether to be reassured that he wasn't a criminal, or worried that he was good enough never to be caught.

And one other thing, I loved the way he winked.

Without another word, he passed me and went into the store. A few minutes later, he returned with a cup of live worms and an apple fritter.

"Nice breakfast," I said.

He nodded, but didn't meet my eyes as he crossed to the side of the porch and picked up his fishing pole.

Later, I noticed his canoe was gone. I didn't have time to worry about what he'd said to the sheriff. The morning was full of work. My alien mailman showed up with his wagon loaded with boxes. It seemed everyone shopped by mail or online now that they knew I'd be here to receive the boxes.

By noon, Timothy had picked up two boxes from Amazon, Mrs. Deals had sent Willie to get her box from Dell, and Mary Lynn had driven over to get her four fluffy packages from the Home Shopping Network.

I was glad Mary Lynn came last. I asked her to join Nana and me for tea on the porch and she accepted as graciously as if we drank out of fine china and not mugs. She talked of her garden and a small greenhouse where she grew plants all winter. Nana told of how her father always made them plant corn by the dark of the moon and potatoes in the light of day.

I mostly listened for any hint of the story the sheriff had told me. But Mary Lynn never mentioned her family or any tragedy.

After she left, I talked to Nana about keeping the coffeepot warming on the counter all afternoon now that the days were getting cooler. Customers could come in and help themselves.

"You're feeling guilty," she said in answer. "You always do when you feel like luck's been good to you."

I stared at Nana, the one person who knew me all the way to my heart. "Maybe," I answered.

Nana patted my arm three times. "You can't always bounce blessings, child. Sometimes you just have to catch them."

She walked away muttering a recipe for cookies she planned to make to go next to the free coffee.

I sauntered through the store, straightening supplies. I was settling in. Getting to know people. Starting to care.

Panic hung like static electricity around me. I stilled, fearing the shock if I moved. If I wasn't very careful, I'd start believing I belonged here, then when we had to move on the pain would be sharper than ever. Sharper even than when we had to leave the farm after Grandpa died. I'd already taken full bolts of sorrow the few times I'd tried to belong. I wasn't sure how much more I could take.

Chapter 16

The next few days passed in a calm haze. I went down to the gas station on the highway and called in an extra large order for Micki to bring out, which included two gallons of teal paint. I had thought of driving all the way into Lubbock and picking it out, but didn't want to leave Nana too long. Cooking, she was great, but when she made change at the store, she couldn't seem to get it right. Though she shrugged it off as always being poor at math, I remembered how she used to balance her checkbook to the penny.

When Micki brought the order on Thursday, I took a few hours off and painted the upstairs teal. Micki told me it looked great, but she was wearing a lime green scarf, orange-trimmed socks, and red knee shorts at the time. I couldn't help but wonder what her husbands must have been like. She looked like she could bench-press three hundred pounds.

We made our weekly trip into town and bought our

dollar-store supplies using money from the tip jar beside the free coffeepot. I told everyone it was free, but they always left a little anyway. I discovered fishermen were an easy lot, slow-moving and friendly with little-boy smiles. For most of them, a day fishing was a day playing hooky from life.

On the drive back home, Nana was silent for a long while, then said, "I always sleep next to Flo when winter comes. She can't keep warm without me there."

"You mean when you were a child?" I knew the past sometimes came back so strong to her that it was like yesterday and not seventy years ago.

"Yes," she said as she stared out at the dry buffalo grass blowing in the wind. "My ma always made us wear socks, but when I'd crawled out of bed in the morning I could still feel the cold floor. We'd dress as fast as we could and run down to the kitchen stove. Many a morning I ate my breakfast standing with my back to the fire."

I took her hand and we drove on in silence. I loved her stories, even the sad ones. They made me feel like I belonged to a small slice of that time—like the memory of it was in my genes, not just in my head.

When we pulled up to the lake, I noticed Paul Madison's BMW parked near the dock. He had on jeans and a dress shirt with the sleeves rolled to the elbows. He'd told me Monday that his cell phone wouldn't work up at the cabin he'd just bought. I broke the news that no one's phone worked around here except Mrs. Deals's, and Willie said she'd turned the ringer off years ago. He said his wife would be writing if she wasn't able to make it from Dallas by the end of the week.

I climbed out of the van, hoping he had no letter in the box left on our porch. Maybe she'd come down tomorrow and they'd patch up whatever argument had made him look so sad.

Paul waved as Timothy shoved off for his day of sitting on the lake, then the businessman turned and walked toward me. He tried to act casual, even offering to help with the groceries, but I saw the worry in his eyes when he glanced toward the porch.

Once we were inside, he poured himself a cup of coffee and watched me sort the mail.

I'd almost reached the bottom of the box when I frowned. Paul Madison had a letter. One in a business envelope. That couldn't be good.

When I lifted it, he set down his coffee and walked toward me. I tried to think of something to say. "Maybe she'll make it out for a little of the weekend."

"Maybe," he said as he took the letter. For a moment he just stared at it, then without looking at me, he walked out of the store.

The wind caught the wind chimes in Nana's kitchen and I heard the familiar tinkle. I moved to the window and watched Paul head toward his car. He couldn't have been more than thirty-six or so, but he seemed to age as he walked.

A pair of fishermen getting an early start on the weekend pulled in and blocked my view of Paul. They climbed out, laughing and wagering bets. One had a hat that looked like a hook cushion and the other's hat had a bite-sized piece missing off the brim. His friend called him Hank, but he looked more like a Herbert to me. Old hats and new clothes. I'd guess these guys didn't know much about fishing.

I stayed at the window, letting Nana greet them and offer coffee. The two men wandered around the store like two children allowed to fill the shopping basket for the first time. Forty dollars of snacks later, they were ready to go.

When they left, I turned and noticed Luke staring at

them from the pass-through window. When he looked at me, he frowned.

"What do you think?" I asked. "Bank robbers hiding out or escapees from that show *What Not to Wear*? Or maybe they are junk-food addicts kicked out of all the towns around?"

"Worse," he answered. "They're drunk fishermen."

I blinked and he was gone. I guessed it would be a waste of time to even bother to look for him. The man reminded me of a jack-in-the-box.

A jack-in-the-box who kissed, I added.

Nana yelled that she was starting bread so I decided to haul our potted plants up to the bedroom. With the walls painted and sheets made into curtains, the rooms upstairs had lost most of the drab they'd clung to.

An hour later, I glanced out the window and noticed Paul's car was still out front. He sat in the dirt beside his passenger door with the open letter in both hands. He wasn't crying, he just stared as if looking at something he couldn't believe was real. I could feel his sorrow so raw I almost looked away. I didn't even know this man. We'd only said a few words. It wasn't my place to get involved in his problem.

But I remembered that first night when his wife had asked for wine and we didn't stock any. Maybe that was the turning point, the last straw, and somehow I was responsible.

While I watched, Mary Lynn pulled up in her rusty Volvo. She drove over the dam road twice a week to see if any of her orders had come in. She'd said she was redecorating, but the mailman swore she must be "one of them compulsive shoppers," because he was always delivering something she'd ordered.

The old maid took a few steps, then noticed Paul. Unlike me, she didn't hesitate. She walked right up to the banker and knelt down beside him.

I couldn't hear what they said, but after a while, Paul stood, dusted off his jeans, and they headed toward the store. I ran downstairs feeling guilty that I'd watched.

"Afternoon," I managed as they came in. "I'll get your package, Mary Lynn."

"Thank you," she said in her polite, shy way. "And would you mind if we had a pot of tea, Allie? I think that might just hit the spot."

"Of course," I said, thinking that we didn't usually serve tea. It didn't seem to go with worms.

But Nana and I managed to find an old steel pot. While she heated water, I stacked Lipton bags on a saucer. We added the old sugar bowl and a small plate of cookies. Nana spread one of her bandana napkins over a cookie sheet and I served tea to our guests sitting in the bay window.

"Thank you," Mary Lynn said. Her gentle smile somehow didn't touch her eyes.

Since she didn't invite me to join them, I moved to the other side of the store. As the afternoon aged, I watched her pour him tea. Neither seemed to talk much. Once I saw him nod when she pointed at something on the lake.

They were still there when the fishermen began to dock for the night. Luke's canoe slipped in just as the sun touched the water. He pulled out a string of fish and walked up the dock.

Without a word to me, he handed the catch to Nana. "Same deal?"

My grandmother smiled. "Same deal."

As they disappeared into the kitchen, I walked over to Mary Lynn and Paul for the first time. "Could I interest either of you in joining us for dinner? Looks like Luke caught twice what we can eat."

They looked at each other, then turned to me and nodded.

Paul stood slowly, like a man finding his footing on new ground. "I'll help him clean the fish."

Mary Lynn looked up at him. "You know how?"

He shrugged. "I've done it a few times."

When he disappeared out the back, I sat down by Mary Lynn. "Is he all right?"

She nodded. "He will be." She hesitated before sharing. "His wife wrote to tell him she filed for a divorce. She said buying a dusty little shack on a nowhere lake was the last straw."

"Why'd he do it?"

Mary Lynn shook her head. "He said he'd always dreamed of having a place, a retreat from the world. He thought she understood."

"He might be in time to stop the sale."

"No. I don't think he wants to. Maybe his life with her was part of the reason he needed the retreat."

I felt like a voyeur looking into someone else's pain so I changed the subject. An hour later, as we sat on the porch eating Luke's fish and Nana's cottage fries, I tried not to act as if anything was wrong even though I guessed this must be one of the saddest days of Paul's life.

He ate little, stared at his plate, and forced a smile when he did look up.

Mary Lynn told us the story of how Jefferson's Crossing got its name. It seemed Jefferson Platt was named after his ancestors who operated a raft so wagons could cross Twisted Creek. When they dammed the water and created the lake, his people stayed on, first with a trading post and later with the small bait store.

Luke backed her up, saying that when he was a kid he'd heard old Jefferson tell the same story. Except for the army, he'd lived his life in one spot.

I tried to picture Luke as a boy. Reason told me he

couldn't have been born six-feet tall and hard as a rock, but I couldn't visualize him younger. Knowing that he'd come here for years ended my worry about him being a drifter, but I couldn't see him living anywhere else. If this were his getaway place, where did he live?

When they'd left and Nana had gone up to bed, I walked out to the campfire Luke had built. Fall drifted in the air, chilling the breeze off the lake.

We sat for a while looking at the flames. I loved to watch the colors dance toward heaven. Once I'd tried to paint the firelight, but I could never make it come alive. An instructor told me that the only way I'd ever make fire look real on canvas was to burn it.

Finally, I could stand the silence no longer. "The banker's wife is divorcing him because he bought a place out here."

He stirred the fire. "Good a reason as any, I guess."

I tried to see his face in the shadows. How could someone who kissed so good show no sympathy?

"That's all you have to say?"

"Would you rather she left him for another man, or because she bankrupted him, or because she had a gambling problem?"

I got the point. "You're right. The reason doesn't matter, I guess, because it's not the real reason. She left him because she doesn't love him anymore." Somehow that sounded so much worse than all the other reasons.

I wanted him to say something like loving someone for even a short time was better than never loving at all, but he didn't. He just turned his back and watched clouds reflecting shadows on the water. I wondered if this quiet man had ever said he loved some woman. Did he understand Paul's pain?

I stood. "Good night, Luke," I said as I started up to the house.

He said good night so softly I couldn't be sure I'd heard it.

When I reached the porch, I glanced back and saw him standing on the far side of the campfire staring out into the lake. His legs were wide apart, his body at parade rest. He seemed to be looking for something. Watching for something.

Chapter 17

Luke noticed a thin line of gray smoke circle and rise against the nighttime sky. He could feel someone or something moving in the night. From patrolling the streets years ago in Houston, he'd learned that evil craves the shadows. As soon as he knew Allie was safely inside, he pulled his backpack from the canoe and began his search with night vision equipment. Today, he'd moved silently in his boat around the shoreline, trying to think like a drug dealer. Trying to guess where they'd set up next.

Smiling, he remembered how his cover of fishing had slowed the search because the fish kept biting. He'd even dropped the hook once without bait and somehow managed to snag a water moccasin. When he accidentally flipped the snake into the canoe he almost dove into the lake to avoid it. Only the fear that the slimy creature might have been traveling with friends kept him from the water.

He'd thought of calling it a day and going into town for a

steak and a visit with the guys at the office. Luke had moved around enough over the years to know men at every ATF office in the state. He also knew they wouldn't be interested in an old man's death on some forgotten lake. Even the proof of three burned cabins wouldn't pull them into his vacation investigation. They'd probably say that on a wild night a lightning storm could cause as much damage.

Luke needed more evidence, plus once he caught the fish he wanted to go back and offer them for supper. If it were another time, another place he might have asked Allie out on a date. Brought her flowers instead of fish. They'd go somewhere nice to eat and she'd be wearing something besides jeans. Who knew, in another world they might even end up in bed—but not in this world. She was as much of a suspect as any of the other nuts around her. Being attracted to her didn't take her off the list.

Reaching his boat, Luke had just pulled on his backpack when car lights turned into the drive and headed toward the store. He ducked down and watched as the two fishermen he'd seen earlier climbed out and stumbled to the porch. The big one he'd heard called Hank almost dragged the other up the steps.

"Drunks," he swore and lowered his pack back out of sight.

Luke moved toward the store as they pounded on the door.

"Help," the big one yelled. "Somebody help!"

Lights flickered on upstairs. Luke hoped Allie stopped to put on clothes. He didn't know if he could take the sight of pink panties again.

"Help! My friend is dying." Hank wiggled his buddy as if showing proof.

Allie pulled open the door as Luke stepped onto the side of the porch. When she flipped on the light all he saw for a moment was blood covering the smaller man's chest.

Hank kept yelling, "You got to help him, lady. I can't."

Allie backed away so pale Luke thought she might faint.

He rushed forward, stepping into the role of an authority as easily as he would well-worn shoes. "What happened here?"

He helped guide the bleeding man inside. The smell of whiskey and blood blended thick in the air.

"I don't know," the town crier yelled. "We was fishing off the bank a little after dark and the next thing I knew he was screaming like the devil had a grip on him."

Luke moved in close, pulling the bloody man's hand away so he could see the wound. His chest was bloodied but no wound visible. Luke grabbed the man by the shoulder with one hand and forced his head up with the other.

Blood dripped in a steady stream from both nostrils. A huge hook pierced the left side of his nose. "It's not as bad as it looks, boys." Luke hoped he was right. "Get me ice, a pot of cold water, and a few towels, would you, Allie?"

She nodded and almost ran to the kitchen. Luke pulled the patient to the first chair in the café area. "Now, tell me again what happened."

The bleeding man took a deep breath and forced words out. "I hooked myself trying to cast. It was dark. Hank thought I was hung up on something so he yanked on the line. When he did, I fell forward on my face."

Hank agreed to his part in the crime. "His face splat against a boulder half the size of a car. Thinking I'd killed him, I fell into the water trying to get to him. I got tangled in the line. I could have drowned."

No one listened to Hank.

"I think your nose is broke," Luke said, more to himself than the bleeding drunk. He'd seen enough bar fights to recognize one. They usually bled sufficiently to stop a fight.

Hank knelt down beside his friend, now that he realized

death wasn't near. He seemed fascinated with the wound. "It's broke all right, Dan. You'll be sneezing in your left ear from now on."

Luke frowned at the drunk's bedside manner. "Take a seat, Hank. I'll get him cleaned up, then I'll drive you both to town."

Allie returned with a pan of cold water and towels. Luke dipped one of the towels, rolled it, and hung it over the back of Dan's neck. The chill might sober him up and slow the blood flow.

While Luke washed Dan's face, he told Allie to search for a pair of pliers. He wasn't surprised when she handed them to him and disappeared. The drunk did look frightening. Blood still dripped. The hook stuck out the left side of his nose and both eyes were starting to turn black.

Luke snapped off the end of the hook and pulled it through the flesh. Then, bracing his fingers on both sides of Dan's nose, he snapped it back into place.

The drunk yelped, then his eyes crossed in pain.

"Can you breathe?" Luke asked, hoping Dan wouldn't pass out.

"Yeah," Dan answered. "That hurt like hell." He sounded as if the pain had sobered him somewhat.

So much for a thank-you, Luke thought, then handed Dan the towel and looked up at Hank. "Are you sober enough to drive him to the emergency room in Lubbock?"

Hank nodded. "Then, I think we'll go home. We've had about as much fun as we can stand for one night."

"Yeah," Dan mumbled around the towel. "And after my wife gives me hell, she'll feed me till I feel better."

Luke walked them to their car and watched until they pulled out on the road. He almost felt sorry for them. Unless he guessed wrong, they were probably both married and were in for a great deal of teasing.

"Want a cup of coffee?" Allie asked from the porch.

Luke knew he didn't have time. He had a full night of hunting to do if he planned to find a meth lab among the hundred shacks and cabins around here, but he said, "Sure."

While she put a pot on, he stripped his shirt and washed blood off his hands and arms. His T-shirt was tight over his skin, the way he wore them when he strapped a bullet-proof vest on.

"You growing lately?" She studied him.

"No," he lied. "I just bought the wrong size."

Allie turned her back to him as she pulled two cups from the shelf.

"You still wearing pink?"

"What?" She followed his gaze down her body. "Oh," she muttered in sudden understanding. "Not that it's any of your business, but my grandmother always buys me under-wear and socks for Christmas. She thinks I like pink."

Luke couldn't believe he'd asked her, but now he had, he was glad she didn't act all offended.

"We through talking about underwear?" he asked as he met her stare.

"Yes," she answered calmly.

"Then, would you mind if I kissed you again? I'd kind of like to know if it was half as good as I remember it being."

She smiled and moved to within an inch of him.

He would have liked to pull her close and feel her body against him, but he'd only asked for a kiss and now wasn't the time to step over the line.

Cupping the side of her face with his hand, he lowered his mouth to hers. For a moment, he thought she tasted of cherry syrup and bubble-gum toothpaste, then only of Al-lie. Sweet, sweet Allie.

She rose to her toes and wrapped her arms around his neck as if she feared he might end the kiss too soon.

Luke laughed against her lips. Moving away wasn't likely to happen. He had no plan beyond kissing her. For right now it seemed enough.

Slowly she leaned into him and the kiss deepened.

Chapter 18

When Luke pulled away, I couldn't think of anything to say. He wasn't the drifter I'd first thought him to be, but— except for kissing me—he gave no indication that he welcomed any personal questions. Happiness seemed rationed in his world. Somewhere an invisible timer sounded and he stopped.

He had simply straightened, kissed my forehead, and vanished, leaving me with a full pot of coffee and no answers. He reminded me of one of those old westerns where a stranger rides in, kisses the girl, kills the bad guy, and leaves without ever saying a word. Only problem was, I didn't know if he played the outlaw or the hero.

I filled my mug and moved to what was quickly becoming my favorite spot—the bay window overlooking the lake. As I passed the office, I retrieved my ledger book and a pencil. I knew it would be hours before I slept, so I began to draw.

First Luke, in silhouette, standing by the fire. I fought to capture every detail of the way he stood. Almost military, I decided, as if he were on guard. The fire came alive in the dancing shadow and light across his body and the dark water formed an inky backdrop.

On the second page I drew Mary Lynn and Paul Madison with the afternoon sun shining behind them as they shared a pot of tea. They sat, the old maid dressed in her frumpy, out-of-style clothes, and the hardened banker with his life shattering around him. There might only be a few years' difference in their ages, but they seemed worlds apart. He probably knew the best places to eat in every city, played handball in private clubs, and read the *Times* in bed on Sunday mornings. She didn't look like she knew who the president was, considered gardening exercise, and had stains from canning berries on her fingers. But somehow, for that moment, they belonged together.

I caught the scene where I'd seen her lean toward him and lay her hand hesitantly atop his in comfort. Mary Lynn had a gentle heart not meant for crisis. Paul was more the type who thrived on a challenge, but not this time—this time he was broken and she'd been strong enough to pull him back.

When I finished drawing, I looked around the store and the tiny café. This world I'd tumbled into seemed small, plain, yet when I had to leave I knew I'd be glad for the sketches. I needed to remember every detail.

I went up to bed thinking of Luke and trying to get the pieces of him to fit together. He'd handled the drunks' crisis like a pro. Where would a man get such training? It occurred to me that I might be better off not knowing. But I fell asleep guessing.

～

Nana woke me a little after dawn. "There's blood in the café," she said without emotion.

"I'm sorry." I sat up feeling like I'd just closed my eyes. The coffee and kisses I'd had last night weren't on the list of recommended sleep aides. "I should have cleaned it up, Nana. Luke took care of a guy with a bloody nose last night."

Nana grinned. "I'm glad I missed that visitor. It wasn't any of us was it?"

I knew what she meant. The Nesters had become our people. "No. Only one of the weekend fishermen. I don't imagine we'll be seeing them again."

I followed her down and cleaned up the mess, then washed Luke's shirt. He didn't come in to get it and that night there was no fire out by the water. I didn't want to admit to myself that I missed him. But I did.

～

The next night, I built the fire, telling myself I needed to burn off some of the driftwood, but in truth I thought it would make me feel less lonely. Not that Luke was much company anyway. Nana said he'd dropped by for a while when I'd gone into town to the bank. Lately she had trouble telling what happened an hour ago from a week ago. For her the days at the lake weren't days of the week or month, but simply days at the lake.

I watched the flames and remembered all the people who'd dropped by since dawn. It had been a busy day. If it kept up I'd be doubling my weekly order and paying for it with profit. When we had to leave—if we lasted the winter—we might be driving away with enough money to make a real start. Nothing big, just the down payment on a little house. A real house. Our own house.

If Jefferson's Crossing wasn't really mine? I was beginning to think it could be. I had stopped watching for the lawyer to show up. My name had been in the will and all the Nesters seemed to know I was coming. Maybe for once Nana and I wouldn't have to pack up and leave.

I almost swore. I was dreaming again. You'd think at some point I'd learn. Where had the dreams ever gotten me? Like all people, I was a prisoner living in a tiny cell. My view of the world was only a small window and the most I could hope for in a lifetime was maybe to see one or two perfect days. Not a winter. Not a year. Happiness doesn't pile up that long. Maybe I should just be thankful for tonight and the fire dancing before me.

"You look like you got the weight of the world on those shoulders."

Willie moved closer. I could smell him before I could see him clearly.

"No, I was just thinking." I tried not to act like he made me nervous. The man had never done anything out of line toward me or Nana that I knew of, but I couldn't shake the warning Micki had given me. She'd delivered a caution along with the snacks that first day, a caution I thought of every time I saw the old man.

"Thinking only leads to trouble, girl. I gave it up for Lent once and found out I could live without it, so I never went back." Without being asked, he sat down a few feet away on one of the rocks.

I smiled at him for his effort to cheer me up.

"Have you seen Luke?" he asked. "I need to talk to him."

For a moment, I thought he'd read my mind. "No. I haven't seen him but Nana said he came by this morning."

Willie stuck his hands out toward the fire as if the night were cold.

I fought the urge to move farther away. "You wouldn't happen to know where Luke stays out here?"

"Sure," he answered, pointing with his head to the left. "He's not yelling close, but his cabin is on the other side of that stand of trees."

"Really?" I'd walked along that beach a few times when the lake was down a few feet and saw no sign of a cabin. "Are you sure?"

Willie looked like he was thinking about whether to tell me more or not, but finally, he said, "I took supplies to his place with Jefferson once when Luke was laid up."

"Sick?" I couldn't imagine Luke with even a cold.

"No. Shot."

If he hadn't smelled so bad I would have jumped over and choked more out of the man, but I figured the air at a closer proximity would kill me before I could cut off his windpipe. "How'd he get shot?" I wasn't sure I wanted to know, but I had to ask.

"Don't know." Willie shrugged as if he'd never thought to ask. "You got any of that bar-be-qued jerky in the store? I like the one that says 'hot and chewy' on the front."

I'd talked to him enough to know it was unlikely I'd get much more out of him. His mind was like a roulette wheel, not likely to circle round to the same topic any-time soon.

A rumble thundered across the lake like a faraway can-non shot.

We both stood up, knowing what we heard wasn't natu-ral. A heartbeat later, flames shot as high as the trees along the far north shore.

"Trouble," Willie whispered. "Big trouble." He turned

and hurried down the dock as fast as his short legs would carry him.

I shouted for Nana to stay inside and ran down the dock in time to jump into Willie's boat just as he shoved off. We headed toward the fire that grew brighter by the second.

Little wind stirred the water, but we were going across the current. I held on tight as the boat bucked what felt like speed bumps in our path.

"Who lives over there?" I yelled at Willie over the motor.

"No one that I know of. That property by the dam has been for sale so long the sign's rotted away. Mary Lynn's place is half a mile down the shore away from the dam. She's the closest neighbor. I've seen a few campers set up near there in the summer, but the road's too bad to bother with when there are better places south."

"Then what is burning?" I leaned over the front of the boat as if I could see better by being a foot nearer. The closer we got, the bigger the fire seemed. This was no campfire.

He shook his head. "There's an old lodge up there by the dam. It's been closed for twenty years or more. I've never been up close, but I've seen the roofs of several cabins surrounding it."

"Should we turn back and call the fire department?"

He laughed. "They won't come all the way out here. And even if they would, by the time we'd get to the gas station on the highway, whatever is on fire up in those trees will be burned to the ground."

We bumped a sandy shoreline. I jumped into knee-deep water and helped him pull the boat to shore. By the time we stood on dry sand, I saw headlights jumping along a trail from the dam road. Judging from the way the lights were bobbing, nothing but a four-wheel drive would make it from the main road.

Willie and I moved closer.

"Smells terrible," he mumbled.

I had to agree. Something more than wood burned.

Paul arrived next, jumping out of an old Jeep. "What happened?"

Willie paid little attention to the cabin burning so hot someone must have set the fire with gasoline. He rushed to Paul and patted the Jeep's fender. "Where'd you get this old relic?"

"It came with the place I bought. Took me all day to get it running."

I stormed up the bank, frustrated they'd stopped to talk cars in the middle of a crisis. "What happened here? Was anyone hurt?"

Both men seemed to remember this was not a midnight picnic and joined me as we cautiously moved closer to the tiny square cabin. The rock front was still standing; a door and two windows had blown open. The roof and other walls had caved into the fire. The flames blazing behind the wall and across the wooden porch made the front of the cabin look evil, almost as if it grinned at us with fiery eyes and a flaming smile.

I stood, staring, hypnotized by the beauty of its horror.

Other men arrived in boats and on off-road bikes. They stomped around the cabin looking for something that might have started a fire on a clear night.

One yelled, "Circle as close as you can, boys. We want to make sure there's no brush that might catch fire."

Another complained that the place stank.

Paul pulled me back to reality. "No sign of life around the place, Allie. If someone started this, they got out fast." He leaned closer to me. "Something's not right, though. I heard the explosion, then saw the flames. Why would any-one want to blow up this place?"

I ran toward the fire, realizing for the first time that someone might have been inside. Maybe it was someone's crazy way of committing suicide.

Willie grabbed my arm and pulled me back. "Careful there, girl."

"But someone . . ."

He shook his head. "No one is in there. No one alive." He walked me back to where the others stood. "But I agree with Paul. I worked construction a few years. I seen a house burn like this once that had a gas leak."

The smoke decreased Willie's fishy smell so I held my ground. "You think it was a gas fire."

Willie shook his head. "These are primitive cabins. No gas, no electricity."

"But could someone have been in there?" I stared at the fire, feeling the heat on my skin through my clothes from fifteen feet away. If someone had been inside, their skin would have melted away in seconds.

"Maybe." Paul put his hand on my shoulder. "But if anyone was closer than we are now, they're gone, so no use worrying." He lifted a flashlight. "I'll circle one more time to make sure it doesn't catch anything else on fire. I don't like a fire being this close to Mary Lynn's place."

Willie shook his head. "The ground and trees are still wet. It's not likely to spread."

We heard other boats pulling to shore. Shouts came from the water as more arrived. Paul, being the first on the scene, took charge. Willie wanted to stay and talk to newcomers, telling all he didn't know to each person who docked.

The fire roared for a while, then having eaten away the rotting boards quickly, began to die. The fiery monster made of rock wall seemed to be closing his eyes.

We all stood around guessing at how, on a cloudless

night, the fire could have started. No one had the answer, but we all agreed that Willie should stay until it was completely out.

The old man puffed up at his new appointment.

Paul offered to drive me home and the night's excitement was over.

Chapter 19

Luke lowered his field glasses and swore. His lead to the drug business had disappeared into smoke; all the evidence was burning up and any clues were being stomped on by curious campers and Allie.

He'd been sitting at this spot, watching the drug dealers for two days. He'd even made up names for each of them as they'd unloaded their supplies and set up a lab.

Sneezy, a little guy whose drug habit was so bad his nose dripped constantly.

Tanker, a big man in black, who wore a shoulder holster and a huge cannon of a gun. He never bothered to talk to the other two unless he had to.

The third Luke called Skidder, for he was constantly in motion. Skidder's clothes hung loose on his thin frame as if he'd lost a great deal of weight in a short period of time. Meth could do that. Unfortunately the teeth and hair disappear along with the weight.

Luke hadn't moved in on them because he knew none was the boss and he'd love to catch the head man. If he didn't, the boss would find three more losers to do his dirty work within days. Luke had too many questions and none of these clowns would know the answers. He had to stay put and watch. Eventually, the main guy would show up to make sure they'd set everything up right.

After sleeping against a tree, Luke was tired and hungry when the three came back to work the second day. Still no boss.

He watched as they hauled all the supplies from an SUV and finished the setup. About sunset, Tanker drove off and returned an hour later with burgers in a bag, and beer. To Luke's surprise, they sat down on the slip of dry sand by the water and ate. He could see them plainly, thanks to the moon and his field glasses. He could almost make out what they were saying. Skidder and Sneezy seemed far more interested in shooting up than in food. While they sampled drugs from their last batch, Tanker ate all three hamburgers, drank most of the beer, and lay out like a beached whale on the warm sand.

Skidder and Sneezy laughed and pointed as Tanker began to snore, and then must have decided to have another round of meth for dessert with their beer.

The night cooled. The druggies left their fat friend on the beach and went inside their newest lab. They had their heads together, obviously plotting something as they walked away. Skidder opened the back of the SUV and took out something before he went inside, but Luke couldn't tell if it was a small suitcase or a can of gasoline.

Luke waited. He knew the rules. His next step was to call in backup. He'd wait a little longer to make sure they were all asleep, then canoe back to his place. From there he'd climb into the car he hadn't used in two weeks and drive until his cell phone could pick up a signal. He'd have a team out in an hour. They'd clear out the three losers and wait for the big boss to show up.

Only he hadn't had time to carry out any plan. Five minutes after Sneezy and Skidder went inside, Luke heard an explosion. Fire exploded across the inside walls of the cabin. He heard screams, and a car door slammed.

"Shit," Luke swore. The two fools must have added sniffing gas to their collection of drugs.

He ran along the shoreline toward the cabin, trying to see past the cloud of smoke that seemed to be doubling by the second. When he reached the spot where their partner had been sleeping on the beach, the big guy was gone.

As Luke rubbed his eyes, trying to see through the smoke, Tanker disappeared near the SUV.

Luke moved closer, trying not to breathe. The sound of cussing and crying circled in the smoke as the SUV's engine roared.

By the time Luke reached for his Glock, the SUV was in the trees heading out. He ran, taking a shortcut to intersect Tanker at the dam road, but the big guy was driving like a madman.

Luke only got one shot off before the SUV was out of range.

Since then, he'd done nothing but watch from the trees. He could have stepped out and made everyone keep clear of the scene, but dressed in his camouflage everyone wouldn't take long to figure him for some kind of cop.

He wouldn't have minded if the Nesters knew, but there was a good chance the boss of this infestation of meth labs would be among the folks standing around. Whoever picked the spots had known which cabins were abandoned. And that person might guess that a senior ATF agent wouldn't be here just taking a vacation.

They might figure out that Luke was looking into Old Man Jefferson's death, too. If someone had killed Jefferson, and knew he was looking, the killer would go so far underground Luke would never find him.

Luke slipped into the night, moving silently to his canoe. No one watching the fire saw him slice into the water and disappear.

Chapter 20

I tried to talk to Paul as I hung on to the side of his Jeep for dear life. He bumped his way along the back road to the bridge, crossed over, and headed for Jefferson's Crossing.

"You think someone set the fire?"

He didn't answer.

"You think it might be drifters? I guess it could be kids." The thought crossed my mind that the only drifter I knew was Luke.

"Willie said sometimes kids come out to get drunk. I guess they could have picked that place." I'd seen a few beer bottles along the beach, but not enough for a party.

I glanced at him. Though too dark to see his face, his body was rigid. "You worried that someone might be inside?"

"No," he almost snapped. "I don't like the idea of the fire being so close to Mary Lynn's place. Think about it: If the wind had been up, the conditions dry, it could have spread, and she doesn't even have a phone."

I agreed without asking how Paul Madison knew Mary Lynn didn't have a phone. If I were a cop, I might have also asked how he got there so fast. That first day when he'd come in with his wife, he'd said their cabin was on the south shore. That would make him farther away from the fire than Willie and I had been, and traveling by road around here was far slower than by boat.

We turned onto the highway, passing the sheriff's car with light flashing. Paul slowed. I could hear him breathing like a man forcing himself to calm. I couldn't help but wonder if he was a man new to emotion of any kind. He reminded me of one of those rich fraternity guys who thought life would always come easy for them. This week, the letter from his wife and the fire seemed to knock the starch out of both the man and his clothes.

"So"—I tried to think of something other than the fire to talk about—"what do you do when you're not fishing?"

He smiled then. We both knew he had yet to buy a pole or bait.

"I work for Wells Fargo. Mostly handling stocks for companies who want to diversify."

I had little idea what he was talking about so I remained silent.

"This is the first vacation I've had in almost ten years." He seemed to calm as he talked. "Since we worked together, Lillian and I traveled together, but it was always business related. I thought we'd buy the place and take some time off for once." His laughter came cruel, like a hard hiccup. "It seems the only time off she wanted was time off from me."

"I'm sorry."

He shrugged. "Since I've pretty much given up sleep, I've had some time to analyze my life. I think our marriage starved to death over the years. I guess I was just more comfortable living with the corpse than she was."

I nodded, trying to understand.

"I'm taking a few months off. I think Lillian will get my job in the settlement. She was always better at it than me anyway."

He didn't sound bitter, only hurt. The kind of hurt that runs all the way to the bone.

When we turned into my drive, I said, "Thanks for dropping me off."

"You're welcome." He pulled near the dock and cut the engine. "You sell any cigarettes?"

"No." I wouldn't have guessed him for a smoker. "But I could make coffee."

"All right." He climbed from the Jeep.

Coffee was probably the last thing Paul Madison needed. He seemed wound tighter than a thin rubber band on a hot day. I got out and followed him up the porch. "Lights on in the kitchen, which means Nana is still up."

"Mary Lynn's car is over by the campsite. She's probably inside, too. When we saw the fire she said she'd drive over and check to make sure Mrs. Deals called the sheriff." He didn't look like he planned to add any more information, but as he held the door for me, he did. "She said whenever there's any kind of trouble, the locals gather here."

I stepped inside. Paul was right: Several of the Nesters were there already. Mary Lynn with her tiny dog, Timothy, and Mrs. Deals. They'd pushed two tables together as if expecting others.

Mary Lynn made room for Paul and asked, "What's happening over there?"

Paul gave everyone the facts while I poured more coffee. Nana must have brought out the leftover fried pies from this morning, but she was nowhere in sight. I sat down guessing she'd be putting on more coffee by now.

"Are you all right?" I heard Paul ask Mary Lynn.

She nodded, but she looked like she'd been crying.

"Things frighten her," Mrs. Deals said matter-of-factly. Then, with a gesture as awkward as if an amateur puppeteer were controlling her movements, Mrs. Deals jerked forward and patted Mary Lynn's hand. "Everything will be fine come morning, you'll see."

"Scared the hell out of me," Timothy added. "I'd fallen asleep out on the deck and for a moment I woke not remembering where I was. I've never heard a sound like that out here."

"It looked like the place exploded, then burned," Paul said as I handed him his coffee. "I wouldn't be surprised if the sheriff wants to talk to us all."

Mrs. Deals frowned. "You think someone could have set the fire?"

Paul shrugged.

Timothy stood. "I'm out of here. That sheriff makes me nervous. I swear my dad pays him to check on me. He stops by my place weekly to harass me and give me advice on how to stop wasting my life." He laughed. "He calls me by my last name, like he's reminding himself who I am. I get the feeling that if he ever forgets, I'll find out about unnecessary force personally."

Mrs. Deals laughed. "I know how you feel. He does the same thing to me. Only he doesn't frighten me."

Timothy looked surprised, then winked at the old woman. "Thatta girl. Give him hell."

Mrs. Deals raised her chin. "Believe me, I do."

Nana pushed her way through the kitchen door with a platter of ginger pancakes. "This is all I could think to cook fast. Who wants some?"

I closed my eyes. I hadn't had ginger pancakes in years. My mouth could already taste them. When I looked up, everyone had already helped themselves and the stack was half gone.

We talked and ate as the night aged. When everyone left I stood next to Nana and helped with the dishes. "Did the fire scare you?" I asked.

She shook her head. "I went out on the porch and watched it for a while. It reminded me of that summer I lived with my brother's wife, Mary. We rented a place on a lake no bigger than this one. She thought it would be cooler than in town, but it was hotter than blazes that July Fourth. Someone started shooting off fireworks and burned half an acre of trees down."

"Did you watch it with Red?"

I was thinking of the boy named Red who took her to a dance the summer she turned sixteen. Her one summer when she felt young, she once told me. That first summer after Pearl Harbor, when she'd been too young to realize the world had already changed and would never be the same.

Nana grinned. "As a matter of fact, I did. The fire didn't seem all that terrible watching from across the lake. He held my hand in the dark and once in a while I can still feel his fingers around mine."

I'd never heard my grandmother say anything so romantic. She might forget who came in the store an hour after they left, but she could still remember the feel of a boy's hand after sixty years.

She folded the towel and brushed her fingers against the wind chime. As the tinkling sounded, she whispered, "Good night, dear."

I walked her through the dark café and hugged her before she started up to bed. "I love you, Nana."

She just smiled and said she knew.

The night had cooled when I walked out to the dock to

see if I could still spot the cabin on the north shore burning, but the fire was out. A chill moved over me. Jefferson's
Crossing had been made of the same materials—old wood
and rocks. It could burn just as fast.

I didn't want to think about losing my place in a fire.
Better to have the lawyer drive up with papers ordering me
out. He'd make some official announcement that he'd
found the wrong Allie Daniels and give me two days to be
off the property. As I packed, I would remind myself that
leaving was far better than losing the place to a fire.

If Nana were here, she'd tell me to stop thinking of
trouble coming. She'd say bad times never need to be
called, they'll come on their own. But for me, thinking of
what might happen—walking through the worst possible
outcomes—helped. Then, I could tell myself I could
survive.

A movement caught my eye. I watched as Luke swung his
powerful body up on the far end of the dock and walk in my
direction. He wore his wrinkled trousers, old work boots,
and a black T-shirt. The T-shirt was the first clothing I'd ever
seen him wear that looked like it might belong to him.

"You see the fire?"

He nodded as he moved slowly toward me.

"I went over for a closer look." I wanted to ask where
he'd been the past two days, but feared he might say that it
was none of my business. "I was worried about you. I
thought maybe you'd been there. I thought . . ."

Without a word, he stopped an inch from me and put his
arms around me. For a moment I didn't react, then I closed
the distance between us.

He just held me, secure in his arms. I hadn't realized
how dearly I needed to feel safe. I wrapped my arms
around his neck and held on so tightly I was surprised he
could breathe.

"You all right, Allie?" he whispered against my ear.

"I am now. I was afraid you'd been in the fire." I knew I was making little sense, but when I'd been over by the fire I could almost feel him near.

He leaned away from me and tugged my face up. "You were worried about me?"

I realized I'd been a fool to even think he might have been in the old place. But I didn't know where he lived and his behavior sometimes didn't make all that much sense.

I thought he was going to tell me he wasn't my problem, but he brushed his lips against mine as he whispered, "It's been a long time since anyone worried about me."

I closed my eyes, waiting for his kiss, but he pulled away gently and disappeared into the night, leaving me turned wrong-side out with emptiness.

Chapter 21

I wasn't surprised the next morning to wake up to the sheriff pounding on my door. Pulling on clothes as I walked, I managed to button everything before I opened the door.

There stood the law, all three hundred fifty pounds of him. "Good morning, Sheriff." I squinted as the sun reflected off his badge.

He frowned. "Don't know what's good about it." As usual, he stormed in without waiting for an invitation. Only this morning his son, Dillon, was right behind him. Dillon looked sleepy and bored so I guessed it hadn't been his idea to ride along in the cop car this morning.

"Have you got any coffee?"

I took a deep breath and said, "I can smell it so Nana must have it ready. We don't usually open the café for breakfast but I could if you need something to eat?"

Fletcher shook his head. "I'm here on official business. I'll take the coffee and then I'll be wanting some answers."

I started to say that answers cost extra, but I didn't think he'd see the joke, so I headed for the kitchen. Glancing back, I remembered his shadow. "You want anything, Dillon?"

The boy looked up, surprised I called him by name. He shook his head.

I pushed through the kitchen door, thinking the boy didn't quite measure up to all his father's bragging, but then if he had, he'd probably be able to walk across the lake.

Luke and Nana had their heads together at the little table. I could tell they'd been laughing about something.

"Sheriff Fletcher's here," I said, knowing they would have had to be deaf not to have heard him. "Why didn't one of you answer the door?"

Nana giggled. "We were just flipping for it."

Luke flipped a quarter. "Best ten out of nineteen."

I frowned at him. "Why don't you go in and talk to him. He said he had a few questions."

Luke stood. "I'm out of here."

"Coward," I muttered as I watched Luke slip out the back door.

Nana sat down with her coffee and scrambled eggs. She didn't like the sheriff and saw no need to greet him. I could smell cinnamon rolls baking and knew if the sheriff wasn't gone by the time they were done we'd be out a few dollars' worth of them.

So when I went back to the store I suggested we talk in the sunshine of the porch, hoping he wouldn't smell the food.

He agreed as he pulled out a pad. "I'd like you to start with a detailed account of what you saw last night. I understand from another source that you were there."

"Not much to tell," I said as I sat on the newly painted

porch swing. "Willie and I saw the fire. We went over in his boat."

The sheriff looked at the chair next to me and decided he'd stand. "Did you see anyone leaving or running away from it?" He set his coffee on the porch railing and prepared to take down my statement.

"No," I said, thinking I'd pay money to see if the lawn chair would hold under his weight.

He took a minute to write something, gulped his coffee, and asked, "Anyone suspicious at all, beyond the nuts who hang around here normally?"

"No."

"Do you have any reason to believe it might have been set?"

"No. Willie suggested kids sometimes come out to drink in the summers, but except for a few beer bottles lying around I didn't see any sign of that."

The huge man slapped his notebook against his leg as he paced back and forth. Then he stopped suddenly and jotted something down.

While he wrote, I asked, "What did you find?"

"Nothing," he said a bit too quickly. "I'm turning it in as a lightning strike. Anything else will bring strangers out here and we'll know no more when they've finished poking around than we did before."

He held his coffee cup up to me as he studied his notebook.

I took the cup, wondering if he did the same thing to his wife when he wanted another cup. If so, and I were his wife, I'd be giving him some serious lumps with his next cup.

I went inside and refilled his coffee, then stood at the door listening to the sheriff talk to Dillon. "There's nothing but nutcases and losers out here, son. Half these people should be locked away somewhere. If the whole place burned down we could write it off as a beautification project."

"What about that Miss O'Reilly? She seemed nice enough this morning."

The sheriff swore. "She's afraid of her own shadow. Couldn't take people in town talking about her family. She'd fall apart if she had to deal with half the shit I have to put up with in this job."

Fletcher lowered his voice. "I'm telling you, son, there ain't nothing out here but losers and misfits. I could haul every one of them in for being a bother to civilization and no one would care."

I missed a few words as the Landry boys' boat puttered by.

"See them two"—Fletcher raised his voice over the motor—"they're the Landry brothers and they don't have a brain cell between them." He laughed. "Some say their mother was a catfish—that's why they're both ugly and dumb."

I heard the sheriff laugh at his own joke, but Dillon remained silent.

Anger boiled in me. Coffee sloshed, almost scalding my hand, but I barely noticed.

It took me a moment to even feel the arm around my waist tugging me backward. Luke lifted me up against his side and walked backward into the tiny office, out of sight, before letting go.

When I turned to face him, his blue eyes were laughing.

"Did you hear what the sheriff said?" I whispered.

He grabbed one of the old towels Nana kept on a shelf to clean up after what she called "leaky fishermen" and blotted at the coffee on my hand. "It doesn't matter," he said. "But I saw murder in your eyes and I thought I'd better pull you back." He took the coffee carefully as if it were a loaded weapon.

I smiled, realizing I had thought of crowning Fletcher with a coffee cup. "You're right. What he says doesn't matter."

I reached for the cup.

Luke held it up. "I'll take it to him."

"But you . . ."

"I know, but I'd rather face him than have to break up a fight between the two of you." He winked. "By the way, if it happened my money would be on you."

I watched as he walked through the door into the lion's den on my front porch. Moving close to the window, I watched, feeling like a driver slowing down to see a wreck.

"Allie said you asked for a refill," Luke lied as he sat the cup on the table beside the sheriff.

For the first time, I realized the sheriff looked a little uncomfortable. "Haven't seen much of you around here lately." Fletcher straightened slightly.

Luke kept his head down, not looking at Fletcher.

"Didn't you tell me last time we talked that you were only here for a short time?" When Luke didn't answer, the sheriff raised his voice. "Seems to me that short time should be about up."

Luke stood, staring at the planks in the porch. His body was as still as stone and his hands hung loosely at his sides, but I sensed he waited, not frightened at all. It occurred to me that he looked like a man playing a role. A role he wasn't naturally born to play.

Nana interrupted the interrogation by stepping outside with a tray of hot cinnamon rolls. They were as big as a man's fist and dripping with icing.

"Good," she said to Luke. "I was hoping you were still here. Would you mind taking a few of these out to the Landry boys? I told them they'd be ready a little after dawn and they said they'd be waiting at the end of the dock."

Everyone, including me, looked down the dock at the two old men in the tiny boat. They sat at either end waiting.

Luke took two of the rolls, wrapped them in waxed paper, and walked out toward the water.

The sheriff started to object, but Nana stepped in front of him. "Now, Sheriff, you have to try one of these."

He didn't look like a man who often turned down food. He tugged a hot roll away from the others and slipped it onto a square of paper.

Nana offered the boy one, but Dillon shook his head.

About the time Nana stepped back inside, I looked down the dock and noticed both the Landry boys and Luke had disappeared.

Fletcher frowned. "You know where that man lives?"

"Nope," I said honestly.

The sheriff licked his thick fingers. "I'm going to have a long talk with him one of these times. That fellow's got trouble written all over him."

"You think he's a criminal?" If so, that was probably higher on Fletcher's list than the rest of us Nesters.

"I don't know. There's something that don't set right with him." He looked over at Dillon. "You learn to tell the make of a man when you've worn the badge awhile. I can tell a druggie a mile off and a thief, he holds his hands out of sight. Before you leave for college next year, I'll teach you a few things you'll never learn down at Sam Houston University, not even if you get your doctorate in Criminal Justice. There's some things only experience can teach."

He turned back to me. "You know where Willie Dowman is?"

"Nope," I answered a bit too quickly.

He stared at me a moment. "You're just a wealth of information, aren't you? Who else did you see out by the fire last night?"

"It was dark. I couldn't see much." I couldn't believe I was lying, but suddenly I didn't want to help. I might be switching to the arsonist's side, but in some strange way it seemed better company.

He must have figured out I would be little help, so he downed the last of his free coffee and headed toward his car. Halfway there, he turned around. "Old Man Jefferson told me once that his niece was bright. He must have not known you well, girl."

"I'm not a girl." I stared at him. "Size doesn't make a woman any more than volume makes a man."

He opened his mouth to say something, then seemed to notice Dillon standing a few feet away.

To my surprise, he tipped his hat and said simply, "Later."

I crossed back into the store thinking I didn't like the sound of that word.

I stood next to Nana and watched the sheriff's car pull out of our drive.

"He's puffed up worse than three-day-old roadkill," she whispered. "My pa used to say a sheriff is only your friend when he's running for office. I never believed him, until now."

Chapter 22

Sunday
September 29
09.30 hours

Luke walked the path back to his cabin, frustrated that he couldn't deal with Sheriff Fletcher the way he'd like to. But after last night it was more important than ever to let everyone believe he was just a fisherman on vacation. Someone who knew the lake well was picking the spots for the meth labs and the sheriff would never catch anyone.

Luke had seen Fletcher's kind of cop before. Go for the easiest answer. Keep the paperwork short. Don't ask questions if you don't want to hear the answers.

One theory was starting to make more sense every day. Jefferson must have learned something about the illegal activity going on. He was the one person who knew everything about the place. He could have watched trouble rolling in like a storm. And, if the drug dealers found out he knew something, or even suspected, they might have helped him make that final step off the dock that sent him to heaven early.

One clue had been echoing in his mind since the day he went into Jefferson's apartment. Why would a man who quit taking his medicine keep the bottles around for months? Why would he even bother to go to town to pick them up? Luke had asked everyone close to Jefferson and none of them had picked them up for him. It was a tiny detail that didn't make sense. A puzzle Luke needed to find the answer to.

Luke stared out at the water, wishing he could see what Jefferson must have seen. Not only seen, but prepared for. It was like he got all his world in order just in case something happened to him—like he knew what was coming. Knew and couldn't stop it.

If he'd only left a clue.

Luke felt a sudden adrenaline rush. What if Jefferson had left something? He'd have to hide it good, someplace whoever killed him wouldn't think to look. But where?

The only logical place was Jefferson's Crossing, and looking for a clue wouldn't be easy with Allie and Nana around, Allie was just starting to trust him.

Smiling, he remembered their kiss. She might not fully know him, but she was attracted to him. He could play that fact to his advantage.

Mumbling an oath, he thought of the problem in his logic. He was also attracted to her.

Luke slipped into the trees and zigzagged his way to his cabin. The place was still dark and cool, but welcoming in an old shirt kind of way. He removed his gun from his boot, locked the door, and flipped up into the loft. Within minutes, he was sound asleep.

The afternoon sun reflected off the lake and into his window when he awoke starving. All he'd eaten the two days he'd watched Sneezy, Skidder, and Tanker set up the meth lab was trail mix and bottled water. He needed food. Real food.

Without giving it much more thought, he crossed to Jefferson's Crossing and slipped into the back door by the kitchen.

Nana looked up from molding a piecrust and said the same thing she always said when she saw him. "Hungry?"

"Starving," he answered.

"How many eggs can you eat?"

"A dozen."

She giggled.

He sat down and watched her scramble up a dozen eggs while she waited for the butter to melt atop bread she'd put beneath the broiler. Luke had been raised by his father and grandfather. Cooking around their house was limited to a can opener and the microwave. Her skill amazed him.

She stirred the eggs, flipped the broiler open just as the butter began to bubble atop thick slices of homemade bread. With a quick shake, she covered the butter with a cinnamon and sugar mixture and slipped the bread back inside.

A few minutes later, she passed him a plate of eggs and toast with a thin crust of heaven on top.

"Thanks." He breathed deeply, tasting the food in his throat before he took a bite.

"I know how you like cinnamon and we ran out of the rolls before nine this morning. Hope the toast will hold you till supper. I made chicken potpies for everyone."

"Great." He took a bite, and by the time he'd finished chewing, a glass of milk sat beside his plate. "Nana, would you consider marrying me?" he said with a cinnamon-sparkled smile.

She shook her head. "I kind of like sleeping with a memory."

He ate as she told him of her day. He'd learned over the

weeks that Nana threaded the past into every day's memory and once she'd called Allie by the name Carla, but he never corrected her.

After she finished and turned back to roll out another piecrust, Luke said, "It might rain tonight. Might be a few who don't come for the dinner."

Nana shook her head. "Nope. Rain or shine, they'll come. We all agreed after the fire. A little storm didn't stop them last week and it won't this one."

Luke agreed. The Nesters were forming a group as loyal as any supper club. If Nana cooked, they'd come.

When he crossed into the café, he found Allie putting fresh bandanas on all the tables. It took him a minute to realize something was different. "Two chairs per table," he said, drawing her attention.

She smiled that open smile she'd started giving him. Dear God, he liked the way he felt when she smiled.

"A few of the reservations are for two tonight," she said as if this were a fine restaurant that took reservations months in advance. "The Landry brothers said they'd come. I think mostly because Nana told them seconds were free. And Paul Madison said he and Mary Lynn would be sharing the same table."

Luke shrugged. "I'm not surprised."

"And . . ."

He laughed. "There is another 'and.' Now I am surprised."

Allie laughed. "Mrs. Deals came in for her cookies yesterday and said she'd asked Timothy to sit with her. It seems she has a few computer questions for him."

"She'll drill him."

"I told him as much, but he said he'd lived with barracudas all his life and Mrs. Deals was nothing more than a catfish—all mean-looking, but toothless."

He laughed as he moved toward the door.

"Do I count you in for dinner tonight?"

"No," he said, "but tell Nana to save me a piece of that chocolate pie." Then he slipped out the door before she had time to ask any questions.

Chapter 23

The wind kicked up, rustling the dried leaves still clinging to the trees along the lake. Each time I opened the door to welcome a Nester, sticks and twigs marched in uninvited.

The mood of our diners had shifted. Tonight, everyone wanted to talk. Most had been interviewed, or interrogated as Timothy called it, by Sheriff Fletcher. As near as I could tell, no one except Mary Lynn had a nice thing to say about him. She commented that he always had his shirt starched stiff.

When I brought the first of the coffee, Paul Madison was saying, "I don't know what happened, but it wasn't lightning." He'd taken the seat across from Mary Lynn, but they still looked as mismatched as ever.

Willie agreed. "There wasn't a cloud in the sky last night."

When Nana and I brought in the potpies they were talking about how the lake wasn't as safe as it used to be. Mrs.

Deals had lived here the longest. She told of a time when the folks had big cookouts and parties for every holiday.

"Time was," Willie said, "the only thing stolen around here was off o' trotlines."

"Maybe we should think about locking our doors." Mrs. Deals didn't look like she liked her own suggestion.

"Or putting the gate back up," Mary Lynn suggested. "I always liked it when I was a kid and came here. We'd have to stop and open that big, gold gate like we were stepping into heaven."

The Landry brothers nodded, but didn't stop eating.

About the time the conversation came around to organizing a way to communicate if there was trouble, Nana brought in dessert. She served each diner a slice of the pie of their choice and disappeared back into the kitchen.

Paul picked up where we'd all paused. "We need to get the phone company out here to run more line. I'm thinking of doing business from my place." He didn't have to say that he had nowhere in the city to live—we all knew. "If so, I'll need a dependable phone and Internet up twenty-four hours a day."

"Maybe we could find a dependable cell service," Timothy added. "Half the time I think the sheriff stops by my place because my dad tells him to check up on me. If my folks could call that might end the visits." He shrugged. "The whole family can't understand why I don't want to join the company. They all think I'm hiding out and will eventually come to my senses and become an accountant." He laughed. "I'd rather die."

Willie jumped in, as usual a few bars behind the chorus. "If trouble came again around here, I could circle the lake and flash a spotlight in everyone's window. Jefferson always kept one out in the shed. I'm sure if we added new batteries it would work."

Everyone talked about the advantages and disadvantages of each kind of warning system. We all agreed none was perfect. Mary Lynn even suggested we buy a bell. She said she'd always liked the sound of a bell ringing.

In the midst of the discussion, Nana brought in a tray of pies. "It's time for dessert," she sang with excitement.

The room fell silent.

"Doesn't anyone want dessert?" Nana asked, the knife in her hand ready to cut.

I opened my mouth to tell her we'd already had pie. She must have forgotten. She'd had a busy day. She . . . How could I say anything without hurting her feelings?

"I'd love a piece," Willie said as he moved his empty saucer aside. "I was hoping you made buttermilk tonight."

I relaxed, seeing him look as excited about this piece as he had been about the last one.

Nana smiled. "I did, I did." She cut him a big slice and handed it over. "Now if that ain't enough, you just let me know."

Willie took a bite and made the same sounds he'd made ten minutes before when she'd served him his first piece.

"I'll take a chocolate, ma'am." Paul stood and stepped to the counter to wait for his piece. "And I think Miss Mary Lynn would like one of those buttermilk slices."

"A small one," she said. "I'm full from the potpie."

One by one everyone ordered and said almost the same words they'd said before. I stared, meeting their eyes and hating what no one said. I'd been ignoring Nana's lapses in memory for months. They didn't have to tell me anything, I knew that I could turn a blind eye no longer. Nana's mind was slipping.

A half hour later, when they all filed out, I hugged Nana so tightly, she asked me what was wrong.

"Nothing," I lied. "I just think you are the best."

"Ditto." She giggled as if she were still a girl.

"How about we turn in and do the dishes tomorrow?"

Nana shook her head. "Luke's in the kitchen eating. I thought I'd have a cup of tea and talk to him awhile, then call it a night. You go on up."

I nodded, not wanting to face anyone else tonight. No one had said a word about Nana serving double dessert, but I knew it was only a matter of time before they did.

And once they did, I'd have to deal with it.

For the first time in a long time, my mother crossed my mind. I wondered if Carla Daniels would come home if she knew her mother needed her. Would she drive in, throw her arms around us, and say she'd help?

I knew the answer and was mad at myself for letting an old dream creep into my mind. The Landry brothers were more likely to help.

The memory of the two of them squeezed into the corner, their hats still on their heads, their forks always moving, made me smile. There was nothing I could do tonight to help Nana remember better, but I could draw. I grabbed my ledger and climbed the stairs. I'd sit by the window and feel the night cool while I tried to catch their likeness on paper.

The Landry brothers . . . who ordered seconds twice and ate every bite.

Chapter 24

2200 hours

Luke ate the last piece of chocolate pie. "That was great."

"I know." Nana smiled. "I'm better than Flo at baking, but we all say hers are good because no one wants to hurt poor Flo's feelings, you know."

"You said you had two brothers?"

"Frank and Charlie."

He could almost see her mind moving back to the present. "They were both killed in the War."

"And Flo?" Luke asked, testing to see if she'd been pulled into the present.

"She died before she had time to marry." Nana looked up at him. "I still miss her, you know."

Luke's big hand covered her wrinkled fingers. "I know. I don't have a single clear memory of my mother, but sometimes I miss her. Kind of like I know there's a piece of me that would have been different if she'd lived. I think about what might have been."

Nana looked younger when she smiled shyly. "I think about what might have been sometimes. It's like there's another life I'm living along a road I chose not to travel. When times get hard, I think about that other place and I go there in my mind."

"I know what you mean," Luke answered. When he'd been shot he'd thought about every time in his career when the path had split and how each time he'd taken the more dangerous way. He'd told himself it was because, unlike some of his friends, he had no family to mourn him, but maybe it was the other way around. Maybe he had no loved ones because he always took jobs involving the most risk. Even his apartment in Dallas, the address he called home, looked more like a hotel than a home.

When Nana stood and said good night, Luke said he'd wash up his plate before going.

She patted his arm and asked, "Could you lock up tonight? Allie went up to bed early."

"She had a rough night Friday night with the fire across the lake," he said. "She must have been beat."

Nana shook her head. "I think she wanted to draw." She laughed as if sharing a secret. "She's drawing again. I've always loved her pictures. When she was little I used to put up postcard pictures of all the great artists and she'd spend hours looking at them. I'll bet she's drawing every detail of that fire."

He walked Nana to the foot of the stairs, then watched her climb slowly. She could work all day, but her age crept in when she had to climb.

After locking up, Luke walked out to the dock and watched a storm moving in. The night chilled around him and fog moved like a shadow across the lake. If it rained tonight, there would be little evidence left from the fire. He'd thought of calling a team in to sift through the ashes earlier, but he knew there wouldn't be much to find. He already knew there had been a drug lab set up in the cabin and he'd bet a month's pay that the tag on that SUV was stolen. His best chance of catching those three was to stay low and wait until they relocated. If they thought no one was investigating, they'd be more likely to move in faster.

Drug dealers were a strange lot. They always wanted to produce more, faster. The longer they were in the business the sloppier they got. He'd make sure they didn't get away the next time.

Standing at the far end of the dock, he began stripping off his clothes. In a few more weeks it would be too cold to swim the lake. His grandfather used to swear that he swam across year-round as a boy. He'd say, "Luke, the Navajo blood is too watered down for you to swim all the way across."

Luke pushed himself for weeks, that summer, before his muscles and stamina developed enough to cross the lake. When he finally made it without stopping to rest, his grandfather hadn't said a word, but Luke had seen the pride in his eyes.

Even five years ago when Luke returned to recover from a wound he'd taken in the line of duty, he'd known he wouldn't consider himself well until he was able to cross the lake. Those first few weeks he swam, Jefferson would follow in the boat with a spotlight tied to the front, ready to pick him up when he could push himself no farther. But each time he made a few more yards before he gave up and crawled into the boat. Swimming laps in a gym just didn't bring him the satisfaction of crossing with the moon and proving his bloodline.

Tonight as he swam, he didn't enjoy the movement of

the water or the night. His thoughts were filled with Allie. She wasn't like the women he usually met. With her there would be no casual affair. She wasn't guarded, dishing out feelings in small doses. She led with her heart. If he had any sense, he'd stay away from her.

An hour later, when he climbed back on the dock, he sensed Allie even before he saw her standing in the shadows by the porch watching him.

Pulling on his clothes, he stepped into his boots and walked up the dock.

She didn't move when he neared.

Maybe it was the night, all dark with rain hesitating just above him. Maybe it was the way his senses always felt stronger when he'd done something he knew the men of his lineage had done for hundreds of years. Maybe need just outweighed reason. But Luke didn't stop to talk.

He walked up to her, lifted her up, pressed her back against the wall, and kissed her hard with need. To hell with having any sense. For one moment in his life, Luke just wanted to feel.

She almost buckled his knees when she kissed him back.

The need for her was something primal within him. Something he'd felt from the first day. She didn't fit in the mold of women he occasionally dated. He liked them tall, sophisticated. The kind who played no games and made no hints about a future.

Allie wasn't like that. She'd want more. Much more.

He could feel every curve of her body. He was half-drunk on her kiss. But he wasn't ready to turn down a road he'd never traveled.

Without breaking the kiss until the last moment, he lowered her and pulled away.

He was gone before she had time to open her eyes or ask any questions.

Ten minutes later, when he lay in the total blackness of his cabin, he could still feel her body against his . . . still taste her . . . still want her.

Chapter 25

Distant thunder rumbled. The sound of rain tapping against the window lulled me near sleep but I couldn't find the off button in my brain. Thoughts danced from one problem to another as if channel-surfing.

I decided I should stop worrying about Willie being a pervert and start worrying about Luke. He was like a phantom kisser. Every time he touched me I went all soft inside, and tonight I'd made it as plain as I knew how that I'd welcome a little more.

But he'd disappeared.

Maybe it was me. Maybe I had some kind of natural repellent when it came to men.

I closed my eyes. I knew little about him, except that he made my toes curl every time he kissed me. I think with men it's not so much about knowing how to kiss, but more about knowing how a woman wants it. Problem is, a woman wants it different at different times. Tonight he got it right.

Hard and hungry with need. I drifted to sleep remembering every detail.

When Nana called me I thought the roof must be leaking. All the years of growing up, no matter where we lived, the roof always seemed to leak. My job was usually to run around the house until I stepped in water. Nana always followed with the pots. Then, we'd go back to sleep with the sound of a tin-can band playing until the rain stopped.

"Allie," Nana said again. "Get up. Someone's at the door."

I glanced at the rainy night beyond my window. "It's too early to open."

"I know, but they won't quit knocking."

I groaned and pulled on my flannel shirt. "I'll see who it is."

Nana waited. She had a few rules no one else seemed to follow. One was she never answered the door after dark. I'd heard her say many times that news coming at night is always bad.

It was a good rule, only problem was if she didn't answer the door . . . that left only me to go.

I reached the ground level and switched on the twinkle lights so I could see my way to the door. All the bright-colored boxes of cookies and snacks sparkled at me, but they couldn't help the fear growing like bindweed around my lungs. No one would come to my door at this hour unless there was a problem—a serious problem that couldn't wait until daylight.

The wind did most of the opening when I turned the knob. Rain blew in as icy spikes against my skin. I stepped aside so Willie could rush in. Even in his parka and hat, I knew his smell. Only now it was a wet Willie odor—kind of like the smell of an old dishtowel and dirt. It would take more than one storm to wash that away.

"What's wrong?" I knew he wouldn't be here unless something had happened. Willie liked to fish after dark, but even he wouldn't have gone out tonight.

"Trouble," he yelled as he tugged off his hat. "I didn't know where else to go. I thought you might could get a fire going out by the dock, but in this rain it's not likely."

"What trouble?" I said the words slow as if I could keep whatever it was smaller.

Willie scrubbed his hand across his face. "I found Timothy's boat bashed against the north shore. The little motor he uses when he's out late was still running."

My first thought was that the boy had finally decided to fall in, but that didn't make sense. He rowed out every day to think about killing himself, Luke said. But tonight he'd used a motor because the water was so rough. A man who had all day to fall in wouldn't hook up a motor so he could do it in the middle of a storm.

Tonight he'd looked happier than I'd ever seen him. He'd even teased Mrs. Deals about getting fat because the old lady had asked for a big slice of the second round of Nana's pie.

"Maybe it just came untied?" I said. The instant the words were out of my mouth I knew they didn't make sense. No one ties a boat up with the motor running.

At least, that's what I think. But, then again, I don't think there is a manual for suicide on water.

"No, it didn't come loose from nowhere." Willie shook his head, swishing water like a dog. "He ties it up here under your dock when the wind gets up as he's afraid it won't stay on that broken-down dock of his. Tonight, he took Mrs. Deals home. I almost offered my motorboat because I could see the storm just waiting on the edge of the horizon and that little motor he has ain't much more powerful than a mixer."

"Maybe he's still at her place?" I glanced at the clock by the register. After midnight. Not likely.

Willie confirmed, "No, I stopped by her place and woke her up. She said he left there hours ago. She said the wind was getting up and she told him to stay close to the shore and circle around the dam instead of crossing the lake."

I nodded as if the plan made sense. "Maybe he flipped the boat and swam to shore."

Willie shook his head. "I checked his house. No one is there. Plus . . ."

Luke came through the kitchen door from the back and finished Willie's sentence, ". . . Timothy can't swim."

The vision of Timothy's sad eyes closing as his body drifted down into black water crossed my mind and I blinked as if I could keep more bad thoughts out. "We have to do something."

Luke nodded in agreement. "Willie, pull a life jacket on and get that spotlight out of the shed. We'll cross to the north shore and start following the path he would have taken."

"Could he have had a vest on?" I could picture him, wet and frightened as he bobbed in the water.

"Might have." Willie pulled his hat back on as he moved to the door. "Mrs. Deals makes me wear one when she rides with me. If he had it in his boat, he may have used it."

Luke met my eyes. "I've never seen him wear one." He didn't turn away, but shared my fears even though neither of us said more.

An old Cadillac pulled in from the road. We all stood on the porch and watched as Mrs. Deals and Mary Lynn climbed out. Mrs. Deals looked like death's grandmother in her black cape of a raincoat and black galoshes. Mary Lynn wore a bright pink slicker and mustard yellow boots over her stretch pants.

Mary Lynn ran around to hold an umbrella over Mrs. Deals as they sloshed through the mud. The rain was coming in sheets now.

"What's being done?" Mrs. Deals shouted as she moved into the store. "We can't leave that boy out in this." She looked straight at me. "Get all the lights turned on in this place, girl. If we can't build a fire it'll be the next best thing."

I jumped into action.

Luke swore under his breath as if he considered the women far more bother than help. "We're going out to search. Don't worry. He probably pulled to shore when the storm got bad and didn't tie the boat down. We'll find him standing somewhere waiting for a ride."

No one believed him.

"If he did, he's somewhere along that stretch where the fire was, and there ain't no one out there." Willie tried the next lie. "There's a good chance if he was following the shoreline that he wasn't in water over his head even if the boat flipped. Most places along the north shore there's fifty feet before the shallow falls off."

"Not at the dam." Mrs. Deals snorted.

I'd seen the dam. The water looked deep there and the dam was too high for a man to pull up on. Anyone in the water along that side would have to swim. Even if Timothy could swim, I wasn't sure he'd be strong enough to cross to land in choppy water.

Luke grabbed Willie's arm and pulled him into the office. I heard him whisper, "We may have another problem, Willie."

I moved closer so I could hear better.

Luke looked at me as if trying to push me back with a stare.

"I'm staying," I said as I straightened, daring him to try to shove me away.

He growled, but continued, "I think that fire was set by men making drugs. If Timothy made it to shore, he might have stumbled upon more trouble than the storm."

To my surprise, Willie looked like he was following Luke's logic. "I got a flare gun in my boat. I'll keep it ready. If there's any trouble of that kind I'll stay out of the way and let you handle it."

Luke nodded once. "Then we go. Drugs or no drugs, Tim might need our help tonight."

He turned to me. "You stay here. If the rain stops, try to find enough dry wood to start a fire."

He moved to the door without looking at me again, but when he passed, his hand slid along my back in a light touch no one else would have noticed.

"Stay put folks, we'll find him." Luke raised his voice to all of us. "Have coffee and blankets ready. If we're not back in an hour, drive over to Mrs. Deals's place and call the sheriff. Tell him we need a team out here."

"I already thought of that. The storm knocked my phone out." Mrs. Deals looked angry. "Find that boy."

Luke nodded once and followed Willie out.

I felt helpless. All I didn't understand would fill a moon crater. Why had Willie said he'd step aside and let Luke handle trouble? How did Luke know about the drugs?

We all huddled around a table and drank coffee. Mary Lynn's dog yelped when Paul pulled up in his Jeep. He'd remembered Willie talking about signaling with a light and came as soon as he spotted it on the lake. With his hair uncombed and wearing an old pair of jeans, he almost looked like he belonged among the Nesters.

As the storm pelted the windows, I washed new thermoses and filled them with coffee. Fishermen drifted in, drawn first to the light on the lake, and then the lights at Jefferson's Crossing. Those who had motors on their fishing boats paired up and headed out to crisscross the lake. All were familiar with the danger of being on the lake, even with the storm dying. All wanted to help.

"I've got to do something," Paul said as the third search team left. "I'm doing no good here."

"No," Mary Lynn whispered. "You don't know the lake well enough."

He touched her shoulder. "I've got an idea. I'll be in no danger, Mary. I can drive back and forth over the dam road. If he did get tossed out of the boat, he probably made it to shore and decided to walk home. I can pick him up along the road and be right back here."

When I handed him a thermos, he whispered, "Stay with Mary Lynn. She's worried about the boy."

"I promise."

Once he closed the door, the air in the store seemed heavy with worry. I sat with the women, feeling jumpy. Finally, my eyes met Mary Lynn's stare.

"We have to help," she whispered. "I know of one place to look that has not been covered by the boats or Paul's car on the road. If Timothy did make it to shore, he might be by the old lodge, and if the men making drugs tried one cabin, they might try another. If he stumbled in on them, they might not kill him, but leave him tied up. Or he could be hurt, unable to see Willie's light or make it to the road to flag down Paul."

She'd thought of even more bad news than I had.

"We could go look, but neither of us can handle a boat across the lake at night, even if we had one," I answered.

"Take my car," Mrs. Deals snapped.

"But that road down to the cabins is terrible. It would probably ruin a car."

She shrugged. "I need a new one anyway. Take it. There are flares in the trunk. Set one off if you find him and the men will see it."

"Then I'm going." Mary Lynn stood.

I ran for my clothes. "I promised Paul I'd stay with you, so I'm going along."

Mary Lynn collected flashlights and a few blankets. "If he's there, he'll be wet and cold at the least."

When I glanced back at Mrs. Deals she nodded once. "Nana and I will be right here when you get back. Don't worry about us."

My last thought before I climbed in the Cadillac was that Luke wasn't going to be happy about us leaving.

Chapter 26

The rain had slowed to a drizzle by the time we reached the north boundary and turned into the area where the dilapidated lodge now haunted the shoreline. The road was as bad as I remembered it, only the Cadillac took the hits like a true fighter.

Mary Lynn hadn't said a word. The blackness of the trees around her must have spooked her as bad as they did me. If we'd been in an old black-and-white horror movie, I had the feeling we were headed straight for the monster's lair.

Finally, Mary Lynn said in jerky little sentences that matched the bumpy ride, "I remember when I was real little. This place was still open. Lots of church groups came out here to sit around the campfires and sing. Kids stayed at the lodge and meeting house, couples rented those tiny cabins. They walked around the lake on group hikes. I'd come over at night when my father preached."

"That must have been fun."

Mary Lynn nodded. "It was. I believed in him then."

"Your father?" I'd heard the sheriff's version of Mary Lynn's heartbreak, but I didn't want to let on.

"Yes," she said. "I grew up believing everything he said, but then he left surrounded in questions."

I guessed she didn't want to talk about it. For a while we were silent. I tried to imagine what that kind of loss could do to a girl. No wonder Mary Lynn was so shy.

We reached the cabin closest to the road.

I jumped out and ran to an open doorway and into a single room. After one wide circle with the flashlight I ran back to the car. "Nothing."

Mary Lynn shoved the Caddy into gear like a seasoned getaway driver.

We hit the next cabin, and the next.

The blackness pushed in on the flashlight's beam, giving me the feeling that something waited just outside of the light. Its foggy breath blurred the light now and then. I fought to keep my hand from shaking.

As we rolled to the next group of cabins, Mary Lynn whispered, "My father said that when he was little they used to have parties here. Big ones as festive as any county fair. He told me that a little circus even stopped here once and stayed a few weeks. Then the Baptists bought out the place and the parties stopped."

I blinked, praying none of the descendents of circus animals lived in the thick trees. I could almost hear them in the roar of the wind. "I wish I'd left my imagination at home."

Mary Lynn laughed. "I know what you mean."

We pulled deeper into the night.

The next cabin's roof had fallen in. I had to climb over rubble, but I did my search, even calling Timothy's name.

Nothing.

When I walked back to the car, I stared across the lake, letting the tiny lights of Jefferson's Crossing ground me.

We moved closer to the water and circled around the burned cabin. I thought I saw Willie's light far up by the dam. The beam moved slowly along the water, telling me he hadn't found anything yet.

The next cabin was farther back in the trees. Mary Lynn got as close as she could and parked. "Should we skip this one, or walk the rest of the way?"

"Walk," I answered, knowing it was unlikely if Timothy were hurt that he'd go so far, but if we were going to search, we needed to be thorough.

We climbed out and held hands, steadying one another as our flashlights bounced their beams off the trees and brush. After about ten feet of eroded path, the ground leveled and we walked the last twenty feet or so to the cabin. Perhaps because it had been protected by so many trees, this cabin looked in better shape than most. Its door and windows were still intact.

I moved to the corner of the porch and shined my beam along the side of the cabin. A little inlet of water fingered into within a few feet of the back steps. The rain off the porch overhang plopped water into tiny sandy pools on the side of the house.

I retraced my steps and shoved on the door. The knob fell off in my hand. The door didn't move.

"Timothy?" I yelled, doubting he would have had the strength to shove this door open after he'd crawled to shore. Thunder drowned out my second call.

"The storm's getting worse," Mary Lynn whispered as if the weather could hear and respond.

"We'd better hurry," I whispered back.

Mary Lynn, standing on her toes, held a light to the only clean pane in the window.

I turned. "Let's try the next."

"No," she whispered. "I just saw something move in there."

I didn't even want to guess what animal might be holing up inside, but I shined my light and yelled above the rain, "Timothy!"

For a second the wind seemed to hush, then I heard, "In here."

Mary Lynn and I rushed to the door and both shoved hard. It didn't budge.

"Let's try the back." I yelled, "Tim, we're coming."

We splashed down the line of sand puddles to the back door.

It was open. A moment later, we were inside.

"Timothy? Are you all right?"

The cabin must have been used for storage because chairs, boxes, and parts of boats were scrambled like some kind of garage sale salad all around us.

"I'm fine," he said, sounding out of breath, "but I think he's hurt."

Mary Lynn shoved her hood back and knelt. It took me a minute to get my flashlight to focus on the floor.

Timothy knelt, fighting to shelter something wet and black that had curled in the fetal position. Rain dripped from a leak in the ceiling.

I circled the beam of light until I saw Tim's face. He shivered, wet and frightened but unharmed.

I moved the flashlight to see what he was shielding. I could hear Mary Lynn stripping off her coat. Her flashlight lay on its side, reflecting a muddy floor spotted with bright red drops of blood.

Shifting the light, I saw legs, then a hand, then a body curled on the floor.

"Hold the light high, Allie," Mary Lynn ordered. "I have to see where he's hurt."

"Who?" I stared at the shadow that was Timothy.

He looked up and I could barely make out his thin face filled with an overload of sadness.

"Dillon," he said calmly. "I saw him jump off the dam." Tim sounded like he'd been crying. "By the time I got to him, he was floating facedown. I pulled him up by the back of his letter jacket. He gulped for air, then went limp again. I couldn't pull him all the way into the boat, but I held on to him and tied a rope around the handle of the motor. I thought I could make it back to Mrs. Deals's house."

"Hold the light steady," Mary Lynn said. "He's bleeding and may be going into shock."

I adjusted my flashlight to shine on the floor by Timothy, but I couldn't follow the beam and see where Mary Lynn worked. I forced myself to keep looking at Timothy.

"I hit a bad spot on the water and flipped the boat. It went wild, circling around and slamming into the dam wall." He sounded as if he'd aged since dinner. "We were in shallow enough water when it all went to hell. I managed to get him here. But something's wrong. Something's really wrong."

Mary Lynn blanketed her coat over Dillon. "Allie, we need help fast. I can't tell how badly he's hurt."

"Can we get him to the car?" Dillon was no small boy. He outweighed Timothy by thirty or forty pounds. I wasn't sure all three of us could carry him, and if we managed it wouldn't be easy to cross to the car without someone to hold the light.

Mary shook her head. "Run to the beach and keep blinking your light at Willie's boat."

I didn't hesitate. I grabbed my flashlight and ran out the

door. For a second, I thought of crossing back to the car and looking for the flares. But there wasn't enough time because even if I found the flares I'd still have to find the path to the shore.

I splashed through the water at the back door. This would be easier and probably safer.

I stepped into knee-deep water and took big steps, hoping I didn't plunge into a five-foot-one–deep hole.

As soon as I saw Willie's big light, I began flicking my flashlight on and off, continuing to move out away from the trees.

The water had reached my waist by the time I saw the boat turn and head toward me. "Help!" I yelled. "We need help!"

I turned and guided them down the inlet. The boat was even with me when we were within ten yards of the cabin's back door.

"What the hell are you doing out here?" Luke said, low and angry.

"Did you find Timothy?" Willie shouted over Luke's comment. "Is he alive?"

"He's fine," I answered as Luke jumped from the boat and bumped into me. "But he's got Dillon and the boy is hurt."

"Dillon Fletcher?"

I nodded as if he could see me in the shadows of the trees. My flashlight was still on, but the beam bounced like a hyper firefly.

Luke's arm circled round my waist and swung me out of the water and onto the porch, then he disappeared into the cabin.

I helped Willie pull the boat as close as we could and the old man cut the motor. He shot one question after another at me without waiting for any answer. "How'd you get out here? Where is everybody else? What was Dillon doing out here? Why didn't he come out?"

I leaned against the cabin, shivering with cold and worry as I tried to offer a steady light, but my fingers were so cold the flashlight slipped from my hand and rattled across the porch.

Willie flicked the spotlight toward the cabin.

Luke stepped into the light of the beam with Dillon in his arms.

Mary Lynn followed. "He needs to get somewhere dry and warm as fast as possible."

"Take him with you, Willie." Luke lifted the boy over the side of the boat. "The fastest way to Jefferson's Crossing is straight across."

Mary Lynn sent Timothy to fetch a blanket from the car while we settled Dillon into the bottom of Willie's boat.

I noticed that while I'd been gone Mary Lynn had wrapped her scarf around Dillon's arm.

"Take care," she fretted. "I don't think he's got any broken bones, but I'll have to have light to know for sure."

Luke helped her into the boat. "Can you keep him calm? Willie will make faster time if he takes just two across. I'll follow in the car with Allie and Timothy."

"Of course. I may not have finished nursing school, but I read all the books." Mary Lynn turned to me, her voice level with authority. "Get a blanket around Timothy and get him back to the store as fast as you can. Just because he's not bleeding doesn't mean he didn't get injured when that boat flipped."

Willie pulled the motor back into action and Luke jumped into the water to help guide them. I stepped in as well, shining my light as they backed out.

Finally, Willie took off across the lake. Luke ordered Timothy and me to the car with a short, angry snap.

Timothy didn't seem to notice. He crawled into the backseat with a blanket and cradled the thermos of coffee. He rattled on with every detail he could remember about what had happened. Then, he told of what he feared might happen if someone didn't find them fast. He was shaken to the core. He repeated several times that he preferred his adventures to be in books, not in life.

Luke drove the bumpy road faster than Mary Lynn had and I was thankful Timothy didn't try to open the coffee. I cranked up the heater and tried to stop shivering. My clothes, from the waist down, were heavy with lake water and my tennis shoes had turned icy.

When we made it to the main road, I took the thermos from Timothy and poured him half the lid of steaming coffee.

He cupped it in his hands and drank in little sips as if the coffee were too hot, but he wanted it anyway. When he finished, I poured the same amount in his cup and handed the rest of the thermos to Luke.

He shook his head, but didn't look at me.

I told myself I didn't care if he was mad at me. We'd found Timothy and Dillon and that was all that mattered. Besides, who was he to order me around?

Chapter 27

We blinked our lights when we passed Paul Madison on the dam road and he circled and followed us back to Jefferson's Crossing.

Dillon and the others were already inside when we climbed out of the Caddy. Paul helped Timothy inside.

I felt like I took my first breath since leaving when I stepped into the warmth of home and saw Dillon sitting on one of the café chairs that had been pulled close to the old stove.

All his wet clothes except his boxers had been removed. While he warmed by the stove, Mary Lynn knelt beside him, spreading antiseptic on cuts along his leg. His nose still dripped blood and the scarf bandage on his arm looked like it might cover a still-bleeding wound.

Before I could relax, I noticed Dillon's eyes. Something was still wrong. He might not look injured, but he didn't look normal. He swayed back and forth and stared with a blank look.

Mary Lynn glanced up at us and smiled. "It's not as bad as I feared. There are no bad cuts or broken bones."

Paul voiced what was on my mind. "Then what's wrong with him?"

Luke moved in closer and pulled the boy's head up. "He's on drugs. I'd say about now he's coming down from a bad trip."

Then he lowered his voice and spoke only to Dillon even though we could all hear. "What'd you take, son?"

"Nothing," Dillon shoved Luke's hand away. "And you're not my old man, so stop trying to act like a cop."

"Answer me. I'm not messing around. You'll tell me or you'll be locked up in the time it takes me to get your ass to jail."

Dillon wrapped in the blanket and slumped low in his chair. "I don't have to tell you losers anything."

"I want to know exactly what you took and when." Luke leaned into the boy's space. "And then, I want to know where you got it."

Dillon turned away, but Luke didn't back up an inch. "Now, Dillon. Right now."

"Go to hell," Dillon shouted.

I glanced at the others. We were all staring open-mouthed at the ungrateful brat of a boy. Timothy had risked his life to save him. If Tim hadn't seen him jump, the boy would be at the bottom of the lake and Tim would have made it home without wrecking his boat. We'd all gone out into a storm, risking our cars and boats and lives for him.

Luke was the only one who didn't seem surprised by Dillon. He placed his thick arms on either side of the chair and lowered his voice to a deadly calm.

None of us breathed, except Dillon, who made a great show of slowing his exhale and ignoring us all.

"You've got ten seconds to start talking, son, or I'm calling your father in."

An ounce of sanity flickered in the boy's eyes. "No," he said. "Don't call him. He'll kill me."

Luke straightened and pulled a chair up. "We've got all night to talk. I'll get us both a fresh cup of coffee, then I'll hear the whole story."

"Sugar," Dillon muttered, then straightened. "I like sugar in mine."

Luke smiled as he moved to the pot. "Sugar it is."

Before he could say any more, Nana clomped down the stairs with a load of blankets. "All right, everyone, out of those wet clothes. I'll not have you all catching pneumonia and the storm is far too bad to go back out."

Mrs. Deals, the only other dry person in the room, nodded her head. "I agree. First things first. Get out of those wet, lake-smelling clothes." She looked at me. "You're all starting to smell like Willie."

I pointed with my head for Mary Lynn to join me upstairs. She looked reluctant to leave Dillon, but Luke assured her the boy would be all right for a few minutes.

We toweled our hair and I loaned her a sweatshirt. She told me that because her pants were polyester, they'd be dry in no time. With her hair all wild and curly and the shirt replacing her librarian clothes, she looked ten years younger.

I slipped out of my dripping clothes and into a dry pair of jeans and a shirt I'd had in college. Since our shoes were wet, we put on slipper socks. Mine had tiny giggle bells at the back of my ankles and hers were red, white, and blue stripes with each toe fitted like a glove.

"You have a lot of these?" she asked as she wiggled her multicolored toes.

"Nana buys them for me every holiday." My grand-mother might never be able to give me a big gift under the tree or on my birthday, but she showered me with small ones.

"You're lucky," Mary Lynn said, and I realized she meant it.

"You did a good job of taking care of Dillon," I whispered as we started downstairs. "You have a gift for staying calm in crisis."

"I've had a lot of practice." She shrugged, then added, "I always wanted to be a nurse, but I had to drop out of school when my folks died. I read everything I can find about nursing and first aid, though. I think in my heart I am a nurse."

"I was glad you were with me."

As we reached the bottom step, I noticed Luke tugging off his shirt and accepting a T-shirt Nana handed him from the store that said "I LIVE TO FISH."

With his back turned to me, he pulled on the dry shirt. I stared at the muscles now clearly defined in the twinkle lights. Muscles and scars. Too many scars.

I closed my eyes, not wanting to think about how many more might be on his chest. Whatever he'd done, wherever he'd been, the road had not been an easy one for him.

Timothy sat by the stove beside Dillon, also wrapped in a blanket. Both young men looked like they'd been through hell and back tonight.

The storm raged suddenly, as if demanding another chance to fight.

I took inventory. Paul and Mrs. Deals were standing by the bay window, watching the play of lightning reflecting off the lake. "Where's Willie?" I asked.

To my surprise, Mrs. Deals answered, "I made him change on the porch. Told him to stand under the drain coming off the roof before he put clean clothes on."

No one said a word, but Luke's blue eyes danced with laughter.

As if we'd taken a silent vote, we all pulled our chairs close to the fire and waited for Dillon and Luke's talk. Luke could forget any thought he might have had of talking to the boy alone.

It crossed my mind that Luke had done this kind of gentle interrogation before. The only question was: What side of the table had he been on at the time?

Once Dillon started talking, he couldn't seem to stop. He admitted to buying drugs from a guy out by the bridge.

"All the team knows about him. Speed for the game, downers after so you can sleep. A few pills that make you forget. A few that make you not care. He sells them all."

"How long has he been there?" Luke raised an eyebrow.

Dillon shrugged. "I don't know. Before old Jefferson died. I've known about him, but I swear this was my first buy. Guy on the team says he's out there around midnight and sells until he runs out of drugs. I came out once with some friends, but he wasn't there."

I was glad Luke didn't ask for a vote as to who believed Dillon.

"After I made the buy, I decided to sit out on the dam and watch the storm move in. Most nights I try to make it in after my old man has gone to bed." His words were slurred a little.

"How much did you drink?" Luke asked, as if they were simply talking.

"A few beers."

"Two, three, six . . ."

He looked down. "Six, I guess. It was a bad day. The coach told me I'm benched for grades and if they don't come up I'm off the team. Before next Saturday, I got to tell my dad that I'm not playing."

No one said a word, but Nana reached over and patted his hand.

Dillon slowly pulled it out of her reach and looked back at Luke. "I was only planning to sample some of the pills I bought. I must have taken too many. I remember it started raining and I just sat there trying to figure out what was happening. Then, I felt sick, real sick. I stood to throw up off the dam and the whole world started spinning. You know, like the world starts circling too fast and gravity starts to give?"

None of us looked like we understood.

Luke leaned forward. "You didn't fall in on purpose?"

"Hell, no." He shook his hair out of his eyes. "I got a date Friday night with Brandy Russell."

His laugh held no humor. "Besides, I'd never have to kill myself—my dad will probably do that for me when he hears I'm not on the team for much longer. You don't know how much it means to him that I play ball."

"Where are the rest of the pills?" Luke changed the subject.

"The bottom of the lake, I guess." Dillon rubbed his forehead, then winced with the pain. "I think the boat clobbered me when we flipped."

"Where do you hurt?" Luke didn't sound too interested. So much for bedside manner.

"Everywhere," Dillon answered. "Look, man, you can't tell my dad. I'll do whatever you say. I'll swear never to take another pill or drink another beer, but you got to forget this ever happened. I'll tell Dad I fell during football practice and got clobbered at the bottom of a pile." He looked up at the people surrounding him and lowered his head in his hands.

I heard him gulp back tears.

"I wish I'd died in that water. I might have survived his disappointment about football, but if he finds out I did drugs he'll think I'm nothing but a loser. He'll never stop lecturing me, or worse, he'll start ignoring me. I'll be dead to him. I'll be just one of the low-life losers who never went anywhere. I'll be worthless. I'll be . . ."

Timothy finished the boy's sentence. "You'll be one of us."

Dillon raised his battered face, bruised and tearstained. His wide-eyed gaze moved from one of us to the other. I felt like a performer in a freak show who always thought she lived in the normal world until catching the first glance through the eyes of a stranger.

Luke leaned forward and laced his big hands together in front of him. "We won't tell." He spoke for us all. "But I know a way you can make your father proud of you that in his line of work might mean more than scoring a touchdown. You can help put whoever's dealing drugs in jail."

Mrs. Deals puffed up like a blowfish. "You're not going to put this boy in any danger, are you, Luke? I'll not stand by and allow you to do that."

"No," he answered. "I promise."

Mary Lynn raised her hand. "I want to help also on this quest. I've got the only house that's near enough to the dam to keep a lookout."

"If she's helping, I'm in, too." Paul placed his hand gently on her shoulder. "From her window we can track every car that goes over the bridge."

"I'm in for a shift. It'll be something to do besides sit on the lake," Timothy answered.

Everyone started talking at once. No one seemed to hear Luke's repeated warning that none of them needed to get involved. Even Willie said he'd run a lookout from the shoreline and Nana started planning the stakeout menu.

As the storm raged, the Jefferson's Crossing army formed

and drafted Luke as our leader. I watched him argue, then debate, then finally give in. They all wanted to help and I think deep down he knew he needed us.

When I met his gaze a few minutes later, I saw acceptance. And something else. Worry.

I had to wonder if we had any idea what we were getting into.

Chapter 28

Monday
September 30
0100 hours
Jefferson's Crossing

Luke stood on the porch and watched the last of his new drug-fighting force leave. A heartbroken banker, a bossy old woman, a Pollyannaish old maid, two kids—one who wanted to kill himself with drugs and another who seemed to be trying just to die before he had to become an accountant. Luke almost laughed out loud when his mind added one stinky fisherman and Nana, who didn't even grasp that there was a problem. If this had been a work assignment Luke would have turned his supervisor in for cruel and unusual punishment.

He'd made the suggestion to Dillon of helping because he thought it might be good for the boy's ego to know that there was more to life than football. The quickly formed plan had been simple: Luke would ask Dillon to describe the drug dealer while Allie drew. With luck he'd have a likeness to work from. Once he caught the snake, Dillon would be proud of his involvement in a drug bust within his father's territory.

But he'd been blindsided by all the others forcing their way in. He couldn't make them understand that this wasn't a scavenger hunt. What he planned to do was dangerous. People got hurt sometimes. *He* got hurt sometimes. If the bullet five years ago had been an inch to the left it would have exploded his heart.

From the moment he suspected drugs, he'd been trying to protect the people here, not recruit them.

But it appeared that heroes come in all sizes and ages. And smells. Luke smiled, remembering the way Mrs. Deals sniffed Willie before she'd let him back inside even after he'd changed into clean clothes.

In truth, it wasn't a bad idea for them all to keep an eye out for someone acting strange. The ATF didn't have enough men to send out agents to this small community in hopes of catching one dealer doing one buy. That kind of bust usually didn't even earn the bad guy more than a few months in jail, if any. With the sheriff writing off the last fire as lightning, there was a good chance no one higher up would send backup even if Luke did turn in a report tonight.

The last time he'd gone into the office, his boss had suggested Luke let the old man rest in peace. The department had cases backed up. Jefferson Platt's death was so far down in the order of importance it would never be investigated—unless Luke took the time. And for Jefferson, he'd do just that.

Luke might be wrong, but he felt somehow the drugs and the fires and Jefferson's death were connected. And in his line of work, he'd learned to trust his gut.

Leaning his head against the wall, he tapped a tin sign. It rattled in his ears like doubts coming to call. He had to be careful. Put none of them in danger. Keep them quiet about what they were doing.

Dillon, of all the people plotting around the potbellied stove, would be the one who might break. He might brag to his dad. He'd gone home sobered with coffee and swearing he wouldn't say a word, but Luke wasn't sure what the boy would do if his father interrogated him. And, after all, Luke had only asked him to give a description of the drug dealer.

How dangerous could that be? Common sense told Luke the sheriff should know; after all, it was his jurisdiction. But something didn't settle right in his mind. Fletcher seemed more about counting the days to retirement than wanting to join in on a bust. A drug deal in his county would look bad, not good for him. No crime gathered more votes than a long arrest list.

The lights went off one by one in the house. Allie and her Nana were going up to bed. He heard her slide one of the upstairs windows open. The storm had left everything newborn and fresh. Luke closed his eyes and breathed deep. The smell of the land and lake seeped into his soul.

Memories of his times with his grandfather here blended as thick as today's problems. Maybe that was why Nana always talked of the past and the short time she'd spent once on a lake. After more than sixty years, she might not be able to remember where the lake was, or how to get to it, but her living out here now brought those few days back, a breath away from reality.

Luke was seven again, learning to fish. He'd stuck a hook so deep in his thumb he'd bled and fought down tears.

He'd just turned ten and his father let him build the fire and sleep out on the sand still warm from a summer sun. The sounds of the lake kept him awake all night.

He was fifteen and had heard that if you grab a water moccasin by the tail and pop real fast you can snap off its head. He'd tried. He'd been sick for three days and still bore the tiny bite scar on his wrist. He'd been fast, but the snake had been faster.

He was seventeen and playing quarters with a group of kids from the Baptist summer camp. The liquor was so cheap it stung his nose when he had to drink. He'd French-kissed his first girl that night, but his tongue was so numb from the drinking he couldn't remember how it felt.

Luke smiled. He'd lived months, years away from the lake. He'd gone to school, worked, dated, yet his memory's core seemed right here. Like everything really important happened with the smell of fresh water in the air.

"I'm told horses sleep on their feet," Allie whispered. "I never thought people did."

He opened one eye and frowned at her. The moonlight played in her damp hair. She smelled fresh from the shower. "I wasn't asleep," he managed to say when he realized she was waiting.

She didn't look like she believed him, but she leaned into the wall beside him, brushing his shoulder as if it were something natural to do. She even crossed her arms over her chest just as he had.

"What were you thinking?" she asked.

"Nothing."

"If you weren't sleeping, you were bound to be thinking."

"I was thinking about French-kissing." He smiled at her reaction. "Don't move away, I've no plans to attack you tonight. I was just remembering."

She didn't close the distance. "I've no plans to attack you tonight either. I don't even know who you are. In there just now, and before with the hurt fisherman, you were different. You wear authority too well not to have had the suit fitted."

"I'm Luke Morgan," he answered. "I thought you knew.

Remember me, I scared you that first day and you thought for sure I was the mad lake killer of your nightmares." He smiled. "Remember me. You love fighting with me, ordering me around when you get the chance, and touching me whenever you're within three feet of me."

He tapped his first two fingers against his own chest. "It's me, Allie, Luke. You've seen me dive off the dock nude. You know me." He couldn't stop the slight change in his voice as he added, "I'm the one you don't bother to listen to when I tell you to stay put. You have to follow Little Miss Muffet out into the storm."

She responded to his tone more than his words. "I don't know you and I don't take orders from anyone."

This wasn't the way he wanted to end the night. He'd thought about her all day—thought about the way they'd kissed. Thought about how she'd felt pressed up against him.

He lowered his voice and rolled his shoulders toward her. "You know me, Allie. You know the feel of me."

He half expected her to storm off, but she shifted to face him. Now their breath mingled in the night. He couldn't see her face, but he knew the anger had left her as quickly as it had left him. "I only told you to stay because I was worried about you. The wind almost knocked me out of the boat during the storm. It could have carried you away."

"I'm not fragile. I can take care of myself," she answered, anger still salting her words. "And I've already been to Kansas so storms don't frighten me." She placed her hand over his heart. "Now, Luke Morgan, tell me about you."

Luke could never remember a woman's light touch affecting him so. Allie made him feel young. Even though he was only thirty-four, he'd felt old for a long time. "I'll trade a fact for a kiss."

"A good fact, not how many fish you caught yesterday."

"A good kiss, no peck on the cheek."

"Fair enough. You start."

Luke spread his hand over her fingers resting on his chest. "I live down the shoreline in a cabin that belonged to my grandfather. When he died, since my father was already dead, I inherited it. It's one room with a loft big enough for one. Two if they sleep very close."

"Fair enough." She stretched up on her toes and kissed him on the mouth. A nice good-night kiss, nothing more.

"I'm not married." He liked the game. "Never have been. Never even close."

She stretched again, only this time the kiss lingered and the tip of her tongue sliced against his lips, but didn't enter.

"I went to college in Austin. Loved college, hated school, but managed to finish."

She waited.

"I majored in girls the first two years and worked as a dispatcher for the campus police my last two years."

This time when she moved he met her halfway and the kiss deepened. For a moment, he thought he'd tell her anything if she'd keep up this game. Then she pulled away and waited.

He tried to remember his own name. All he could think about was kissing her. Correction. After that kiss he could think of a great deal more to do with her. "I . . ."

"Brain damage?"

"Something like that." Surely he could think of one thing that wouldn't give too much away. But for Luke his work was his life.

"We'll continue this game some other time. I have to go up."

She turned to leave and made it two steps before he caught her and pulled her back against him. When she opened her mouth to protest, he leaned down to her mouth.

The game was over. No more questions, no more talking. His kiss was hungry with need as he crushed her between the wall and his chest. She reacted as he knew she would, wrapping her arms around his neck and pulling him closer. They might not know all about each other, but he knew Allie Daniels was as attracted to him as he was to her.

He felt himself melting into the softness of her, taking in the feel of her, the smell of her, the taste of her. His hand slid down her back and over her hip as he pulled her close. Her fingers dug into his hair and she moaned as he kissed her like a man dying for the nearness of her.

When they were both out of breath and panting, she lowered her head and rested against his shoulder. "You're not what you seem, Luke. And knowing your name or where you went to school isn't knowing you."

"Maybe not," he whispered, "but what's between us is real. This attraction I feel for you, this need to be near, goes all the way to my gut. On some level, I already know you and you are part of me. You believe me, Allie?"

She nodded.

"When the trouble on the lake is over, we'll sit down and play your damn questions game all night, but right now I want you to know that . . ." He brushed her mouth with his. ". . . this is not a game. What is between us is authentic. Maybe the most real thing I've ever felt in my life."

Chapter 29

I walked inside with the feel of Luke still on my mouth. Much as I hated to admit it, he was right. Deep down I did already know him. I think I had from the first. But I'd fallen enough times that I'd learned not to trust.

I grabbed the ledger book I'd come down for twenty minutes ago and went back upstairs. I curled up by the window and began to draw the Nesters sitting around the stove. Everyone had slicked back wet hair, except Mary Lynn. Hers, long and curly, tumbled around her face and down her back, tiny ebony rivers of curls.

When I drew Paul, I drew him staring at Mary Lynn.

Dillon didn't look so tough. I drew him huddled by the fire with one of Nana's mother's old quilts wrapped around him. He'd put on a pretty good act when he'd been with his father, but now my sketching reminded me of how young he was.

Timothy, though four years older than Dillon, was

smaller in build. He'd fought hard to save the kid. I hadn't heard Dillon thank him.

I drew Timothy with his legs stretched out toward the stove. He looked as thin as ever, only his eyes didn't seem as sad. He'd saved someone's life tonight. Maybe there was no need for Dillon to thank him. The satisfaction on Tim's face may have been enough for him.

I flipped the page and drew Luke leaning against the side of the store, his arms crossed, his eyes closed. The shadows across him kept me from filling in details and I wondered if it were me or the knowledge of how little I knew about him that kept the drawing from looking finished.

Nana brushed my shoulder.

I looked up and smiled. "I thought you'd already gone to bed."

"I did, but I got to thinking." She brushed my hair back over my ear. "Tomorrow would you watch me and write down how I make the cinnamon rolls?"

"Sure."

She patted my arm three times and turned back to her bed. I wanted to ask her if she wanted to make sure I learned the recipe in case she died. But I knew why she asked. She knew she was forgetting things. Cooking was a part of who she was and Nana knew that memory was slipping away.

Part of me wanted to run and crawl in bed with her like I used to do on cold mornings after I heard my grandfather leave. I wanted to hold her and tell her everything was going to be fine. Everything would stay the same.

But I couldn't lie. And I couldn't frighten her more with the truth. If she thought writing down her recipes would hold the memories, then I'd write them all down.

Chapter 30

By full light we were in the kitchen. Nana cooked and I wrote down all the ingredients. The morning air seemed to have cleared her mind. She wanted her recipes taped to the inside of her cabinet doors.

"My mother had a big ceramic bowl with a crack in it that she made biscuits in every morning." Nana talked more to herself than me. "She didn't have to measure a thing, she just knew how high to fill the bowl. Then as she sprinkled flour over the dough, she'd stir it around with her hand until it made a ball. We never washed the biscuit bowl, just set it up out of the way, still floured and ready for the next morning."

"What happened to it?" I couldn't remember ever seeing such a bowl.

Nana smiled. "Carla, your mama, took it with her when she moved to New York to set up housekeeping. Said she just had to have it. I figure it was because she was going to be all those hundreds of miles away and wanted to have something passed down through the generations. Something her mother and grandmother, and maybe even great-grandmother handled."

I couldn't imagine Carla Daniels being sentimental about anything, but maybe I was wrong. Most of my memories of her were of her waving good-bye.

About the time Nana pulled the last batch of rolls from the oven, the local fishermen started dropping in for their free morning coffee. They seemed to have learned that Nana never cooked more than the day before, so if they wanted breakfast they needed to show up before nine.

This morning most seemed in no hurry to move on. They sat in the café, munching on rolls while they talked. I didn't mind. Though they knew nothing about Dillon and the drugs, they talked about the fire and the storm.

Willie came in, but he passed right through the swinging door with his free coffee. When I looked across the pass-through, he and Nana were sitting at the little table in the corner.

The rolls and the fishermen were gone by the time Luke showed up. I didn't look him in the eyes. I didn't know if I could take those blue depths this morning. He'd made it plain last night that the few kisses we'd shared weren't just a flirtation. He might not have said the words exactly, but I thought I heard a promise in his voice.

"Morning," he said. "I guess I missed breakfast."

Nana looked up from where she'd been wiping the counter and smiled. "I saved you one. I was guessing you'd be by."

"I told Dillon I'd be here when he could get away. I thought I'd have him describe the drug dealer to Allie so she could draw."

I knew he looked at me, but I acted as if I had no part in

the conversation. I didn't look up until I heard the swinging door swish and knew they were in the kitchen. *Don't
start dreaming again,* I warned myself. *Don't build your
hopes on something he almost said.* My bad luck would
hold, just like it always did, and he'd disappear. He might
not be the lake bum I first thought he was, but what were
the chances he was my knight in shining armor?

I heard an engine out front and moved toward the door.
Most of the weekday fishermen owned their own boats, but
now and then a weekender would come out to sneak in a
fishing day during the week. When that happened he'd usually use the dock for quick access.

An emerald green Mercury pulled up with no boat behind. Whoever came to call was not planning to fish.

I stood at the door, letting the screen hide me from view
as I watched a woman climb out. Long legs in four-inch red
heels. An expensive-looking bag with letters on it. A skirt a
few inches shorter than I'd seen on most business suits. A
jacket that fit her waist tight and emphasized her breasts.
The hat that matched hid her face.

I'd bet every fishing pole I had in the store that this
shopper wasn't here to buy bait.

She made it two steps toward the porch before I saw beneath her hat and turned to stone.

Carla Daniels walked right up to the screen door,
peeked through at me, and said in a voice dripping with
honey, "Aren't you going to let your poor mother in, girl?
I've been driving for hours."

The familiar sound of her voice slid along my spine,
thawing every muscle. Over the years I'd gotten so used to
her "What do you want?" greeting that anything else
sounded out of place.

I slowly opened the door and looked at her without
smiling. "I'm surprised you found us."

She shrugged as though she hadn't expected a warm greeting from me. She walked past me without a hug. "This place looks like a trash heap from the road."

I tried to remember when I'd grown so cold toward her. As a kid I couldn't wait for her visits and letters. Except the visits became more and more infrequent and the letters less personal and never directed toward me. My affection for her must have died on the vine sometime before my teens. After that, I used coldness as a shield.

She looked around the store with only mild interest. "Where's my mother?" she asked.

"In the kitchen," I said and pointed. I followed her, thinking I should at least be civil to the woman who gave birth to me. "How have you been, Mother?" She was no more important to me than I'm sure Nana was to her. In this family, the word "mother" was not an endearment.

"I'm fine." She turned and smiled her perfect, capped-tooth smile. "I was promoted last year. That darling car"—she waved one manicured finger in the direction of the front door as if I might get her car and another on the lot mixed up—"was a bonus. I'm doing well, but working far too many hours. It seems I'm the only one who knows anything around the office. They all depend on me."

I'd never known what my mother did. Some kind of secretary, I think. She always traveled with the boss, but the boss's name changed from one letter to the next.

"How'd you find us?" I knew the lawyer in Lubbock had called her when Jefferson died. She hadn't bothered to call us and I hadn't called her when we moved here. For once I thought it would be a waste of time.

She raised a perfect, painted-on eyebrow. "It wasn't easy. When Garrison Walker didn't call me back after a few weeks, I guessed he must have gotten in touch with you about the property I inherited."

"You?"

Nana came through the swinging door and Carla turned without acting like she heard me. "Mother!" she screamed as if they'd been separated by a war.

Nana blinked, then smiled. "Carla, dear, you've come back."

Carla gave her a Hollywood hug, all breasts and pats, no holding or kissing. Nana smiled as if Carla were one of the kids she used to cook for in the cafeteria.

"It's so good to see you." Nana pulled her neck back like a turtle and waited for Carla to finish patting on her.

"It's been too, too long." Carla looked like she gave a second's thought to crying.

Luke swung through the door with a tray of cups.

Carla took one look at him and straightened to a pose. "And who are you?" she asked as she sized him up. "Let me guess. Too old for my mother. Too much of a man for my baby, but definitely prime-cut."

I tasted bile in my throat. My mother was playing Goldilocks. I expected her to say that Luke looked like he was just right for her.

Luke's blue eyes darkened, more with suspicion than interest, and I fought the urge to run over to kiss him. My mother drew men like flies to watermelon, but Luke didn't look like he planned to be her next victim.

"I'm Luke Morgan. I've got the place next door." He didn't offer his hand or waste a moment longer than necessary looking at her.

Carla glanced back at me. "That"—she pointed at his back—"could make things very interesting around this dull place." She turned a full smile to Luke as he glanced back. "I'm Carla Daniels, and it looks like we are going to be neighbors. Feel free to come over any time for a cup of sugar or something."

I looked down, not knowing how to explain my mother to him and not wanting to explain him to her.

He leaned close to me. "Where do you want me to put these, Allie?"

He knew where the cups went, but the brush of his arm against mine made me look up. I saw understanding, not judgment, in his eyes.

"Over by the coffee."

Carla made a show of taking off her gloves and hat. "This place isn't much, but it will do. I knew that old man would leave it to me. He was tickled to death to meet me. Couldn't stop asking me all kinds of questions."

I turned back to Carla, wishing a house would fall on her. If it did, I'd gladly take her ruby shoes. "He didn't leave it to you. Jefferson Platt left it to me."

She shrugged. "Oh, that was just a mistake. He meant to leave it to me. I'll get it cleared up with the lawyer."

If she hadn't said my greatest fear, I might have ordered her off the property, but deep down I'd known owning this place was too good to be true. I'd known it was a mistake from the first.

"Don't worry," she said as she walked around taking inventory, 'I'll let you and Nana visit whenever you like. At least until I sell this place. The store isn't much, but the property should be worth something."

Nana picked up the empty cups left scattered on the tables and said simply, "I'm not leaving." She disappeared into the kitchen before Carla could answer.

"Oh yes you are." Carla stormed toward the door. "I've no plans to take in freeloaders."

She made it three steps before Luke's arm shot out and stopped her.

Carla fought him for a moment, then stilled. "Let go of me." Anger melted away any progress makeup had made against age. "Or I'll call the police and have you arrested for assault."

"We don't have a phone," I answered with far more composure than I felt. "The only one around here is up at Mrs. Deals's place and it went out during the storm last night."

Carla didn't seem to hear me. She was trying to stare down Luke.

"Look, I don't know who you think you are, but this is my place and I'll not be manhandled by you or anyone else."

"I think you'd better leave," he said in a voice that was so calm it made even me nervous.

Carla's eyes darted to me for help. She found no ally. Though Luke held her arm, most of her anger had shifted to me. "You're making a big mistake. You can't just come in and squat on my property. I'll have you and the old lady arrested and carried off if I have to."

When she finally took a deep breath, Luke let go of her arm, but didn't move out of her way. He studied her with interest, but not anger.

"This is my place." I finally managed to put words together. "My name was on the will."

Carla straightened her clothes. "I know, but it was just a misunderstanding. You see, I visited Jefferson Platt here years ago. I told him about you and Nana and he must have gotten our names mixed up."

"I knew him all my life and I never heard him mention you," Luke said. "He talked about Allie all the time. There was no mistake. Everyone on the lake knew he'd be leaving Jefferson's Crossing to her one day."

"You're wrong. It's mine."

"It's Allie's place," he said again as if he were talking to a child. "Nana and her belong here."

"Like hell." Carla flashed that wounded, little girl look that didn't quite work on a woman in her forties. "It's mine, and if I have to I'll go to the lawyer and the sheriff to prove it."

"Go ahead." Luke didn't even seem bothered by her threat.

Carla glanced at me. "Nana will give it to me if I ask. You know she will. If I tell her I really need it, she'll just hand it over."

"I've already told you, Nana doesn't own this place. Allie docs."

Carla steamed. I could almost see the curl falling out of her dyed hair. "We'll see about that."

Before I could say a word, she stormed out, climbed into her emerald green car, and scattered rocks as she drove away.

"She'll be back." I leaned against the door frame. "Even if she doesn't want the place, she'll try to take it away from me."

Luke rested his arm just above my head and moved close. "Why would she want to hurt you, kid?"

"Because she blames me for ruining her life. She has since the day I was born. She left me with Nana when I was three and never came back for me." I looked up at him, not knowing whether to be happy or sad. "Until today I think a part of me always thought she would remember that I was around and magically turn into a loving mother."

"And now?"

We heard Nana singing a hymn in the kitchen. "Now I'm glad she never came back for me."

He leaned closer and kissed me on the nose. "You know, Allie, I think you're a wonder in this world. After knowing Nana and you, I think I'd make that woman driving away take a blood test to prove she's part of the same family."

I laughed. "I'll ask her that next time. From what I can tell, Nana's given her everything she could and it was never enough." I closed my eyes. "And now she wants this place."

"She won't get it."

Willie waved as he putted by in his little boat. Luke straightened away from me and I wished we'd had another moment alone. One more minute and he might have had me believing his words.

Chapter 31

Dillon showed up after school. He said his folks wouldn't expect him home until after football practice and since he was benched he didn't see any problem with skipping.

The bruises from the night before had darkened to almost black, but his eyes were clear of the drugs. He was a boy on the edge of becoming a man. I wasn't sure if keeping last night a secret would help him or hurt him.

We circled our chairs on the porch where the afternoon light blinked bright through trees almost bare of leaves.

Luke asked me to try and draw as Dillon described the man who sold him drugs along the bridge road. I never knew how hard it would be to draw another person's memory. Police artists always seemed to have an easy job in movies. Dillon said the man was average height, thin, and over thirty.

"How much over," Luke prodded.

Dillon shook his head. "I don't know. People over thirty

pretty much look the same to me until they hit the old level and start to mold into shades of gray."

"How thin?"

"Thin. He didn't seem much more than a hanger for the clothes he wore. I'd bet anything the guy never worked out."

"Do you remember the color of his clothes?"

"No. It was dark and I wanted to make the buy and get out of there as fast as possible. I drove over the bridge, then about another hundred yards and flashed my lights twice. A guy at school said most nights he's not there, but if he is, he'd flash back from the trees."

Dillon shivered. "I almost jumped out of my skin when I saw a small light blink back at me, but I put the car in park and waited. He came up to the window and we didn't waste any time talking."

The boy looked up and saw Luke still waiting. "His clothes were dark, I guess. I probably would have noticed if he'd had on white. I do remember his hand looked dirty, black kinda, but not oily."

I got nothing.

Luke had him start with one feature at a time. Round eyes, thin nose, wide mouth. Jeans, maybe. Dark baseball cap with the brim out of shape. Boots, not tennis shoes, maybe. Dillon kept repeating that he really didn't look.

My drawing looked like an alien with a hat. The only good it did was when Nana walked by, she laughed.

Luke stood and stormed away, probably trying not to show his frustration, but failing.

I offered Dillon a cookie and waited while he ate. "You're doing great," I said. "Most people don't really look at other people. Sometimes I think it's more a feeling we get about folks than the facts about how they look. When I draw, it's usually a feeling I'm chasing, not a likeness."

Dillon nodded. "This guy seemed more nervous than me. He was downright jerky."

Luke, who'd moved over to pour himself a cup of coffee, looked up. "Skiddery, like those bugs that skim along the top of the water in summer?"

"Yeah," Dillon agreed. "You know anyone like that?"

Luke frowned. "No, but I've seen him. Could his hands have been burned and scabbed over instead of dirty?"

Dillon shrugged. "I didn't look that careful. I just remember them being black, like they were caked in mud."

We talked on, but learned nothing more about the stranger. Dillon finally stood and said he'd promised to drop by over at Timothy's place before he headed back to town.

"You've been a great help." Luke stood.

"You won't tell my dad about what I did?"

Luke offered his hand. "You have my word, if I have yours that you'll keep quiet about this. The only way we're going to catch these guys is by surprise. Don't tell a soul we've talked."

"I promise." He took Luke's hand. "You know, my dad's wrong about you all. Dead wrong."

Neither Luke nor I said a word. The boy had to figure it out for himself. Sheriff Fletcher might not be doing much of a job, but he was still Dillon's father, and letting the sheriff believe his boy was perfect didn't seem like much of a crime.

We stood on the porch and watched him drive away. The late-afternoon sun danced on the water, turning it to shimmering silver in spots. I folded my ledger book. "I'm sorry I wasn't much help."

"You were more than you know." Luke didn't look directly at me and I had the feeling he was a million miles away.

"What are you going to do?"

"Wait," he said. "And watch. I might even drive over the bridge late tonight and flash my lights. Maybe the bad guy will come right to me."

The mail truck rattled down the road and pulled up a few feet from where we stood.

"Running a little late today, Fred." Luke didn't sound too interested in the mailman's answer. He was just paying a greeting, like when folks ask how you are and then walk away before you answer.

In the weeks I'd been here I'd never thought about asking the mailman his name. He seemed only the unfriendly alien mailman who complained about delivering our mail and drank all the free coffee he could hold as fast as possible.

"I have a special delivery. For what they paid to get this delivered, I thought I'd bring it out fast."

I studied Fred. Tall, thin, over thirty, hat. He almost fit the description of the drug dealer. Only Dillon would have noticed his long fingers.

Fred handed me a wide, white envelope. "It says I have until noon tomorrow to deliver, but I had to make another delivery out near here so I brought it along. I don't like the pressure of last-minute things."

The mail was addressed to me. I'd seen the return address before: Garrison D. Walker, Attorney.

For once Fred didn't stay for coffee. "Got to run. The wife and kids will be waiting supper on me."

Luke wished him well. I just stared at the envelope.

After the sound of his rusty blue hatchback disappeared, Luke whispered, "You got to open it, Allie, to know what's inside."

I smiled. Nana always said the same thing. I made up my mind. "It can wait until after supper. Want to join us?"

"I'll see what all she's cooking." He smiled and I knew it didn't matter; he'd love it.

As we went back inside, I dropped the envelope on the shelf in the old office that had become the catchall for things that belonged nowhere. Duct tape, pencil sharpener, old towels too ragged to carry upstairs.

I glanced at the receipt boxes I'd never bothered to toss and decided it would be more interesting to follow Luke to the kitchen than to clean.

When I pushed the swinging door open, Nana was frying up fish Willie had given us. The old man sat at the kitchen table reading last week's paper aloud, and for once he didn't seem to smell.

As always, Luke had disappeared without saying goodbye. I wasn't sure if he planned to eat with us or not, but I pulled down four plates just in case. Willie and Nana debated for a few minutes on whether to have Dr. Pepper floats or Cherry Cokes for our evening's fine wine.

I pulled out the glasses and silverware, then wandered back to the store. While I counted out the cash drawer money, I listened to Willie read to Nana. If he was a pervert, he was sure taking his time to show his colors. Near as I could tell, he was just a lonely old man looking for company.

When Luke returned, he'd changed into dark clothes and wore a black Windbreaker. His dark hair and short beard added a look of danger about him. He wore his black jeans and boots like a uniform and his shoulders were no longer relaxed. A man on a mission, I thought, wondering what he planned to do once the lake grew dark and still. And if he were fishing for trouble, what did he plan to do with it if he found it?

We moved one of the tables near the bay windows and ate watching night drift across the lake. Fish, coleslaw, and hush puppies made with sweet onion chips inside tasted like heaven.

Willie told stories of his years at the lake—storms, snakes, and wannabe fishermen doing crazy things. He related the year a bunch of drunk college kids had a party and decided to steal all the boats Jefferson rented by the hour. They tied a string of canoes together behind a powerboat. The rope got knotted up and the students were tossed out in the middle of the lake. "None of them could swim worth a lick. If it hadn't been for the beer coolers, a few might have drowned. Jefferson and me was fishing for college boys half the night. Come morning, he made them pay twelve hours' rental for every boat."

We all laughed and I tried not think of the letter in the office waiting to be opened.

Nana told of her first time on a lake. "It was like this one, only not near as many cabins or people. I had just turned sixteen and couldn't drive. It was my first summer more than fifty miles from Hollis, Oklahoma. Mary, my sister-in-law, was pregnant and thought she had to get away for a few days. We got in the car and drove until we saw a little sign that said CABINS FOR RENT. She let me go watch the fireworks with a boy I'd met at the swimming hole. He was all legs and arms and red hair. We spent almost the whole night sitting on that cabin porch talking.

"The night was hot and full of the sounds of the lake." Nana smiled as the memory surrounded her. "He won me that wind chime at a little fair we passed."

I caught the last of her story. She'd never told me about the wind chime. I guess, since it had always been in her kitchen, I never considered where it might have come from.

"What happened to him?" Willie asked.

Nana shook her head. "We wrote for a while, then

toward the end it was just once a year. I know he went to the war after that summer. He told me he was going to lie about his age and join up. I got postcards sometimes even after I stopped writing."

I changed the subject to how pretty the lake looked with the trees turning. Another month and it would go from brown to dead-looking. I was afraid Nana might tell the story of Poor Flo, or worse, start talking about Carla. Nana didn't mention my mother often, but since she'd shown up this morning, Carla might be on her mind tonight. Nana didn't seem to have many stories about Carla, and a few she'd told of late were stories of me that she'd just gotten mixed up in her memory.

Carla's words crossed my mind. What if Uncle Jefferson had meant to put Carla and not me on the will? After all, he had put her as the one person to call when he died. What if my mother was right? A month ago I wouldn't have cared, but suddenly losing this place would be like cutting a piece of my heart out.

When Willie and Nana collected the dishes, Luke leaned over and whispered, "You got to open the letter, Allie."

"How did you know I was thinking about it?"

"You've glanced toward the office a dozen times tonight."

"I'll open it." I knew it was bad news. I just knew it. Bad news could wait. "Want to go for a walk?"

He raised an eyebrow. "The night's cool."

"I'll get my coat."

He waited for me out by the dock while I went upstairs, then faced my demons in the office. I wanted to open the letter alone and steel myself against the pain before I faced anyone. I read the letter, squared my shoulders, and walked out to meet Luke without emotion.

When I stepped close, he offered his hand without turning to look at me. "Where do we walk?"

Pointing in the direction of his place, I waited to see if he'd back away.

He didn't hesitate. He jumped off the side of the dock, then turned and caught me as I dropped onto the damp sand. The lake was down enough tonight so that the normally muddy beach in front of the willows was almost dry. It wasn't the direction we should have picked for a walk, but I wanted to catch a glimpse of his place.

I could tell Luke had never taken a walk for pleasure in his life. He marched down the beach as if on a mission.

"Slow down." I tugged my hand away from his grip.

He stopped, retraced his last two steps, and placed an arm on my shoulder. "Sorry."

"I don't see your place," I said as casually as I could.

"It's in the trees. After dark, unless I light a lamp, no one would ever find it."

"Do a lot of entertaining?" I tried to sound funny.

"No." He laughed. "Last week I did have a possum. She ate all my crackers and left."

We moved at my pace for a while before I blurted out, "I opened the letter."

He stopped and turned me toward him but didn't say a word. The night was cool and a gentle wind whispered in the pines that marked the property line between my place and his. They made a whining sound.

"Garrison Walker wanted to inform me that there would be an inquiry about Jefferson Platt's will."

Luke relaxed and took my hand again. "He probably had to notify you." We walked on.

I followed for several steps before I gulped back a cry. "She's going to take it away from me."

"No she's not."

I wanted to pound on his chest and make him understand. My mother always got what she wanted. Nana never stood up to her. Even when she'd dropped by for the funeral of Henry, Carla had talked Nana into giving her half the cash we had so she could cover her gas.

"Allie," he said with more caring than I'd ever heard him use. "She's not going to take Jefferson's Crossing away from you and Nana."

I stopped, not able to look up at him even in the shadows. "Nana will give it to her."

Luke rubbed his warm hand against the cold side of my cheek. "Nana doesn't own it. You do. That may be why Jefferson left it to you. Maybe he guessed that you'd be the one taking care of Nana and you'd need a place. Maybe he figured you might be strong enough to hold on to it."

"How would he know that?"

Luke laughed, his breath close against my face. "Carla said she came by and talked to him. Thirty minutes with that woman would teach a man a lot about what not to do."

"But she is pretty. She's always looked like a dress-up doll to me. Everything matching. All fitting perfect. All smelling of roses."

He hugged me close. "There are a lot of men who don't care for that kind of pretty."

"Yeah, Willie." I laughed against his shirt and hugged back.

"And me," he whispered, leaning down to kiss the top of my head.

When his hug tightened, I moved into his warmth, needing the solid feel of him tonight.

My arm connected with the cold steel of a gun just below his armpit.

I jumped back. "You're wearing a gun."

Luke swore.

He reached for me, but I took another step backward. No lake bum, no fisherman wore a gun strapped around his shoulder.

"It's not a gun, Allie, it's a Glock 9mm automatic." He swore again, realizing he wasn't calming me down by being more specific. "I told you I planned to go out by the dam tonight and look for our nervous drug dealer."

"You didn't tell me you planned to shoot him." I took another step backward. The man I cared about, the quiet drifter with the bluest eyes in Texas, wasn't the kind of man who went hunting for another. "I don't know you at all," I said, thinking of the dumb kissing game we'd played earlier. Maybe I should have asked if he'd killed anyone lately or what side of the law he walked on.

The pieces of him began to fit together. Willie said he was shot once. He lived out here all alone. He avoided the sheriff. He carried a gun. All he needed was a neon sign saying OUTLAW and I might be able to figure it out.

"Allie. Let me explain."

I headed back toward the dock. "Never mind. I don't want to know." I didn't think I could handle learning that he'd killed before, or that his picture was in every post office.

If I left now, if I moved fast enough, maybe I could outrun the heartache that I'd fallen for a criminal. The first man I'd been attracted to since college and he had to be a Glock-toting, unemployed drifter. How many "wrong for you" signs did I need?

It took me a few breaths to realize he was matching my steps.

I glanced over. He wasn't even breathing hard. The guy was in shape, and for the first time it dawned on me that he might not keep so fit just so he could race the moon at night.

"You going to slow down and let me explain?"

"No." I didn't want to hear anything. Every time I'd been interested in a man I'd hung around until he cut me up into little pieces. This time I was getting out while I could still stand. What would there be next—pills in pockets, a picture of his kids in his wallet?

"Allie?" His voice was cold, hard. "You will listen."

Maybe he was going out to the dam to kill the drug dealer because the skiddery guy was moving in on his territory. Maybe Luke had this county scwed up. That would explain a few things, like maybe why he was in my house when we'd arrived. He had to check me out and make sure I wouldn't interrupt his drug trafficking.

"Allie?" Luke's hands closed around my arms as I reached for the dock. In one sweep, he lifted me up and sat me down hard on the boards.

I looked down at his blue eyes and waited. At half his weight, I couldn't fight him, but that didn't mean I had to listen or believe.

"I should have told you earlier, but I didn't know who to trust. I've been a special agent with the Department of Alcohol, Tobacco, and Firearms for ten years. When I heard Jefferson died, I decided to come home and check it out. It didn't make sense that a man who spent his life on the lake would accidentally fall in one day and die."

"You work for the government?"

"Yeah, I'm like a cop only I work mostly undercover. I came out here to see what I could find out, not as an agent, but because Jefferson and my grandfather were friends." He lowered his head and swore. "I couldn't believe I didn't pick up the clues that someone was running drugs sooner. I thought they were just using abandoned cabins for meth labs. I didn't know someone was selling out here. Dillon could have been killed."

"Why didn't you tell me earlier?"

"I didn't know who I could trust. Except Willie, of course. He and Mrs. Deals are the only two out here who know what I do for a living."

"Willie! You told Willie? What about me?"

"I didn't tell Willie, my grandfather did years ago. But that doesn't matter. You stood to gain the most from Jefferson's death. You were my most likely suspect."

"What?" I scrambled to my feet. I felt his big hands sliding along my body as I moved, but he didn't try to stop me. "When were you going to finally trust me? When I lost the store and Carla became number-one suspect in your book?"

Luke had the nerve to laugh. He jumped up on the dock and caught up to me. "No, I knew you didn't kill him. And of course I let Nana off the list as soon as I learned she could make homemade cinnamon rolls."

He was trying to be funny. I wasn't buying. How could I even think of getting involved with a man who didn't trust me? No, worse—thought I might be a killer. I shoo spiders outside.

We reached the door to the store and he whispered, "I couldn't figure out how to tell you, Allie. Telling people what I do is not something that's ever come easy for me. My safety in the field depends on it."

"How did Mrs. Deals find out?" It was a dumb question that didn't matter, but I asked anyway.

"Her only child was an agent. He disappeared years ago while working undercover." Luke forced words out as if each came hard. "I met him when I was a boy out here and looked up to him. He got me the job, then vanished a month later. He was a good agent. When he didn't come in, we all knew he was dead, but officially he was missing."

I faced him. "She doesn't act like she knows you."

"I know. I can't tell if she thinks it should have been me who disappeared, or if facing me reminds her that her son is gone. Last night, with everyone around, was the first time she'd even looked at me."

He straightened before me, no longer with the rounded shoulders of a man trying not to be seen. "I've made more enemies than friends, and the few people I know when I'm off-duty don't know what I do."

I looked at him, needing time to get away and think. "Your secret's safe with me, Officer Morgan." My words seemed to freeze the air between us.

"It's Agent Morgan and it's time I went to work."

He shoved away from the door frame and disappeared into the night before I could think of anything to say.

One tear worked down my face. I was going to lose this place, this home I almost believed I had. Nana and I would be out on the streets again. But worse, I'd already lost what I thought I had a chance of having: Happiness.

Luke had been friendly because I was a suspect and I'd been fool enough to think it might be love.

When would I ever stop turning those corners looking for a better world on the other side?

Chapter 32

Luke stormed through the pine trees to his place, frustrated at the way he'd handled Allie. Or, more accurately, not handled her. A moment before she'd touched his shoulder holster, he'd been thinking about bringing her back to his place and going a hell of a lot further than kissing.

He wanted her so badly he couldn't sleep. All through dinner, she'd played a game of brushing his leg, then looking away like nothing happened. He'd been so turned on he could have been eating part of the table and he wouldn't have noticed. When they'd stepped out on the dock he'd known it was time for him to go, but he'd wanted just a few more minutes with her.

That few more minutes had cost him her trust. If he'd just told her who he was before she found the Glock, she might have understood him and his reasons for hanging around. He could have counted on her to help him piece together the last few minutes of Jefferson Platt's life.

Now he wasn't sure she'd ever speak to him again. He'd spent too many years being nobody, saying nothing. Now the silence that had always protected him had cost him dearly.

Luke reached his cabin and grabbed his gear. He knew the three stooges from the other night were probably setting up another lab somewhere right now. This time when he found them, he'd call in and wait for backup.

He moved soundlessly to his canoe. If he didn't spot the new lab by midnight, he'd come back, store the canoe, and drive across the bridge flashing his lights twice. Luke reminded himself he was an expert trained to do a job. In his gut he had a feeling the drugs on this lake and Jefferson's death were connected. He'd find the meth lab first, then go back and face Allie.

Luke smiled, knowing he'd picked the easier of the two jobs to do first.

Chapter 33

I tried everything to sleep, but my eyes were broken blinds stuck on open. Nana snored from the other bed. She'd had a busy day, what with Carla coming and then cooking a big meal, but her love for this place grew daily. This morning she'd even mentioned that she planned to have a garden next spring.

I'd read the letter from Garrison D. Walker twice before I finally turned off the light. It was all official, but I couldn't help but feel it had been hurriedly written. My mother wasn't one to waste time, but this seemed more than that. This speed seemed near panic. I could imagine her rushing into Walker's office crying so hard she didn't notice the first two buttons of her blouse were undone. She'd plead until he agreed to look into the matter and then, before she left, she'd demand he inform me. In my mother's mind, she probably thought the letter would frighten me off the land.

Grinning, I remembered something Nana might have said if she'd understood the problem. "Well," she would say, "Carla better have another think coming."

In my mind, I flipped through all the things my mother had said. One kept rolling around in my thoughts. She'd said she'd been promoted and the car was a bonus. Judging from the stream of lies she'd told me since birth, I could almost bet that she was lying about the promotion, and maybe about the car. Also, I could never remember her coming to check on us. Once, when I'd called to tell her we were out of money, she'd responded, "How is that my problem?"

There wasn't a mothering bone in Carla Daniels. She'd come for the place and nothing more. But she'd lived in Boston and New York. Why would she want a little nothing house on the lake?

All I could come up with was that Carla must need money bad and she needed it fast. I felt sick to my stomach realizing that Nana would give it to her if she could. Carla blamed everything bad that happened to her on Nana. I even heard her blame Nana for having me. Carla had said if Nana had watched her closer, she wouldn't have gotten into trouble. I'd figured out a long time ago that Nana thought that if she kept on giving, at some point Carla would give back.

I saw no hope of that ever happening. Something must have twisted in Carla years ago and no amount of love from Nana would turn it back.

I was no longer a child who had to stand and watch Carla take next month's grocery money when she left. I'd been on my own long enough to be strong. If she wanted anything from me, she'd have a fight on her hands.

About two A.M. I got up, pulled on my jeans and sweater, and went for a stroll along the same stretch of beach Luke and I had walked earlier. I listened to the water lap the shore and could feel myself growing older by the minute. Part of me mourned the parents I never had. Part of me thanked God I had Nana. Most of me just wanted to live in a world for a while that wasn't constantly changing.

I let my body relax as I walked. I loved the way the shadows crowded the lake at night, turning the edges to velvet black. I'd thought winter would be an ugly time here after the color of fall, but it wouldn't be. Winter had its own special beauty out here, I was sure. And the autumn sunsets might not hold the warmth of summer, but the colors glowed gold and orange, spreading out in a long farewell. And the willows and pines turned to ink sketches over gray skies, reminding me of Georgia O'Keefe's early work done of New York City's skyline at night.

A light flickered in the tree-blackened darkness a hundred feet from where I stood. I wouldn't have seen it except that I stood on the beach straight in front of where the light blinked.

The beam blinked again and I moved closer. The moon was high enough for me to make out Luke's big frame lifting a canoe from the water. He carried a backpack across one shoulder and a flashlight clipped to his belt that pulsed light as he moved.

He headed inland.

I followed.

Within a minute we were in too many trees for me to see him moving, but I followed the flicker of light that dotted the ground in front of me. I heard the canoe drop against wood and then the creak of boards as if he'd stepped onto a porch. The night was so black, I couldn't make out a cabin. I sensed it more than saw it. I hurried closer and caught the light reflecting on a door. The hinges sounded as the door swung open and I heard the thud of what I guessed was the backpack hitting the floor.

I moved closer, stumbling twice over roots. When I reached the porch, my tennis shoes made no sound as I stepped up.

A low light came on from within the cabin. Taking one step closer, I watched Luke from the open doorway. He'd pulled off his jacket and was unbuckling his shoulder holster. Soundlessly, I stepped over the threshold. I watched him tug off his shirt and shoes. Suddenly, he froze, and I sensed I was in danger.

I didn't even breathe when he turned slightly and stared at me. I had the strong instinct that if he hadn't been able to see me clearly I would already be dead.

He shifted, straightening, moving his hand away from the butt of his Glock. The pale glow of a single light flooded me as he stepped out of its way. "What do you want, Allie?"

I could tell by the tired tone in his voice that he hadn't had any more luck on his quest than I'd had in getting to sleep.

I took one step into his neat little cabin. A living area with a sofa that probably doubled as a bed and one reading chair by the fireplace, a wall that must act as a kitchen, and a table for one by the window.

He watched me. The silence saying more than if he'd yelled at me.

"I don't want to argue," I managed. "I don't even want to talk."

He didn't move.

"I can't sleep. Would you consider not saying a word and just holding me for a while?"

He looked away for a second and I let out a breath, realizing that I'd closed a door earlier. Part of me was still angry and I guessed he might be also. How could he have thought I had anything to do with Jefferson's death? Part of me didn't care right now. I just didn't want to feel so alone.

The light blinked once and was out. The cabin was as black as the night outside. I turned to where I knew the door was and wondered if I trusted my memory enough to try to make it back to the shoreline. From there the moon would light my path.

Before I could take a step, I felt Luke's arm go around my waist and pull me to him. He pressed against my back, feeling like a wall, strong and protective. I leaned into him and rested my head on his shoulder.

"I don't want to talk," I whispered. "I don't even want to think. I just don't want to be alone."

He lifted me up and carried me to what felt like the old couch I'd noticed. Luke sat down, pulling me into his lap and wrapping his arms around me. He didn't try to talk or kiss me, he just held me. The kind of hold a little girl feels from her dad when she's sad and then spends the rest of her adult life looking for just that kind of safe hold again. Only I'd never had a father hold me in such simple safety.

I nestled my face between his neck and shoulder, loving the smell of him and the slow pounding of his heart. I told myself what he did for a living didn't matter. He was still my Luke. The same Luke who had been near every time I needed him since we'd arrived.

Slowly, the sounds of the lake whispered in the night. I closed my eyes and fell asleep.

Dawn woke me. Sometime during the night we'd shifted and spread out across the length of the couch. Luke's arm rested just under my breasts and his knee trapped both my legs.

I wiggled.

He pulled me tighter.

There was no way I could slip away gracefully and act

like this had never happened. After debating my options—none—I poked him in the chest.

He opened one eye, then went back to sleep.

I poked harder.

He opened both eyes and stared at me as if he couldn't quite remember why I was in his cabin.

I shoved at his arm and he let me go.

I stood, straightened my shirt, and looked for one of my tennis shoes that had fallen off. Hopping around to put it on, I kept an eye on Luke as he slowly sat up and plowed his fingers through his hair.

"We still not talking?"

"Right," I said more because I couldn't think of how to tell him how lonely and frightened I'd been last night than because I was still mad at him.

Running out of the cabin, I made it ten feet before I glanced back. He was standing in the doorway watching me go. I thought of backtracking, but he hadn't trusted me with the truth and I'd be nuts to get involved with a man like him. He was a man who obviously liked being alone. I not only came with my own luggage, I came with Nana's as well. Besides, Luke hadn't offered involvement.

I followed the sound of water until I reached the shore, then I stomped back to the dock.

Willie was there, tying up.

"Morning," he said. "Early for a walk."

I just nodded. The last person in the world I wanted to talk to about my problems was Willie . . . except maybe Carla. I'd die of thirst before I told my mother I needed a drink.

As if my thought of her caused her to materialize, the Mercury pulled off the main road and headed toward the store. It didn't look quite as shiny as it had yesterday and there was no smile on Carla's face as she stepped out. Her clothes seemed worn, as if she'd slept in them.

I waved good-bye to Willie and walked toward the store. It wasn't full light yet and I decided this day could not get any worse.

Chapter 34

As I walked toward my mother, the thought crossed my mind that I could run and keep running. Maybe if I disappeared she'd never find me again. After all, I was fifteen years younger than her. There was a good chance I'd outlive her. Another thirty or forty years in hiding didn't seem so bad if it meant never having to speak to her again.

But I couldn't leave Nana, so no use thinking about it.

I walked straight toward Carla Daniels, mentally shoving aside all the dreams I'd had of her coming home and caring about me. Once the dreams were gone I realized there was very little about my mother that I liked.

"Good morning, Carla," I said as I stepped on the porch.

She pouted. "What happened to 'Mommy' or 'Mother'?"

My smile was no more real than hers. "I've often wondered that."

She smoothed her skirt and straightened as if preparing

to make a sacrifice. "Look, Allie, I've come to offer you a deal that I think will help you out."

I waited, trying to decide what she was up to.

"I know that I'm the one Jefferson meant to leave this place to. I'm sure he didn't even know about you until I told him." She kept her voice soft, almost caring. "I don't want to have to fight my own daughter. Garrison Walker said it would be hard to prove the truth, but he's willing to take my case for a fee. He seems to think I have a good one since I'm the only one who talked to Jefferson."

I knew she was lying, or maybe Walker was lying to her. If Carla believed she had any chance of winning, she wouldn't be offering me a deal.

She didn't give me time to say anything. "So, because you are my daughter and Nana is my mother, I'm willing to split the sale of this place with you. You and Nana will get forty percent and be able to go wherever you like."

"How much is this place worth?"

"Walker called around and he thinks we can get over a hundred thousand for it. If it were cleaned up and fixed up it would be worth twice that, but I vote for an immediate sale."

That prickly feeling in the back of my brain sounded again. Carla wasn't playing straight. She reminded me of a child cheating at Monopoly. "I'm not interested in selling."

"But you only have forty percent of the say. I'm the majority holder here." Carla wiggled her head back and forth slightly as if I didn't know the facts.

"Wrong. I own this place. All of it. And I'm not selling."

"I could get the sheriff to remove you. Walker said if we fight over it we'll both lose because the lawyers will get the biggest piece of the pie."

Now I knew she was lying. Walker wouldn't try to get her to settle. It wasn't to his advantage.

"We'd both end up with nothing and you wouldn't even get forty percent. So, my dear, I'm through discussing the matter. We sell."

"Not when the deed is in my name." I walked past her into the store and began opening up for the day.

She followed me in, all sweetness gone from her voice. "You don't know what I'm capable of, Allie. If I have to I'll . . ."

"No." I fought to keep from yelling. "You don't know what I'm capable of."

I held the remains of yesterday's coffee in a twenty-cup pot. She backed away as if I had flashed a weapon.

"You ungrateful brat."

It crossed my mind for the first time that my mother still saw me as a child. She hadn't been around enough in the past ten years to realize I'd grown up. I almost felt sorry for her. I'd bet she still told people she was in her mid-thirties, and if so that would make her having had me when she was nine.

Like a chameleon, she shifted. "Think, Allie, you wouldn't even have this place if it wasn't for me. I'm the one who came here to talk to Jefferson."

I sat the coffeepot on the counter and asked, "Why did you come here, Mother? Was the search for a new 'boss' getting harder as the wrinkles came?"

"Stop it," Carla snapped. "I won't put up with you running me down. I came out here to make you a fair offer. I wanted to help you both out. But I can see you're as self-centered as always. Even when you were a baby you were selfish."

"You left when I was three," I pointed out.

"I'm surprised I stood it that long."

We both stared at each other in silence as we heard Nana's footsteps on the stairs.

"Morning, girls." Nana always sounded cheery in the morning. "I've got to get biscuits made and sausage fried for the men." She glanced at Carla. "You'd best get that cow milked."

Chapter 35

After Carla stormed through the door, almost taking the screen off its frame, I thought she'd left for good, but when I stepped onto the porch to sweep, I found her waiting for me. She looked out of place in the old green lawn chair, her high heels making her knees reach almost to her chin. She'd been staring at the shed and not at the lake.

I knew she had more to say, so I took a seat opposite hers. The sooner I heard her out the sooner she'd leave.

"What's wrong with that woman?" She didn't look at me, but her voice was raw, not with worry, but with rage.

"What woman?" I said just to aggravate her.

"Nana, you idiot." She twisted to face me. "I thought something was strange yesterday, but I don't think she knew who I was this morning and I'm pretty sure you two didn't buy a milk cow."

I shrugged. "You've been gone so long, maybe she forgot you."

"A mother doesn't forget her child."

"You did."

Carla's face wrinkled, showing every age line. "Don't be smart with me." She stood and paced, her high heels tapping against the wood. "Something is not right. I never thought Nana too bright, but she seems to have slipped a notch even for her standard."

"Nana's getting old." I almost felt sorry for my mother. The one person Carla could always twist around her finger wasn't there to be twisted. Carla mentioned once that her father quit listening to her about the time she started school.

After two more laps through an obstacle course of chairs, she stopped in front of me. "You're not saddling me with a crazy old woman. So don't even think of leaving without her. I'm young. I've got my life. I . . ."

It crossed my mind to argue that she wasn't the only one who was young, but Nana mattered too much. "She's not crazy. She just forgets sometimes. I'll watch over her."

Carla relaxed a little. She straightened her suit. "Well, all right then, I'll give you fifty percent of the sale of this place, but Nana stays with you."

Before I could question who was crazy, Luke stepped onto the porch. He'd given up all signs of being a fishing bum. His hair was combed, he'd shaved, and his clothes fit perfectly. I couldn't help but smile. I'd seen him nude, diving into the lake, and even in the shadows I'd swear there wasn't an ounce of fat on him.

Though Carla frowned at his arrival, I didn't miss the way her eyes ate up every detail of him.

He frowned back at her and gave me a wink.

I don't think she saw the wink. If she had, I have a feeling she would not have handled it well. She was a woman used to being center stage around men.

"Before you start waiting on customers, Allie," she

began with a glare in Luke's direction, "you should think over my offer."

I turned from Luke to Carla. "I have thought about it. I'm not selling and we're not partners." Then, I added, "And Luke is not a customer, he's a guest. Nana invites him to breakfast every morning."

"You'll never survive in business giving it away."

I forced myself not to comment.

"I'll be in Lubbock when you come to your senses. Walker will know where to find me."

"I won't be calling," I whispered.

"Then it will be your loss, dear. I'll give you a little time to think it over. You'll wise up or suffer." She said the last word as if it were a curse. Plopping down on one of the metal chairs, she stared at the lake, but I knew she wasn't really seeing it. If I could paint my mother's mood, it would be a black canvas.

Luke and I left her on the porch. A few minutes later, I heard her car drive away, but I knew we hadn't seen the last of her. If she thought she could get something out of us, she'd be back. I thought of my early days when I'd waited for her, excited that she was coming home. I remembered she never brought presents and sometimes, after she was gone, Nana cried.

The memory shadowed my soul for only a moment, then I heard Luke saying good morning to Nana and bragging on how the kitchen smelled like heaven. Nana's laughter made me smile. It was always so easy to brighten her day. I wondered why Carla never tried.

Luke found me in the little office counting out money for the cash drawer. Today would be busy. Mrs. Deals would be in for her cookies and Micki had said she was dropping off new stock within the hour. The shelves would be full, even though as the days cooled fewer people came out.

I looked up to find Luke watching me.

"I tossed the letter from Garrison D. Walker in the trash." I guessed what he might be thinking.

"Your mother's gone for good?"

I shook my head. "She'll be back, but I'll be surprised if the lawyer takes her case. If she thought she had a chance of getting this place she wouldn't be out here trying to make a deal."

He took a step closer. "You still mad at me?"

"Right. I forgot. I'm not talking to you." He was three feet away and I swore I could feel the warmth of him.

"Good." He smiled and closed the distance between us.

His kiss came hungry and wild. A midnight kiss of promise, not a good-morning kiss at all.

For a moment, I just stood there letting all the passion wash over me. His hands gripped my arms and held me tight, his body pressed hard against mine. The man who'd agreed to simply hold me last night was gone with the morning.

I reacted as I always did to Luke. I kissed him back. No. It was more than a kiss. Kisses are for people who are teasing, learning, preparing. This was none of that. This kiss was need—liquid and raw. The kind that makes you forget to breathe.

I wrapped my arms around his neck. He was wrong for me. Not the right kind of man for me. But deep down I needed him more than I had ever needed a man. In the core of me, where none of the layers of who I pretend to be matter, I was already his.

Luke seemed to read my mind. His hands moved over me with a boldness that I should have been shocked by. When I didn't stop kissing him, he shoved his hand beneath my blouse and spread his fingers over my breast.

He groaned with pleasure, and passion washed over me

like steaming water on a cold day. Every cell in my body came alive.

"You feel so good," he whispered as his mouth moved down my throat.

The screen door slammed.

Luke caressed my flesh one last time, then pulled an inch away.

I would have tumbled to the floor if I hadn't been holding onto him.

He kissed my nose and smiled, but his eyes were still full of fire. "At this rate I never want to talk to you again. Stay mad at me, Allie. It allows us to communicate in other ways."

I stared at him, wondering how he could make me feel so completely lost in lust. "I agree." I had a hundred questions to ask him, about his job, his past, his future, but they could wait. "I don't want to talk either."

"Good," he whispered. "I'll meet you at the dock after midnight."

"Great, a date." I tried to act more sophisticated than I felt. "What should I wear?"

"I don't care," he said against my ear. "You won't be wearing it long."

I heard Micki banging through the door with this week's orders. "Allie," she yelled loud enough for half the lake to hear. "You up yet? I'm early this morning, but I got a double load to deliver down the road so I thought I'd start here."

"Come on in," Nana shouted from the kitchen. "The first batch of biscuits is cooling if you got time for one. I set out butter and honey."

"I'll be right there." Micki must have let the dolly fall because the rattle echoed through the building.

I looked at Luke, who blocked my way out of the office. "I have to go."

"I know. Me, too."

We stood, neither wanting to look away. Both remembering what had just happened between us.

Then, with a groan, he turned and walked away. I stood, needing time to step back into my life. A life of forgetful Nana and hateful Carla and running a store hoping to make enough money to keep going.

A life of waiting until midnight so I could step into another world. A world with Luke.

Closing my eyes, I hid away the anticipation and walked out of the office.

"Brought the jerky you ordered," Micki mumbled as she ate a biscuit. "And the wool socks and extra popcorn."

"Good." I tried to act normal, but I couldn't help but wonder if she saw "been kissed recently" written all over my face. "Nana says she's going to make popcorn balls and hand them out every Saturday in October as a pre-Halloween treat."

"You won't get many, if any, kids out until Christmas break."

"I figured that, but the fishermen can eat them or use them as bait."

Micki agreed, wiped her fingers on her trousers, and started counting out supplies. She was still there when Timothy came in.

"Got any coffee yet?"

Nana motioned him toward the kitchen and he followed.

Micki leaned over toward me. "Don't get too close to that boy. He's trouble. I hear he's going to kill himself any day. That's the way with kids who have too much. His dad owns a big CPA firm in town and he stays out here hiding so he doesn't have to work for the old man."

She waited for me to add to the story. I looked at her and saw her clearly for the first time. If I stayed long enough, she'd eventually tell me something bad about everyone. I'd allowed her to color my reactions to Willie, but not Timothy. Not a boy who'd risked his life to save someone he hardly knew.

"Thanks for making the delivery early," I said, watching her flicker of disappointment when I didn't add to her story.

She shifted. "Oh, you're welcome. I know business gets bad in the winter. I hope you and Nana will be able to hold on to this place."

Fishing, I thought. "We'll be fine," I said. No catch here. Micki will have to go somewhere else for her gossip.

She folded up and moved to the door. "Looks like we're in for good weather for the next few days."

I joined her as she moved onto the porch. "Yes, it does."

She waved and climbed into her truck. I went back inside and joined Tim at the bar for breakfast. I was glad he'd been in the kitchen when Micki talked about him. "You're up early, today," I said as I pulled a biscuit open and watched steam lift out.

"I'm heading over to Mrs. Deals's. She says I've got to teach her how to use her computer or she's tossing it into the lake to confuse the fish." He smiled. "She's tough as an old boot, but I don't mind. One good thing about growing up around my dad, I lost all fear of people. I used to think my dad would murder me in my sleep and eat me for breakfast if I didn't do everything he said."

Tim grinned. "He threw a fit when I moved out here, but he's been out twice this month and hasn't said a word about it."

We ate for a few minutes in silence, then he added, "Mrs. Deals told me I reminded her of her son."

"How many children does she have?"

"I don't think she has any anymore. I think her only boy died. You know what else she said?"

"What?"

"She said I'd make a good teacher. Imagine that." He ate the rest of his biscuit and mumbled between bites, "You know, I think I might like that. High school maybe. I liked talking to Dillon."

I decided old Mrs. Deals had done something no one else seemed to be able to do. She'd given him a direction.

Willie banged in carrying two fishing poles he claimed washed up near his place during the last storm. He dropped the poles like he thought I ran the local Lost and Found. "Morning, Tim." He sat down on the other side of Timothy at the bar. "You going out to the middle of the lake this morning?"

"No," Tim answered. "I'm heading over to Mrs. Deals's. I hoped I'd see you here. Any chance you could give me a ride? I won't get another boat out before Monday."

"Sure, be glad to."

"Should you take her cookies over?"

Both men said no at once.

Willie spoke first. "Mrs. Deals doesn't want to admit she has a sweet tooth. Jefferson always said she wanted to come in and be treated like a stranger when she was on her weekly cookie runs. Like he wouldn't notice she bought the case one bag at a time."

Nana handed Willie two biscuits wrapped in waxed paper. I didn't miss the way he touched her shoulder in a silent thank you.

Willie thanked me for the coffee and followed Tim out.

I slipped my arm across Nana's shoulders. "Willie's a nice man."

Nana put her arm about my waist. "That he is."

I hadn't been fair to the old man.

Chapter 36

Tuesday
October 1
2100 hours

Luke strapped the small Colt to his ankle. He'd spent the day piecing together theories about the operation at the lake and talking the agents in Lubbock into believing the threat was worth checking out.

"Ready?" He glanced at Nathan McCord, a young agent out of the Lubbock office. Nathan was runner-thin and would be able to keep up no matter what they faced, but his inexperience worried Luke. He'd spent most of his two years since the Academy doing office work.

"Almost." Nathan tugged on his bulletproof vest. "I think you're on to something big here, Morgan." He muttered as he worked. "That guy you call Skidder sounds just like a man we hauled in a few months ago but couldn't get enough evidence to make a charge stick. He kept saying his boss would flatten him if he so much as said 'good morning' to a cop. When we asked who his boss was, he went all wild-eyed and crazy."

"Did he have a record?"

Nathan shook his head. "Funny thing, three years ago he was a respectable car dealer. We don't know how he got messed up with drugs, but we could trace the slide. His business went to shit, then his wife left him. Six months ago he lost his house and disappeared off our radar. Word on the streets is his habit is so big that he works for product."

Luke had seen it a hundred times before. Once they started to fall, there was only one of two endings: prison or death. A few make it through rehab, but only a few.

"If he's the one blinking the light in the trees, we'll pick him up." Nathan went over the plan one more time. "Nobody will probably miss him for a few days, and by then he'll be needing a fix so bad he'll tell us anything we want to know."

"I want the top man on this." Luke wasn't in this for a quick, small-time bust.

"We'll get him," Nathan promised.

Luke hadn't told them Dillon's last name when he'd related the story about the high school kid falling in the lake. He'd learned that the Lubbock office had had reports of drugs at the lake before and every time the sheriff had said he'd handle it. This time, the ATF would go around Sheriff Fletcher. They couldn't wait until some kid died driving back from the lake with drugs running in his blood.

"What time is it?" Luke asked.

Nathan grinned. "What does it matter? You got a date tonight?"

"Something like that." He'd had no time to let Allie know that they'd decided to go in tonight after last night's search had turned up nothing. If she'd had a phone, he would have called. As it stood, if this went down as planned, he'd be lucky to get back to the office and finish paperwork by breakfast. She'd be madder than hell at him.

He smiled. She'd probably be so mad she wouldn't talk to him.

There was a chance they'd find no one in the trees. If so, he might just make that midnight date with her. Otherwise, he'd explain everything to her later.

"Ready?" Nathan said as he lifted his pack. "You sure we have to use the canoe to get there? I've never been comfortable in water."

They moved out of Luke's cabin and toward the lake. "Anyone hiding in the trees by the dam would see a car go over the road. In a boat we can slip in behind him and catch him by surprise."

A few minutes later they were in the water. Nathan got the rhythm of paddling and they silently crossed the lake. Luke went over the plan in his mind. Paul Madison and Mary Lynn had told Willie that they had spotted a car crossing the dam bridge just before dark, but it never passed Mary Lynn's place. There were no occupied cabins between her place and the dam. So the chances were good Skidder, or one of his friends, was in place.

Luke grinned. Or else they were about to scare the hell out of kids coming out to make out in the woods or some fisherman who didn't want to buy a state license and thought he could fish near the north shore without anyone noticing.

The canoe slid against sand and Nathan jumped out like he couldn't wait to get out of the water. Luke slid the canoe out of sight in a cove he'd found a week ago while Nathan checked the gear. They didn't know what they'd find here so they were going in well-armed.

Luke took the lead as they moved into the trees. He knew most of the areas around the lake better than this one. Even as a boy he'd always found the campground and lodge around the old Baptist retreat spooky. Maybe because when he'd visited here as a boy the campers had always told ghost stories after evening services.

Stories so frightening he still looked behind him now and again.

The big, old lodge peeked over the trees, its roof spotted with dark holes where the tiles had blown away over the years. It reminded Luke of what a place would be like if houses had acne. Pitted and scarred. The little cabins huddled around it as if for warmth, but Luke felt only the stale stillness of neglect.

"When was the last time this place was open?" Nathan whispered as they circled on forgotten trails between the buildings.

"Twenty years, I guess. But even then it was falling down with neglect."

"Looks like they would have fixed it up. I'd think this property would be valuable."

Luke nodded. "The church who owned it folded after their preacher was killed in a hotel room with a woman he'd hired for the night. It seemed everyone left the church at once with no one claiming any part of it, including this land."

Nathan moved closer so that his voice only carried a few feet. "I remember hearing about that from some of the guys. The couple was blown away with one shotgun blast. Some thought the preacher's wife did it, but if I remember right, she killed herself with pills less than a month later."

Luke didn't like to talk about the murders. Maybe because he knew Mary Lynn and knew what talk had done to her. If he'd been her, he would have run so far away he'd never hear the story again. But she'd stayed, hiding because of the sins of her parents. Preferring loneliness to questions.

Nathan shook his head. "I think someone said that the only name on the deed to all the church property was the dead preacher's, so his daughter inherited all church holdings."

"We're coming into range." Luke didn't have to say more. They both knew from now on they'd be moving silently, using light only when absolutely necessary. A night wind camouflaged their steps, blowing dried leaves around and stirring the water against the uneven shoreline.

After half an hour of crisscrossing through the trees and around abandoned cabins and campsites, Luke spotted what looked like the black SUV he'd seen at the cabin fire. Nathan moved left. Luke took the right side. Neither made a sound as they circled the vehicle.

The side door stood open. Luke held his gun ready and flicked on his flashlight. The one he'd called Sneezy jumped with the light, but before he could say a word, Luke closed the distance and clamped his hand down hard on his mouth.

"If you don't make a sound," Luke whispered against Sneezy's ear, "you just might be alive at dawn."

Sneezy's eyes bugged out. He nodded in panic.

Nathan moved close, sliding his knife back into his boot. He didn't have to say anything, they both knew that whoever remained out here wouldn't be going anywhere. The hissing sound of tires going flat blended with the rustle of dried leaves. It wasn't procedure, but with drugs on the seat and the rest of the dealers missing, it seemed a necessary precaution.

Nathan cuffed Sneezy and patted him down while Luke tried to get him to talk. It was hopeless. Judging from the state he was in it was no wonder his friends had left him in the vehicle. His mind was so messed up he couldn't even remember his own name, much less what he was doing out here in the dark. He had enough drugs on him to put him away for a long while.

They gagged him and carried him to the porch of one of the cabins about a hundred yards away.

Luke leaned to within an inch of Sneezy's face. "Stay here and stay quiet or the bears will find you. We'll come back."

The little man rocked his head back and forth as if to say he didn't care one way or the other.

"If he was in the backseat then there are two more." Nathan tied Sneezy to the porch rail.

"Or three," Luke whispered.

They backtracked to the SUV. No sign of anyone about.

Luke pointed toward where the trees thinned near the road.

Again Nathan moved left and he crossed right. Luke was still deep in the trees, moving as soundlessly as possible, when he spotted the big guy he'd named Tanker, who'd slept on the beach the night the fire started.

Tanker obviously stood guard as before, his weapon crossed over his arm at the elbow, his feet planted wide apart.

Luke knelt down and studied the shadows. After a while, he spotted Skidder pacing about ten feet from the road. If possible, he looked even thinner than before. His hands and arms were moving as if he were doing sign language at warp speed.

"Be still," Tanker ordered. "Ain't nothin' going to happen tonight. We'll make the sale then get the hell out of here."

"I don't like it." Skidder kept pacing. "The buy's too big for us to handle."

Tanker lifted an automatic. "That's why I'm here. To make sure nothing goes wrong and you don't start eating into the profits."

A car bumped its way across the dam and Skidder

jumped back into the trees. Tanker stood perfectly still. The old Jeep passed without slowing or blinking any lights.

Luke followed the headlight's beam along the tree line and spotted Nathan standing far too close to the edge of the trees. Then in the blink of lights, the rookie made a second mistake—he moved.

Tanker must have thought he saw something because he yelled, "Get back! Someone's out here."

He raised his weapon and in rapid succession fired off three shots following where the car lights had passed. Luke dove out from behind the big man, trying to stop the shots.

Luke hit him solid in the back, but didn't take the giant down.

Tanker swore and whirled on Luke. He got in one good punch with the butt of his automatic before Luke sent the mountain of a man to ground with a swinging blow that almost toppled them both.

Tanker, hurt and angry, scrambled for his gun.

Luke dropped his knee into the man's back and pushed the barrel of his Glock against Tanker's head. "Move and you're dead."

Tanker stilled.

Luke knew he was in great danger. Skidder was somewhere in the shadows and if he was armed Luke would be an easy target. Chances were good the frightened little man would run, but Luke didn't like betting his life on it.

Luke slapped handcuffs on Tanker, then removed every weapon. The big guy wore an arsenal. As Luke worked, he listened for any movement around him. All he'd have was a second if the click of a gun sounded near.

As soon as he had the prisoner in check, Luke flipped on his flashlight and scanned the area. There was no longer any need for darkness. Skidder knew he was there. The only question was: Where was the jittery little man?

Luke pointed the light to the trees where Nathan had been.

Nothing.

"Nathan?"

No answer.

Using a plastic tie to bind Tanker's feet, Luke thought of dragging the man back to the porch, but he wasn't sure he could pull Tanker that far. At least bound, if the thug went anywhere he'd have to do so hopping.

"Stay put," Luke ordered. "I'll shoot if you so much as raise your head off the ground. I'll be within sight of you."

Tanker swore, but he didn't move.

Luke crossed to the spot where he'd seen Nathan standing and tripped over him.

Flipping on his light, he saw the younger agent lying on his back, almost as if he were asleep. Only sleeping men don't have blood dripping out of them.

Luke knelt and moved his hands over Nathan's chest, smearing warm, sticky blood as he checked for wounds.

One bullet had caught Nathan high on his left arm. By the time Luke tied a handkerchief around it, blood had completely stained the white cotton red.

Nathan had taken another hit on the vest dead center of his chest. He'd be bruised, but the vest saved his life.

The third bullet had clipped his neck, brushing along the skin just deep enough to cause bleeding.

Groaning, Nathan opened his eyes and tried to sit up. "I'm all right," he lied as he touched his bandaged shoulder.

"I got the shooter." Luke helped him to his feet. "He's tied up."

"And the third guy out by the road?"

"He disappeared."

"Go after him. I can make it back to the SUV." As

Nathan said the words, his knees buckled and he was out cold. Luke grabbed him before he tumbled to the ground.

"Nathan?" he tried.

The young agent didn't move, but his breathing came in a steady rate and his heart pounded a solid beat.

Luke lifted him over one shoulder. "I'll get Skidder later. Right now, I'm getting you help."

He plowed a wide path through the trees to where they'd left the canoe. The fastest way out would be across the water, then he'd get Allie to drive Nathan to the hospital and he'd go back after Skidder.

For a moment, he thought he'd gone to the wrong place. The canoe was missing.

Luke backtracked along the beach, breathing heavy with the load he carried. No canoe. He left it in the same spot every time he crossed to this site and he made sure it was well out of the water.

So, where was it now?

A slow dread crawled into his heart. He looked out over the water and saw Skidder trying to paddle.

Panic shot through him. He had to get Nathan to safety. An agent was down, bleeding enough for it to be life-threatening. That had to be his first priority.

But the drugged-out criminal was heading across the lake to Jefferson's Crossing. By the way he paddled, Skidder wouldn't make good time. It would be midnight by the time he reached the far shore.

Midnight.

Allie would be standing there waiting. The only person between him and freedom.

Chapter 37

I leaned back on my elbows and watched the moon. Funny how when you live in the city you don't really notice the moon—it's like an accent or a painting stuffed in a corner. But out here, where there were no artificial lights to destroy the view, the moon became a centerpiece of the night.

I'd built a fire when I'd first wandered out after Nana went up to bed. The flames had turned to mostly smoke and crackle. It didn't matter, Luke knew his way.

All day I'd thought about what tonight might be like. Tonight, when we didn't have to worry about someone interrupting us. What would happen when we had time for more than a stolen kiss?

I had been holding back passion all my adult life, thinking it was something I'd never express. When he touched me, Luke made me want to taste it fully.

Giggling, I decided that Luke didn't have to even flirt. I

was ready. I'd probably frighten him. Part of me felt like a fish trying to jump into the boat.

Closing my eyes, I listened to the faint sounds of a paddle hitting the water. Luke was coming, just as he'd promised.

Jefferson must have stopped renting canoes years ago. I couldn't help but wonder if Luke's was the last survivor. It was the only canoe I saw regularly on the lake. Most of the fishermen preferred to row, or use a motor.

Smiling, I wondered if he'd notice that I wasn't wearing pink underwear. I'd made a trip to town before supper just to buy new black panties and a small bottle of the perfume I used to love in college. Now the smell of it vanished into the smells of the lake. I'd wasted my money.

I laughed, realizing I didn't care. It had felt so good to be able to buy one thing that wasn't a necessity. I'd bought Nana a white shawl so she could sit on the porch these cool nights and watch the sunset. She told me it made her feel like a queen.

The sound of the paddle grew closer and I tried to think of what I'd say to Luke. That I was still mad? That I missed him all day? Maybe I wouldn't say anything at all. We seemed to be progressing nicely in our current pattern of not talking.

When the canoe hit one of the dock's poles beneath me, I jumped. Even in the dark I would have thought Luke had more skill. Many more knocks like that and the sole surviving canoe would be at the bottom of the lake.

Standing, I walked over to the edge and waited for him to swing himself up. But he didn't.

I waited, then thinking he must be walking beneath the dock, I searched along the line of planks for him to appear. It was far too dark and too late for him to be playing games. Besides, Luke wasn't the kind of man who'd try to scare me.

Five inches from my tennis shoe one blackened hand

flapped onto the dock. Then another. The one lamp threw enough light for me to see that the hands were thin and scabbed.

"Dirty kind of, black but not oily," I whispered Dillon's description of the drug dealer's hands.

I backed away. Luke was not below. He hadn't been in the canoe. Someone else had. Someone I didn't want to see out here alone at this time of night.

The dock squeaked beneath my steps as I moved backward. I searched the lake, looking for another boat. Praying I'd see Luke heading toward me.

The hands disappeared. I froze, listening to every sound. I hoped whoever crawled beneath the dock would stay there. Every muscle in my body wanted me to run, but if I ran, I might be heading right toward him.

I heard only the lapping of the water against the boards below. He could be anywhere below. Footsteps in the sand wouldn't make a sound.

I forced a slow breath, telling myself I'd fallen asleep waiting for Luke. The hands had been nothing but the remnants of a nightmare.

Just as I turned to walk back to the house, my nightmare reappeared. A black, scabbed hand shot up and grabbed my ankle, pulling me down hard on the wet dock with one violent jerk.

I scrambled and kicked as the grip tightened and a fiend of a man worse than any of my under-the-bed monsters appeared. He dragged me across the dock as he used my leg to pull himself up.

His hands and arms were gross with blackened, burned skin that was healing at different rates. In the light I saw pink new underflesh and hanging dead skin that hadn't yet let go. The rest of him was thin, bony, reminding me of a deformed crawdad as he crawled up on the dock.

If his body hadn't frightened me, his face would have. His eyes were wide and hollow, his mouth twisted from his effort. Brown hair grew across his chin in patches. Madness flooded his stare.

"Let go of me!" I screamed, kicking at his hands with my free leg.

I connected, my tennis shoes landing hard against the side of his face.

His eyes registered no pain, only fright—like a wild animal gone mad.

His grip tightened, dragging me to him.

I braced to kick him again but his free hand caught my arm and pulled me against him. His body felt fever-hot against me and jerked in tiny panicky movements.

"Help!" I yelled, knowing no one would hear. "Someone help!"

His grip was stronger than I'd expected and I couldn't break free. As he struggled to his feet, he planted his knee on my captured arm and pulled a knife from his belt.

The cold blade slid beside my throat deep enough to cut into the first layer of skin.

"Be still. Be still, lady. You got to be still," he rambled, his rank breath polluting the air. "I don't want to hurt you. I just want to borrow a car. I ain't going to hurt nobody. I didn't shoot nobody. I just got to have a car. A car." He pushed the knife a fraction deeper into my neck. "You got a car?"

His hand was unsteady. I tried not to breathe for fear he'd jerk slightly and cut into an artery.

He stood, pulling me up to him, then pressing his body behind me. "Take me to it, lady, and I'll leave you be. I just got to go. Got to have a car."

We walked like Siamese penguins down the dock. I could feel his body shaking. If possible he seemed more nervous than I was. Frantically I tried to think of something, anything to say. Nothing.

I thought of saying, "Don't kill me," but I didn't want to give him any ideas. If I turned around and looked at him, he'd probably think he had to kill me. He was the one with the knife. He should have been the one in control, but he didn't seem to know it.

We moved slowly toward the porch. His grip eased a bit, but the knife remained. "Are you here alone?" he hissed in my ear. "Where's the car? You got a car. Anyone else here?"

"Yes," I lied. I wouldn't put Nana in danger. "I'm alone and I have a car. You can have it. I'll just have to reach inside the door and get the key."

"Good." He seemed to think for a moment, then asked, "Why are you here? I've been here before once. This ain't your place. Why were you out by the dock?"

"I'm Jefferson's niece."

We stopped at the first step. "Jefferson's that old guy who used to own the store? I seen him once. He didn't look like he liked me. You his kin?"

"Yes." I started to nod, then remembered the knife. "Did you know him?"

"No, but I heard he was a nosy old guy." He removed the knife and pointed with it to the van. "That your van?"

His grip on my arm warned me not to move. "Yes."

He poked the point of the knife against my back. "Give me the keys. I don't mean you no harm. I just got to get away from here."

I stepped on the porch, reached inside the door, and lifted the keys from the nail just above the light switch. As I pulled the keys away, my hand brushed the switch and twinkle lights blinked on.

He jumped at the sudden dots of light and I saw near insanity in his gaze.

Shoving the keys at him, I yelled, "Here, take the van." All I wanted was him gone.

He stared at the key, then at the lights, and shook his head as if he thought I was trying to trap him. "No, you come, too." He turned, shoving me off the porch and onto the steps. "If I leave you here, you'll call the sheriff and he'll be real mad at me."

"No," I said, deciding I'd rather be killed here than along the dark road somewhere. "I'm not going with you." My words came out in frightened hiccups. "I'm staying right here."

He pushed the knife until the point cut through my blouse. "You're coming with me. You have to."

I stumbled forward off the last step just as Nana barreled through the door.

"What do you think you're doing, scaring my child?" She puffed up like a baby horned toad preparing to spit.

I took a step to block him from getting to her.

She grabbed his arm and the knife slid across my back as Nana twisted him to face her. This was the Nana of my childhood, strong and always willing to fight for me. For an instant I saw myself as a young girl, when Nana had been my only warrior, my only harbor no matter what the storm.

He swung wildly, the knife connecting with flesh.

Nana screamed but didn't back down.

I jumped into action, grabbing one of the lawn chairs and slamming it into the stranger's head as hard as I could.

He wavered as though deciding which way to fall. I hit him again.

The knife flew. The monster crumbled.

I dropped the chair and ran to Nana. Her arm, from wrist to elbow, had been cut deep.

"Stay still. I'll get a towel."

She nodded, pain showing in her wrinkled old face. "I'll sit on him while you're gone."

Running to the office, I grabbed towels and duct tape from the catchall shelf. One of the file boxes tumbled and pictures scattered across the floor. The mess barely registered. Nothing mattered now but Nana.

Nana sat waiting for me, holding her arm tight against her. I wrapped towels around it as tight as I could and bound it with duct tape. "I've got to get you to the hospital."

She looked down at the stranger. "What do we do with him? I don't think he belongs here."

I grabbed the duct tape. "We'll leave him for Luke. He'll know what to do with him." In seconds, I'd wrapped his hands and feet.

By the time Nana walked to the van, I knew my attacker wasn't going anywhere. One last round of tape secured him to the porch. I grabbed Nana's shawl and ran for the car.

As I drove the van faster than I thought it would ever go, Nana sat beside me, hugging her arm.

"I'm cold," she whispered.

"We're almost there."

The night passed by with blinking telephone poles flickering in the moonlight. I told myself that Nana would be fine. Stitches, that's all she needed. In a few minutes it would all be over and Nana and I would have a story to tell around the coffeepot.

But a worry wormed its way into my thoughts. If the drug dealer had Luke's canoe, where was Luke?

Something the drug dealer said kept picking at my brain like an embedded thorn.

He'd said he didn't shoot anyone.

I shoved the gas pedal to the floor and tried to focus on one crisis at a time.

Chapter 38

2300 hours
North Shore

By the time he reached the gate at the back of Mary Lynn's old Mission home blood burned in Luke's throat with each breath. He shoved the wrought-iron gate open, popping vines of dried morning glories as he charged.

A light spilled into the garden from the picture window that overlooked the dam road. Luke trudged across flowerbeds packed for winter, not caring what damage he did to sleeping bulbs.

"She's home, Nathan. Just a few more steps now." Luke pushed harder. "I see a light. We'll have you on your way to the hospital in minutes." Mary Lynn's skills at first aid were far better than his. Luke had seen that firsthand the night Dillon had been hurt. She'd take good care of Nathan.

Luke felt responsible for him. None of the other agents had shown much interest, but Nathan was on board from the first. There should have been four or five seasoned men in the field tonight. Luke should have insisted. He had enough pull to make it happen, but for once he'd misjudged the situation.

That fact bothered him more than he wanted to think about. A supervisor once said that when you start making mistakes it's time to get out. One way or the other, you will. The only question is, do you walk or ride?

Right now Luke needed to think about the three places he should be at once. First, with Nathan. Second, back rounding up the two drug dealers before the lowlifes gnawed out of their chains like wild animals in traps. And third, he should be standing next to Allie in case Skidder made it across the lake. If the wiry little man had no plan when he stole the canoe, with his bug-sized brain he'd be drawn to the firelight. And Allie would be in his way.

Luke looked up and thought he saw movement on the balcony. "Paul! Mary Lynn!"

"Luke?" a male voice yelled back. "Luke, what's wrong?" Paul ran down the circle of stairs as he shouted, "We thought we heard shots."

"You did," Luke answered, allowing himself to slow his pace for the first time since he'd lifted Nathan half a mile ago. "I've got a man hurt."

Paul reached them and shouldered part of Nathan's weight as they hurried into the open archway beneath the stairs.

Mary Lynn flipped on lights. "Who's hurt?"

"Nathan, my partner. The drug dealers shot him."

Rushing to Nathan, she rested her hand on his throat. "Get him to the couch."

She checked for more wounds as they walked. She had the gentle touch of a healer.

Paul took most of the weight as they shifted Nathan onto the white couch. The half-mile run in sand with a hundred-fifty-pound man across his shoulders had sapped

Luke's energy. He sagged into a nearby chair, testing the capacity of his lungs with each breath.

Paul handed Mary Lynn a stack of kitchen towels. She pulled a first-aid kit from beneath the windowsill and began to clean wounds while Paul tugged off the vest.

Nathan, half-conscious, swore and tried to shove her away.

Mary Lynn calmed him with low, even words. "Roll with the pain, Nathan. It'll be better before you know it. Conserve every drop of that energy. I'm going to help you get through this."

Luke, as his breathing slowed to normal, told them what had happened in short, choppy sentences.

Neither interrupted with questions. When he finished, he leaned back in the chair, feeling his energy returning.

Paul handed him a glass of water, then walked to the deck that overlooked the lake and began flicking the light on and off.

"What are you doing?" Luke asked. "There's no one on the lake this time of night. We've got to get him to the hospital."

"Soon as Mary has him ready to travel, we'll move," Paul said. "Until then, I'll send the signal. Willie told me he and the Landry brothers sometimes run a trotline after midnight. If they're out on the water, they'll come."

"He never told me that." Luke frowned. So much for thinking he knew what was going on at the lake. Speaking of knowing, it was pretty obvious what had been going on here. Paul didn't have his shoes on. Mary Lynn's hair looked like it had been put up hastily with one pin. A half bottle of wine. Two glasses. Luke frowned. Not likely. There must be some other explanation. He'd think about it when he had time. Right now he had calamity line-dancing in his brain.

"I've got the shoulder tied off better, so he won't lose so

much blood. He's lost a lot and the cut on his neck will be infected soon if we don't get it cleaned out. They can do that far better at the emergency room." She looked up at Luke. "Let's go."

Luke stood and lifted Nathan. Mary Lynn grabbed the pillows from the couch. Paul grabbed his shoes. They followed Mary Lynn to the carport.

As Luke transferred Nathan to the back of her car, Mary Lynn braced the young agent with pillows.

Luke heard Willie's boat docking and glanced behind the carport to see the old man jumping out with the ease of a man thirty years younger. The lake air must agree with him.

Paul laughed nervously as he handed Mary Lynn a blanket for Nathan. "I told you he'd be here. Sometimes I think Willie never sleeps."

Luke put his hand on the banker's shoulder. "Can you get Nathan to the hospital? I've got to find the drug dealer who got away."

Paul nodded. "I can. We'll take good care of him. You do what you have to."

They'd shown no surprise when he'd told them he was an ATF agent and Luke couldn't help but wonder if every Nester on the lake knew it. He wouldn't be surprised. Keeping secrets around here was like storing wine in a colander.

"And be careful," Mary Lynn said as she climbed into the passenger seat. "I don't want to see anyone else hurt."

Luke grinned, knowing the old maid believed saying the words would somehow keep him safe. "I will." He watched them drive away, thinking that in some strange way they belonged together, the banker with his sad eyes and the old maid with her unused heart.

Willie reached the carport and pointed at the taillights with his thumb. "Where are they going this time of night?"

"I'll tell you on the way. How fast can you get me over to Jefferson's Place?"

"Fast as I can get the Landry brothers out of the way." He jogged beside Luke down the steps to the lake. "They came to help and they'll be disappointed if you don't let them. I'll be hearing their complaining for weeks."

Luke had never known the Landry brothers to talk to anyone, much less help in a crisis. Nana's cooking must be affecting their brains. "I've got a tough job. You think they can handle it?"

Willie laughed. "They're old oil field workers. I think it was Larry who told me he was a shooter, handling dynamite for twenty years. His brother was a rigger. I reckon they can handle anything you throw their way."

Luke glanced at the pair waiting in their chipped green boat. They looked no friendlier than usual. For the first time he noticed their broad shoulders and muscular forearms. He'd thought of them as old men, but now he realized they were far more. They were part of his troops, if only for the night.

A few minutes later, when Luke asked the Landrys to round up the two drug dealers he'd left tied up, one brother picked up a huge flashlight and the other lifted a monkey wrench like a weapon. Without a word, they climbed out of their boat and marched off toward the lodge.

Luke decided Willie was right. The Landrys could handle Tanker and Sneezy. He climbed into Willie's boat and the motor roared before he had time to sit down.

Willie didn't bother asking questions as they raced across the lake. Luke felt his muscles tightening as if he were in the water swimming, pulling the boat along. The moon reflected off the lake, making the world seem timeless. A heavy anchor settled against his heart.

He couldn't see Skidder. If he wasn't on the water, there would have been only one place he'd try to dock.

With each buck of the boat across the water, they were moving closer to Jefferson's Crossing. Luke didn't even blink as he scanned ahead of him for his canoe and the third drug dealer.

Nothing.

The anchor over his heart doubled in weight. Skidder must have made it to the opposite shore.

When Willie tapped the dock, Luke jumped out of the boat and onto the dock as if someone had fired a starter gun in a race. He made it to the end of the dock before Willie tied up.

Luke froze five feet from the door. He took it all in at once.

Twinkle lights stretched through the open door and onto the porch and the steps. Lawn chairs were scattered and broken in the dirt. Blood dripped from one step to the next as if slowly leaving the scene.

"Something happened here," Willie stated the obvious. "Something bad."

Luke studied every detail as if it were a map. It took a moment, but he finally registered something in his peripheral vision.

"Hell!" Willie breathed his thoughts. "What is that?"

In the flashes of tiny lights reflecting off silver duct tape, Skidder looked like some kind of half-alien, half-human on display.

Luke tried to grab a handful of hair to raise Skidder's head. The balding man screamed as if he were being tortured. "Turn me loose. I'm hurt. I was mugged by an old woman. She jumped off the porch and attacked me for no reason. I was just asking to borrow their car. I wasn't doing nothin'."

Flipping on his flashlight, Luke ran it the length of the drug dealer. Whoever had tied him up had been in a hurry, but they'd done an effective job with what looked like half a roll of tape. Every time Skidder moved, the tape tried to rip away flesh.

"I think the other one gave me brain damage." Skidder's eyes reflected wild in the twinkle lights. "The world's spinning like crazy. I think I'm dying. Even the lights are blinking on and off like stars."

"He's bruised," Luke mumbled. "Not bleeding."

Willie's face twisted in anger. "Ask me if I care. Selling drugs to kids. He should be left here to rot. You mind if I hit him a few times for Dillon's sake?"

Luke barely heard the old man's suggestion. He looked back at the splatters of blood on the porch. "If that's not his blood, whose is it?"

Willie didn't have to answer. They both knew there would have been only two people at the place this time of night.

Luke nodded toward the old man. "You look around out here, I'll check inside."

Willie nodded and stepped into the night.

Luke rushed inside. He checked the kitchen, noticing only the wind chimes moving. Nothing upstairs. Nothing in the store or café.

Flipping the light on in the little office, the memory of kissing Allie flooded his senses thick and rich.

As if his thoughts had conjured her, Luke looked down and saw a dozen pictures of her scattered across the floor. He knelt. School pictures, clippings from the paper when she won an art contest, a snapshot of her waving good-bye in front of what looked like a college dorm. Each was carefully dated.

Luke noticed the old box that had sat on Jefferson's

shelf for as long as he could remember was on the floor as well, and he knew—these weren't Allie's or Nana's keepsakes. These were Jefferson's.

"The van's missing," Willie yelled from outside. "If one of them is hurt, the other's driving. They got to be heading to the hospital."

Luke tucked a picture of Allie at about eight in his pocket and hurried out of the store. "They'll be right behind Paul. Let's go."

Willie stepped on Skidder's foot as he passed, then apologized with no sincerity in his voice.

"My truck's not far." Luke headed toward the trees, walking the hidden path by memory as he rushed into the shadows.

"I'm right behind you." Willie's words were clipped and clear as if somewhere long ago he'd followed orders without question.

"What about me?" Skidder whined from the porch. "I'm the one dying. I should go to the hospital. They got to give me something for this pain in my head."

"Don't worry," Luke yelled back. "The Landrys will pick you up when they come."

"Landrys? Who are Landrys? What are the Landrys? They better not be some godawful bug or alligator that lives on this stinking lake. I'm high, but I ain't moving down the food chain, you hear."

The crunch of dried leaves brushed away Skidder's oaths as Luke moved toward his place. He'd always been careful not to leave enough of a path so that anyone could accidentally find his cabin, but now he didn't care. Allie or Nana was hurt. Maybe both.

He had to get to them.

Chapter 39

I'd always hated hospitals. Saw them as cold, impersonal, and full of people long past caring. To me they seemed like a place where the dead went to be told the news. I avoid them if at all possible. The last time Nana and I went into one, we'd followed the ambulance carrying my grandfather. He was DOA, but we still got a bill from the hospital.

University Hospital in Lubbock wasn't what I expected. When they helped me get Nana out of the van, not one of them asked if I had insurance or could I pay in advance.

By the time we got to Lubbock, Nana's lap was full of blood and I was long past panic. I drove right up to the door and started screaming for help.

Nana held my hand as tight as she could all the way to the examining room. People in scrubs moved around us, doing all kinds of things to her. I kept my eyes on her face, not wanting to see the knife wound. Not wanting to see the blood.

Nana looked like she might pass out, but she didn't say a word about the pain. I took over answering all the questions I could, mostly feeling like an idiot. How could I have lived with her all my life and not know her blood type or if she was allergic to any medicine? I couldn't even remember her mother's maiden name, but did have enough sense to wonder why they asked.

I did my best to give them the facts as they hooked her up to tubes.

"We've given her something for the pain," a large woman, who could have been an Amazon in a past life, said. "She'll relax and probably fall asleep soon."

I glanced up at the woman with no makeup, but kind summer green eyes. "She'll be all right, won't she? She won't feel a thing when you stitch her up? That's all that is wrong—a cut. Just a cut."

The woman in scrubs looked sad. "She'll need a little more than stitches, but don't you worry, we'll take good care of her." I was afraid to ask more.

She turned to Nana. "Now if you'll lie down, dear, we're going to help you rest for a while. The doctor is on his way and the operating room is on ready."

"I have to start the bread for the rolls at five," Nana answered. "You can't hurry yeast. It has to take its good time."

"We've plenty of time." Amazon Nurse glanced at me, then back to Nana.

"The kids like my rolls." Nana leaned back as if she didn't notice the room was crowded with strangers. "I put cheese in them, you know." She grinned and closed her eyes. "They do love my rolls. I had one little boy ask if I'd go home with him and teach his mother to make my rolls."

"That's nice, dear." The nurse checked her vital signs. "Just relax."

Nana slowly let go of my hand.

The nurse slipped an oxygen mask in place. "If you'll wait outside, someone will let you know as soon as we're finished." The nurse touched my back, directing me out as the others wheeled Nana away.

She pulled her gloved hand back and stared at fresh blood. "I think we'd best see you now. You should have told us you were cut as well, dear."

Amazon Nurse seemed kind, but I wasn't sure I liked being her next "dear."

I followed as if walking in a dream. The cuts on my back and neck didn't hurt. My whole world was shifting. I could feel it as plainly as if I were standing on a fault line. I don't think I would have noticed if all the blood had run out of me.

Nana had looked so fragile, so old. All my life she'd been old, but when had she shrunk to frail? Her hair was thin and mousy white. Her fingers twisted, almost deformed. Her arms spotted with age marks.

I wanted to run back and hold her one more time. I wanted to see her through my child eyes, the way she'd been when I was little. I wanted to tell her how much I loved her. I wanted to know that she heard me. That she understood.

"If you'll have a seat right here," the nurse said, unaware my world was spinning.

How could I explain that in the operating room a few feet away lay the only person who loved me, the only one who had ever believed in me? The one person on Earth that I didn't have to prove anything to, or earn her love. Nana just loved me, she always had.

"The cut's not deep." The nurse lifted the back of my blouse. "I'll bandage it for you. Try to keep it dry for a few days, then you can take the bandage off."

I nodded as if I understood.

"Would you like to wash up?"

I looked down. Blood covered my best blouse and left darkened spots on my jeans. The ones I'd worn for my date with Luke. Our midnight date seemed a million years ago.

"No," I said thinking that I'd toss these clothes on the fire out by the dock. I'd watch them burn and forget all about what happened tonight.

"You could leave and go change. Your grandmother will be in surgery for an hour or more. Then she'll be in recovery for a while."

"I'll wait."

She nodded as if she understood. "Is there someone you'd like to call who could wait with you? A relative, maybe?"

My mother crossed my mind. She hadn't left her number with us, only saying she could be reached through the lawyer. If I could have reached her, she would probably say the same thing she had said the time we ran out of money, "Now how is that my problem?"

The nurse leaned down, her voice soft and caring, "Is there someone who might need to know you're here, dear?"

"Yes." I looked up for the first time and she smiled, knowing she'd finally gotten through to me. "I'd like to call Mrs. Eleanora Deals, but I don't have the number. She's the only one who has a phone out at a place called Twisted Creek."

The nurse nodded. "In a few minutes the doctor will be in. As soon as he checks you out, I'll try to have the number for you." She rotated up the top half of the table I was on, and with a gentle tug on my shoulder, leaned me back. "Just rest here until he signs you out."

I leaned back and closed my eyes, wishing I could hear the water at the lake. Wishing I was home.

I must have dozed off. It only seemed like a few minutes after the nurse left, but the clock in front of me read 2:30 A.M.

"Sorry." Amazon Nurse rushed in with her hands full of paperwork. "All the doctors have their hands full with a big fight coming in from one of the bars. I finally caught one to get him to sign for you to leave."

"Have you had any word from my grandmother?"

She stepped farther into the room. "I'm sorry, I thought someone already told you. She made it through surgery about half an hour ago, but her heartbeat is irregular. They rushed her into ICU. They'll probably be wanting to keep her a few days. She lost a lot of blood and for a woman that age it's always a concern."

"I understand," I said, even though I didn't. "When can I see her?"

"Take this to the desk and they'll point you in the direction of ICU. They are pretty strict about visiting hours, but they might let you see that she's resting nicely if you promise not to wake her." Her smile reached her summer green eyes for the first time. "Oh, and I told your family to call Mrs. Deals."

I thought she had me confused with some other patient, but I was too tired to question. I took the papers and thanked her.

When I walked out of the emergency doors, Willie, Mary Lynn, and Paul Madison were waiting for me.

I smiled. The nurse had thought they were my family.

Chapter 40

Wednesday
October 2
0145 hours
En Route to Lubbock

Luke drove like a madman. Paul and Mary Lynn probably had at least half an hour's head start on him, maybe more.

Lubbock had several hospitals and he didn't know the town well enough to know which one Allie and Nana would go to. Willie said he guessed Mary Lynn would be heading to the big University Hospital, but he didn't know where Allie would go.

Luke didn't see Willie as the county tour guide for hospitals, so he punched in the police code and asked the dispatcher to find out. He spelled out Nathan McCord and Nana's last name, then hesitated.

"Edna," Willie offered. "Her first name is Edna."

"Edna Daniels," Luke repeated into the phone.

"I'll get right back to you," she said, then ended the call without another word.

Luke held the phone a moment longer before he lowered

it. "How'd you know her name? I've never heard anyone call her anything but Nana."

Willie was silent for almost a mile, then he said, "I used to hear Jefferson talk about her. Once I came on him when he was sitting all sad like on the porch. He said that Edna was raising Allie all alone now."

Willie looked out the window. "He never said nothin' more except to mention how old Allie was or that she'd be taking over the place after he passed on. Once he said that Edna would look after her till then."

"Did you ask who Edna was?"

"Nope." Willie wasn't one to pry.

Concentrating on driving, Luke finally let the silence bother him enough to ask, "How long did Jefferson know Allie and Nana? Did he write them or call them?" It made no sense that he could know and talk about them and Allie wouldn't have ever heard of him.

Luke thought back to the first day when Allie told him she didn't know Jefferson Platt, but she knew for sure he wasn't her uncle.

But Luke had seen the pictures of Allie's childhood. She might not know about him, but he'd obviously kept up with her over the years. "Someone had to be letting Jefferson know about them."

"Don't know." Willie sounded bored, as if it didn't matter. "Never asked Red about it."

Luke swore, frustrated. He liked facts to fit together. Surely the old man would say more if he waited Willie out. He'd been at the lake for as long as Luke could remember and as far as he knew Willie mostly kept to himself. Willie, like his grandfather, must have known Jefferson when his hair was still red and not white. No one else had called Jefferson "Red" in forty years.

Finally, Willie broke. "Your grandfather and Jefferson

were tight. They talked almost every night. I asked your grandpa once who Allie was. Since as far as I knew Jefferson didn't have no kin. Your grandpa said she was like his niece and not long after that Jefferson called her that."

"But how could she matter so much when she didn't even know he existed?"

Willie shrugged. "Never asked, but Jefferson told me once that he put her birthday in as the combination to that old safe."

"You know the combination to that old safe? Why didn't you tell me? I spent one summer when I was a kid trying to figure it out."

"You never asked." Willie laughed. "We all figured it was something to keep you busy."

Luke saw the lights of Lubbock. "When this is over, Willie, you and me are going to sit down and have a talk and I'm planning on asking about everything."

"Ain't no gossip, son." Willie shook his head. "Never have been."

"That's the truth." Luke's phone rang. "Hello."

The squeaky voice of the dispatcher identified herself, then told Luke that both his inquires were at University Hospital.

"Got it," he said, "thanks." Without a word to Willie, he dialed his headquarters and reported in.

Once he'd told all the details, including where to pick up the three drug dealers, Luke turned to Willie. "There will be men at Jefferson's Crossing to pick up the three and deliver them to jail. I'll worry about them in the morning. Right now, I have to check on the wounded."

Willie shook his head. "I hope they don't get the bad guys mixed up with the Landrys. Old fishermen and druggies pretty much have the same dress code."

"The agents will know." Luke thought about it a minute,

then called the office back and described the two men who would be holding the prisoners.

He swung into the parking lot and a moment later raced toward the emergency entrance.

A sweet but unenlightened girl at the desk told him Edna Daniels was in surgery, and Allie Daniels was being treated and would be out soon. Nathan McCord, however, was in recovery. When Luke questioned her about the extent of their injuries, she flashed him a clueless look.

He tried again, but she only repeated, "You can wait over there. I'll let you know as soon as there is a change posted on my computer."

"Thanks," Luke managed even though he wanted to yell for her to go back behind the door marked "Authorized Personnel Only" and find out.

Luke nodded to Willie, who took a seat in front of the admitting door. "I'll check on Nathan and be right back. If Allie comes out, you take care of her."

Willie pushed his muddy boots beneath the chair and leaned back. "I'll be here."

Luke ran for the elevator and headed up to the recovery area. He'd been reassured that Allie wasn't hurt badly by the girl's comment that she was being treated and would be out soon. If she was hurt but walking out of the hospital tonight, he told himself he could deal with that.

Paul Madison and Mary Lynn were standing in the hallway when he stepped off onto the third floor. Their heads were almost touching as they talked in whispers.

When they spotted Luke, they both smiled. A good sign, Luke thought.

Luke didn't have time to say anything before Paul started talking in his quick, all-business manner. "Your friend is going to be fine. They took the bullet out of his arm and cleaned up the wound on his throat. It'll leave a scar, but he's conscious and telling all the nurses of his adventure."

Mary Lynn nodded in agreement. "It seems he's quite the hero. A lawman who survived three bullets in a drug raid."

Luke smiled. He would not destroy this for Nathan. "They're right. He is a hero. If he hadn't distracted the guy with the automatic, I might not have gotten close enough to jump him." If Nathan was going to have the scars, he might as well get the glory.

"Did you get the third one?" Paul asked.

"Yes, but Nana and Allie ran into him first. They're downstairs now. Willie's waiting for them to come out."

"Nathan doesn't need us." Paul took Mary Lynn's arm. "We'll be downstairs when you finish here. If they are both injured, Willie may need our help."

"Good." Luke turned and took three steps toward Nathan's room before he glanced back. They were at the elevator. "Thanks," he said. "Thanks for being there."

Mary Lynn smiled. "You're welcome, but there is no need to thank us. They're my family, don't you know."

Luke collided with a nurse coming out of Nathan's room. She frowned at him, looking up and down from dirty boots to bloody shoulder.

"I hope you don't think you are going in this room," she snapped.

"Yes, I do." Luke prepared to fight. If he had to he'd move her out of the way.

She placed her fists on her ample hips and seemed to widen like a fullback preparing for the snap. "Visiting hours are over."

If Luke hadn't been so tired he might have tried charm, but charm was never his strong suit. The memory of another fight he'd had with an emergency nurse in Houston flashed through his thoughts. He'd insisted on seeing to one of his men and she'd had him barred from the hospital.

"I have to see him." Luke tried to think of something to say that would get him past this dragon.

"Then I suggest you clean up first."

"Look, lady, I carried him . . ."

"Morgan?" Nathan yelled. "Morgan, you made it."

The dragon nurse melted as if she'd been wax. "You're the man who got him out. Nathan's told us all about you, Luke Morgan." She stepped out of the way. "He said you jogged a mile with him on your back."

Luke relaxed, his anger gone. "More like half a mile. Can I just see him for a few minutes?"

"Of course." The dragon fullback nurse now reminded him of a grandmother type in a cookie commercial. "But he's had a sedative, so he won't last long talking."

Chapter 41

0215 hours
University Hospital
Lubbock, Texas

Luke took his time filling Nathan in on every detail of what
had happened after he was shot. The kid would be out of the
hospital tomorrow and probably insist on working the case.
It was his home office, he'd take the lead. Nathan would go
to work with his arm in a sling and a bandage on his neck.
Every man in the office would want to hear the details.

No matter how much Luke wanted to get downstairs to
check on Allie and Nana, he'd do his job. He owed it to
Nathan.

Finally, when they were the only two in the room,
Nathan said, "I wasn't standing in enough cover. I'd stepped
out too far. The lights of that car caught me before I could
step back."

Luke gripped Nathan's good shoulder. "The lesson almost cost you your life."

Nathan nodded. His voice shook slightly. "I won't make
that mistake again."

"You're a better agent now than you were four hours ago." Luke could think of a few hard lessons he'd learned over the past ten years. "Don't beat yourself up about it. I could have made the same mistake. In that blackness it was hard to tell how far away from cover you were. If the car had been going the other way, its lights would have flashed on me."

"You think so?"

"I know so," Luke answered. "If I'd been caught in the light, you'd have been the one who made the jump toward the bad guy and then you'd have had to carry me."

"I would have," Nathan answered without hesitation.

"I know. That's why I'd partner with you again, anytime."

Nathan looked tired and still in pain, but he smiled. "Thanks, Morgan."

Luke straightened. "Anytime."

They talked for a few more minutes, then Nathan, almost asleep, said he'd see Luke tomorrow.

Luke saluted a sleeping comrade and left the room.

He forced himself to walk slowly down the hall even though he wanted to run. It seemed a hundred years since he'd kissed Allie in the tiny office this morning. The longing for her was an ache deep inside. Reason told him she wasn't hurt bad. She'd driven to the hospital. She was being released tonight.

But reason could be wrong.

When he stepped off the elevator, his blood pressure jumped at the sight of the empty chair where he'd left Willie less than half an hour ago.

Luke walked over to the chair and stared. Not only Willie, but Mary Lynn and Paul were gone.

"Looking for something, mister?"

The girl at the desk had been replaced by a blonde looking five years younger than the one before, but no brighter.

"I'm looking for my friends."

"Old guy who smelled like fish?"

Luke raised an eyebrow, wondering if hospitals kicked people out for smelling bad. "Yes," he said as he walked closer. There couldn't be two men running around hospital halls after midnight who fit that description.

The blonde grinned like she'd just gotten a question right on *Jeopardy!*. "He left with a couple." The emergency waiting room was empty but she busily sorted papers.

"Any idea where they went?"

"They followed a woman we released. Oh, yeah, the old man said they were going to ICU."

Luke didn't bother to say thank you. He stormed down the hallway not caring that his boots echoed off the walls. Two left turns later, he spotted a sign pointing to ICU. Willie slept on a bench beneath the sign. Paul and Mary Lynn waited just outside the door a few feet farther down. They all turned as he neared as if they expected him.

"What's wrong?" Luke asked the question, but he wasn't sure he wanted to hear the answer.

Mary Lynn spoke. "We're just waiting for Allie to come out. Even though it's late, we finally talked the nurse into letting her just look in on Nana. Allie promised not to make a sound and the nurse said she'd allow it if only Allie stepped in."

Luke faced the closed door and stared through a tiny window, his tired gaze searching for Allie amid the equipment-packed hallway.

She stood thirty feet away, staring into a glass room. He couldn't see Nana. He didn't have to. He could see Allie's heart breaking. Her clothes were dirty and torn. Her hair wild. Her face wet with unchecked tears. Her world was splintering and she stood all alone.

Every muscle in his body tightened. He wanted to rush

to her and pull her into his arms and tell her everything was going to be all right. Deep down he felt the need to protect her, but he knew he couldn't. He blamed himself for what had happened. He knew she'd blame it on the bad luck she thought followed her. She wouldn't understand that if she hadn't been waiting on that dock, Skidder might have run right past Jefferson's Crossing. Allie wouldn't be bandaged and Nana wouldn't be in ICU if he hadn't made the date.

Paul stood beside Luke, giving him the facts in a low voice. "Allie's only got a few cuts. She's fine. Nana lost a lot of blood, but they're just keeping her here for a few days to run some tests."

Luke braced his hands on the door frame, fighting not to shove his way through. He knew if he held her now, he'd never be able to let her go and he still had a job to finish.

Luke shoved away from the door. "Can you get Allie and Willie home?"

"Of course."

"I need to file a few reports and have a talk with the men being brought in."

"I understand. Don't worry about Allie." Paul hesitated as if knowing his question was anything but simple. "Don't you want to stay to talk to her?"

"No," he said, trying not to sound as tortured as he felt. "I'll get the work done first. Tell her I'll see her later."

Walking away was the hardest thing Luke had ever done in his life.

Chapter 42

I don't remember the drive home or the shower I must have taken. I don't remember falling asleep, but I think I cried until I had no energy left to worry about being lonely.

The morning blinked into my bedroom and I rolled over, welcoming the day for a moment before I realized Nana wasn't with me. I forced myself out of bed and dressed without paying any attention to what I wore. Then, finding comfort in routine, I went downstairs and made the coffee.

The kitchen didn't feel right without Nana and the wonderful smells of her cooking. I flipped the first cabinet door open and began following her recipe for buttermilk biscuits.

She'd always made it look so easy, but it wasn't. I had to roll the dough into a ball and start over three times. The first time it stuck to the counter because I forgot to put flour down first, the second I rolled it almost pizza-thin. By the third try the dough felt leathery, but it at least looked right.

I'd forgotten to write down how to cut the biscuits. I

knew she used an old glass, but which one? The juice glasses looked too little, the tumblers were too big. I finally settled on an old glass Nana always called the snuff glass, even though I'd never seen snuff. I used a little bacon grease from a can Nana kept on the back of the stove to oil the pan, flipped the biscuits over in the thin film of grease, and shoved them in the oven.

If I keep busy, I told myself, *I won't think about all that happened last night.* The hospital told me not to show up until nine, so I had a few hours to kill. I promised myself I wouldn't spend them crying.

I fried up sausage patties and slipped them into the hot biscuits, then set a tray on the counter ready for customers.

When I opened the front door and looked at the dried blood on the steps, the night's horror came back to me with sledgehammer force. I grabbed the mop and ran water so hot it steamed when I stepped out into the cold morning air.

As I scrubbed the blood away, I remembered a story Nana used to tell me about when she and Flo had been playing once. Flo had fallen and cut her knee. Nana said she cried twice as hard as Flo did. Nana said, "I wished I could take the hurt from her. I wished it had been my blood pouring out."

I knew how Nana felt. I'd give anything if this was my blood, not Nana's, on the steps.

I glanced over at the railing where we'd taped Skidder last night and wondered what happened to him. I remembered Mary Lynn said something about Luke taking care of him last night. She said he would be all night questioning the three drug dealers, but he told her to tell me that he'd rather be with me.

I wasn't sure I believed him. Pieces of Mary Lynn's words drifted into my mind in no particular order.

There had been three, not one on the north shore last

night. Skidder had been one more than I'd wanted to see. I couldn't help but wonder what damage the other two had done.

As I tossed the water from the bucket into the morning glory vines at the side of the porch, I heard a car barreling down the road. It swung into my graveled drive.

The sheriff looked like a drag racer as he took the curve, then scattered rocks as he corrected, heading like a torpedo toward me.

I stepped back, fearing he didn't have enough time to brake. Two feet from the steps, he stopped.

The sheriff jumped from his car with more speed than I thought the big man could produce. He stormed the steps of the porch like a raider. Three feet from the door, he looked up, saw me, and frowned.

"What happened here last night?" He spit the words at me.

Before I could answer he added, "Why didn't someone let me know? This is my territory. I'm the one who should have been called, not the ATF."

He jerked off his hat and wiped sweat from his face.

I glanced at the door, trying to figure out if I could run inside and bolt it before he could block me. Probably not. Even if I made it, he'd just bust the lock and follow me in.

I took a deep breath. "A man tried to steal my van. He held a knife on me and cut Nana bad."

Sheriff Fletcher huffed and puffed. "I don't give a damn about that, what about the drug bust? The dispatcher said there was a report of arrests out here last night. Said an agent was shot."

I shook my head. "I don't know anything about that."

"Of course you do. Every one of the fleas who hang out on this dog of a lake comes here to talk."

I knew I should tell him all I knew, but in doing so I'd have to mention his son and I didn't want to be around when Fletcher got that news. "Mary Lynn told me Luke had them locked up and planned to question them."

Fletcher leaned in closer, glaring at me. "Luke who?"

This I could tell him. "Luke Morgan, the ATF agent who lives next door." I pointed to the stand of trees. "You've met him."

"That bum is an agent." The sheriff's face seemed to sunburn suddenly. "I knew something wasn't right about that guy." He turned and stormed toward his car. "I'll straighten him out. I'm the one who should be questioning any troublemakers, not him. Luke Morgan is going to have some explaining to do."

He glanced back at me. "I'll want to talk to you later, so stay put."

I hated his whole attitude. "Am I under cabin arrest?"

"Don't get smart with me, girl, or you'll be sorry."

"I'm not a girl." I almost wished he would arrest me and take me along. I had a feeling when he finally caught up with Luke, the sheriff wouldn't be walking so tall.

He swore and climbed back in his car.

Suddenly, I could wait no longer. "Stay put" wasn't in my vocabulary. I ran into the store and left a note by the biscuits. I grabbed the van keys Paul had left on the nail after he'd followed Mary Lynn and me home last night, and headed for the hospital.

Thirty minutes later, I walked into the ICU waiting room and spotted my mother pestering the volunteer at the help desk.

Carla looked up and saw me. "There." She pointed to me, but spoke to the volunteer. "There is my daughter. She'll tell you I'm kin to Edna Daniels."

I slowly crossed the room to the desk, but didn't say a

word to anyone. A man stood with his back to me. When I reached the desk, I recognized Garrison D. Walker, even without his too-many-teeth smile.

"Pardon me." The woman at the desk with a name tag that read "Miss Deanne" looked up at me. "Are you Allie Daniels?"

"Yes," I said.

"We allow only immediate family in, and on Mrs. Daniels's chart, we have only your name. This woman says she's your mother."

Miss Deanne looked uncomfortable. Family feuds were not in her job description.

"That's right, she was." I smiled at the volunteer. "She gave me up when I was three."

Now Deanne looked like she was considering turning in her volunteer smock.

Carla braced like she was preparing to slug it out to get in to see a woman she hadn't cared about in years.

Bless Garrison D. Walker's heart, he stepped between us and said in a voice perfect for the courtroom, "Is there a place we can talk in private?"

Miss Deanne jumped up, happy to move the problem away from her desk. "Follow me. We have a family room."

I thought of commenting that Carla and I didn't belong in such a room, but I figured I'd made enough of a scene. With Deanne leading the way, we crossed the waiting room.

I was at the door when I glanced back and saw Luke storming through the crowd toward me. He didn't seem to see anyone in the room. He walked right up to me and lifted me off the ground in a huge hug.

I melted against him. The first good thing since dawn had just happened to me.

He finally lowered me back to the ground, but his arm stayed around my shoulder. "Are you all right?"

"I just had a scratch last night." I brushed my hand over his shirt. "How about you?"

"I'm fine." He winked. "A little tired from banging heads together." He leaned down and kissed my nose. "I missed our date last night."

I shrugged. "It's okay, things get in the way." I tried to keep my words light, but there was nothing casual about the hold I had on him.

Carla's sharp voice sliced through the air. "Can we break this up? I've got a few important things to talk about with my daughter." She glanced at Luke from his muddy boots to his stained shirt. "If you and mud man can pull apart long enough for me to have a few words with you."

My hand slid down Luke's arm to his hand. "He's staying," I said simply as I stepped into the room.

Garrison Walker seemed to think he had been appointed referee. He paced between us for a moment, then said, "Now, Miss Allie, I realize I've led you to believe that the lake property is yours, but your mother has brought a few facts to light that I didn't consider before. It seems she is the only one of the two of you who ever met Jefferson Platt and he did name her as the person to be notified when he died. So, I feel it only fair to consider the possibility that Mr. Platt meant to leave the place to her. At his age, a mistake like that wouldn't be impossible."

"I don't think so." I made up my mind that second that I'd rather see lawyers get every inch of Jefferson's Crossing than allow my mother to take it from me.

Walker remained calm. "She said Mr. Platt wouldn't have even known of you if she hadn't spent the day visiting with him. I'm sure there is some arrangement we can come to here that will be fair to all."

I couldn't stop myself. I had to ask, "Why'd you stop at

his place, Carla? Surely it wasn't by chance." The fact that she'd been there had bothered me since she mentioned it.

She smiled smugly, as if giving away a secret. "Do you remember those dumb postcards Nana used to get now and then? The ones with paintings of the masters on one side and only the word 'remember' written next to her address?"

I closed my eyes, seeing the cards taped to the inside cabinet door. I never thought to see if anything was written on the back. That must have been where I first began to love art. I don't remember her ever getting them in the mail, but she might have because every now and then a new one would appear.

Carla looked haughty. "My father finally made her throw them away. He said they were just clutter. But I found one she'd stuck in her Bible. I took it, thinking it must mean something to her because you know how Nana always was about her Bible. I stuck it in my high school yearbook because if she looked for the card she'd never think to look there. A few years ago, I found it, but this card didn't just have 'remember' written on the back."

She paused for effect, like some small-time actress overdoing the scene. "It had a route number out of the Lubbock post office. I figured it had to be some old family friend or relative, so I dropped by the next time I was in Dallas. I told him my father had died and my mother was all alone and having to take care of you. He seemed real interested until I told him I wasn't sure about your address. I told him you and Nana were moving around like gypsies and I didn't have time to keep up with you. After that, the old man almost tossed me off the place."

I grinned. "I always knew Uncle Jefferson was a fine judge of character."

"He was a bum," Carla snapped. "Some friend of the

family, he showed no interest in investing in a plan I had that would have made us both rich. All he wanted to do was ask questions about you and Nana."

I never met Jefferson, but I could almost see him talking to Carla long enough to figure out what she was and then asking her to leave.

"So you see, Allie," Walker said as he turned to me, "if it wasn't for your mother you wouldn't have this place."

"I disagree," Luke said from behind me. "I think Jefferson Platt knew and loved Allie all her life. He just lost track of her at some point."

"Stay out of this," Carla snapped. "This is none of your business."

Walker raised an eyebrow at Luke. "Who are you, sir?"

"I'm Luke Morgan." Luke reached around me and offered his hand. "Sorry for the outfit, but I've been dealing with a gang running drugs out at Twisted Creek. I'm an agent for the Department of Alcohol, Tobacco, and Firearms." Both Carla's and Walker's mouths dropped open. "But I'm here as a friend of Allie's and because my grandfather and Jefferson were best friends." He let the introduction sink in for a moment before he added, "I have proof Jefferson knew Allie all her life."

"I'd like to see that." Carla folded her arms. "The old guy never said a word to me."

Luke tugged a picture from his vest pocket and handed it to Walker. The edges of the picture were worn and stained slightly from years of handling. "I found this, along with others, in Jefferson's office."

With Walker and my mother, I stared down at a picture of me in the third grade. I hadn't seen it since the year it was taken. Nana had made me a plaid dress the week I had school pictures made. We thought I looked grand, but Henry saw no need for wasting money on pictures. This had to be the one that came free, clipped to the outside of the envelope.

"The pictures show that he kept up with her all through her childhood. He must have lost track of Nana and her when Allie's grandfather died. I've a dozen people from the lake who remember hearing Jefferson talk about Allie." Luke turned and stared at my mother. "You only filled him in on how they were. When you didn't know where to locate them, he was finished talking to you."

"You're making this up," Carla started, but Walker put his hand on her arm.

"I don't think I'm prepared to call Agent Morgan a liar." He straightened and picked up his case. "You'll need to seek other counsel if you plan to continue."

Carla wasn't used to losing. If she couldn't win, she could hurt. "Well, fine, take my property, but you'll spend it all taking care of Nana. Something is wrong with her, real wrong." She followed Walker out the door and slammed it hard for good measure.

I closed my eyes and said good-bye to the woman who'd never wanted to be my mother.

Luke's arms circled me from behind and held me. He didn't say anything. He just held tight.

Finally, I turned to face him. "Did you really find years of pictures of me?"

"I may not tell all I know sometimes, Allie, but I never lie. After the nine o'clock visit with Nana, come back to your place and I'll show you."

"Aren't you going to stay around and go home with me?"

He shook his head. "No. I'm going home to clean up. Then we'll talk."

He kissed me gently and set me away from him. "I'll be in Jefferson's office waiting for you when you get home."

I knew he was right. We had to wait. My first concern had to be Nana right now.

Luke walked me to the doors going into ICU. Without a word, I went inside. When I looked back, he was gone.

I checked with the nurse, then went into Nana's room. She looked so weak, almost held captive by machines. The nurse told me she'd had a good night and was scheduled for tests all morning. She also said that by evening, if all went well, she might be in a regular room.

I wrapped my fingers around her arm just below the bandages and watched her sleep. "I need you so much," I said, wondering if she could hear me.

Without opening her eyes, she covered my hand with hers and patted three times.

I smiled as tears ran. "I love you, too."

Chapter 43

0945 hours
Jefferson's Crossing

Luke spread the pictures of Allie out on the old Hunter desk in Jefferson's office. Twelve pictures, each dated, looked back at him. He also found a few letters, notes really, telling about how grand Allie was.

He read each carefully, feeling like he was trespassing on someone else's memories. Nana had signed each note "forever, e." Nothing more. Carla had said the postcards were signed with the same word. Maybe that was all either of them needed to say. Maybe they both knew. This was no wild affair. This was simply a shared memory, never forgotten, always cherished.

He heard Allie open the door, but he didn't turn around. The rainy-day air blew in around him, but he could feel her warmth before she brushed her hand along his shoulder. Luke smiled, knowing he'd never tire of her touch.

"I still don't understand," she said as she moved around him and stared at the pictures.

"It took me awhile to put it all together," Luke whispered, as if invading Jefferson's privacy by discussing it. "I think it was Willie mentioning that my grandfather used to call Jefferson 'Red' that made the pieces finally fit together. I'd heard Nana tell her story of her week at a lake with a boy named Red. She told me over breakfast about how they'd talked until sunrise. She couldn't remember exactly where the lake had been located. They'd met that summer and kept in touch by one note and one postcard a year."

"Odd. Nana never mentioned anything about keeping in touch with anyone from her past. If she did, I don't think Henry even knew about it. The postcards were just there once in a while."

"It's more than that." Luke closed his fingers gently over her shoulder. "I think they lived a lifetime together in their hearts."

"No." Allie stopped, then whispered, "Maybe."

"Jokingly she told me once that she couldn't marry me because she was sleeping with a memory." Luke pulled Allie against him. "I think they fell in love that week but life kept them apart. She wouldn't leave your grandfather or maybe Jefferson wouldn't ask. First she had to raise Carla, and then you. Or maybe they were both happy with the way it was. For them, they had sixty years of being sixteen in their memories."

Allie smiled up at him. "I wish such a thing could be true. It would have made my Nana's life so much richer. But it can't be, and these few pictures prove only that she knew him and wrote him once in a while."

"They might not have written hot love letters, but she wrote him of what she loved—you. They shared that." Luke knew he was sounding like a poet, but he saw the truth. "In a way, she gave him a little part of what she loved most. She gave him you."

Allie shook her head. "I can't believe that. Maybe he knew Nana. Maybe he was the boy who took her to the fireworks and the fair when she was sixteen, but that was all. He had no other relatives. I was just a name to fill in on the will."

Luke took her hand and tugged her over to the old pot-bellied stove. He knelt down by the safe everyone used as a stool. "What's your birthday, Allie?"

She told him.

He entered the numbers and twisted the dial. The safe clicked open.

Allie dropped to her knees beside him and looked inside. A wind chime exactly like the one her grandmother had lay inside.

"Still think you were someone he just wrote down?"

Allie pulled the wind chime out. "But why me?"

"Maybe he knew that you'd bring Nana back here where she'd always been in her dreams."

Luke left her staring at the wind chime and walked to the door. He locked it, then flipped off the lights. Without asking, he lifted her in his arms and carried her up to her bed. There, he lay down beside her, and pulled the covers over them both.

She was silent for a long time, then she began to talk, piecing the story of Edna and Red together as if it belonged in a love story. The wind chime and the postcards were all Nana had of him, yet she'd tossed the cards away when Henry said they were clutter. Maybe she didn't need them as a reminder. Maybe she just knew he was still thinking of her.

Allie talked of how hard it must have been on her to slip one letter a year to him. Henry never talked much, but Allie said she had a feeling he wouldn't have stood for it. He was older than Nana and always treated her as if she were his child when he talked to her.

Finally, Allie talked herself to sleep and Luke drifted off beside her. His last thought was that maybe he understood about the way Jefferson felt about Nana because he knew he felt the same about Allie. It wouldn't matter if they were separated tomorrow, she'd still remain in his memory.

Chapter 44

I awoke to an afternoon of rain tapping on the window. Glancing at the clock, I counted down two hours before I could go back into ICU and check on Nana.

Suddenly, I smiled. I'd always thought of Nana as being alone, even when Henry was still alive, but now—now that I knew about Jefferson—she didn't seem so alone. The thousand times she'd brushed the wind chime in her kitchen window she must have been thinking of him. Maybe even living a parallel life in her mind with the boy she'd met the first summer after Pearl Harbor. A boy who'd taken her to a fair and won two wind chimes so they'd have the same music in both their worlds.

I straightened, stretching. The feel of the man next to me was all too real. I shifted so that I could see his sleeping face. I had a hundred questions I wanted to ask him about what had happened last night, but I couldn't bring myself to wake him. Deep down I knew I'd sleep with this man and make wild, passionate love to him for years to come, so right now it was enough just to know he was near.

I cuddled closer. He laid his arm over me, keeping me safe even while he slept.

A tapping sounded from below. I didn't move, hoping whoever it was would go away.

The tapping came again.

Luke groaned. "Tell them to go away," he muttered.

I giggled when the tapping turned to a rap.

"I'm not moving," he said, sounding more awake even though his body hadn't shifted an inch.

I slipped away. "Good, you stay here. I'll see who it is and be right back."

He tried to snag me with his arm, but I jumped out of bed and hurried downstairs. I knew if I looked back I'd forget about who kept rapping.

When I opened the door, Mrs. Deals stood before me. "I'm sorry to keep you waiting," I said as I ushered her in. "I forgot today is your cookie day."

She folded up her umbrella. "I didn't come to shop. You got a call from the hospital and I came to deliver the message."

I held my breath and waited.

She took a moment to snap the strap around the umbrella, then continued, "I'm to tell you that your grandmother is being moved to a private room and you can bring up a few of her things if you like."

"Thank you, Mrs. Deals, for coming all this way to tell me."

"You're welcome," she said without a smile. Then she added in a yell as if I'd gone suddenly deaf, "I also have a message to deliver to Luke if you see him. Tell him they have Sheriff Fletcher in custody."

I turned to see Luke at the top of the stairs. His hair stuck up on one side and his shirt was unbuttoned. He looked exactly like what he was—a man who'd just crawled out of bed. My bed.

"I can hear you just fine, Mrs. Deals. You don't have to yell."

She crossed her hands over her chest and looked quite satisfied.

"How'd you know he was here?" I asked without thinking.

"I just guessed." Mrs. Deals smiled. "I knew if he had any sense he'd be here. And if there is one thing Luke Morgan has always had it's sense."

Luke walked down the stairs. "Thanks." He nodded once. "Is that all you know about Fletcher?"

Mrs. Deals shrugged. "Willie told me you and he guessed the sheriff might be behind the drug trafficking on the lake after you found out he always made personal deliveries of Jefferson's medicine. You didn't know it for a fact until he showed up at the jail demanding to talk to the three snakes you caught last night."

"The sheriff was connected with the drugs?" No one seemed to hear me. "He delivered Jefferson's medicine?"

Mrs. Deals's gaze never left Luke. "He picked up the medicine, but didn't bother delivering it until after Jefferson was dead. Everyone knew the old man was forgetful about taking it, but if it wasn't there to remind him, Jefferson probably didn't notice the months passing without it."

Luke shrugged. "We'll never be able to prove that the sheriff hung on to Jefferson's medicine, but I bet he knew the old man sometimes lost his balance when he didn't take it. I don't guess it matters now. We've got enough to put Fletcher away for the rest of his life. Two of the three guys we rounded up last night have already turned on him."

Mrs. Deals stared at Luke. "Good work, Agent Morgan."

"Thank you," Luke said. "I was trained by the best."

She smiled. "That you were."

Something silent and deep passed between them. An understanding. A forgiveness.

Finally, she turned to me and said, "Since I'm here, I think I'd like a box of Milano cookies, if you have any?"

"It just happens I do." I grinned.

She walked out without another word. Willie and the Landry brothers rushed in before the door closed. While they drank coffee and talked about every detail that had happened the night before, I walked around the store trying to think what I could take to the hospital to make Nana feel more at home.

In the end, I packed two things.

～

An hour later I sat on the edge of her bed and used a razor to cut out the sketches in my ledger.

Luke hung the wind chime by the window, then we taped up each picture. The lake at night. The clouds reflecting over the water. Luke by the fire. The Landrys waiting for their breakfast by the end of the dock. Timothy sitting all alone in the middle of his boat. Mary Lynn and Paul having tea. Nana making bread. Willie and Nana snapping peas on the porch. The first night's dinner with the tables set for one. The Nesters circling Dillon as he huddled near the stove.

Our life on the lake covered her walls.

About the time the doctor asked me if he could talk to me in the hallway, the Nesters started pouring in. Nana told them all she was fine, but they fussed over her anyway. They all brought gifts. Mary Lynn and Paul brought flowers. Mrs. Deals brought a book of poetry. Timothy brought a CD player for her and the Landry brothers brought rocks from the shoreline so she could still feel close to the water.

I stepped out and listened to the doctor tell me the details of patching her up in words I didn't understand. In the end, he added, "We'll need more tests, but I think you know that your grandmother is slipping into dementia."

I'd known. As slow as one grain of sand falling at a time in an hourglass, her memory had been slipping. "How long?"

The doctor shook his head. "I can prescribe medicine that will slow the progression, but it will still come. What would you like to do? I can suggest some care facilities."

I smiled. "I'd like to take her home. We'll care for her there for as long as we can."

He nodded as if he felt sorry for me. We talked on until his pager went off and he had to go. I went back into Nana's room and sat on the bed next to her, listening to everyone talk about all the excitement on the lake.

When visiting hours were over, Luke stepped out to walk everyone to their cars and suddenly I was alone with Nana.

I hugged her. "I have to go, too. Will you be all right here tonight?"

She smiled at the drawings. "You're a great artist, Allie. I'll feel right at home."

I kissed her cheek as she curled down into the covers. "Good night," I whispered thinking I'd never have a more important showing of my work than right here.

"Good night, Flo," she answered, and I knew she was slipping again into another time and another place.

I smiled down at her, brushing her hair lightly with my fingers. "I'm here, Nana. You're home. We're all home."

It crossed my mind that maybe all of life isn't lived in the present. Maybe a tiny part of it is lived in the heart.